MY BROTHER'S KEEPER

BEWITCHED AND BEWILDERED

ALANEA ALDER

www.sacredforestpublishing.com
P.O. Box 280
Moyock, NC, 27958
Digital ISBN- 978-1-941315-08-8
Print ISBN- 978-1-941315-09-5
Sacred Forest Publishing

Cover Design and Interior format by The Killion Group http://thekilliongroupinc.com

DEDICATION

~*Omnia Vincit Amor*- Love Conquers All~

To my parents,
stop worrying that I won't finish the book on time.
Look, see, all done :)

To my brilliant PA Brenna,
who keeps me on track, sorry for making you crazy.
(But not really too sorry ha ha)

To all my readers, new and faithful stalkers,
I hope you enjoy this one. Thank you for letting me
into your hearts and into your lives,
your support keeps me going.

PROLOGUE

Three weeks ago

She always looks so sad.

Kendrick watched the pale, blonde woman tenderly wipe the soup from the stubbled chin of an elderly man. Though she smiled, her eyes told a different story. With infinite patience, she managed to get the older man to eat an entire bowl of soup.

"That was wonderful, Dad. You finished the whole bowl! Before you know it, you'll be harassing Ethel down at the Duck In," she teased.

"Never mind me, girlie. When are you going to move on with your life? You can't babysit an old man forever," the man grumbled.

"Don't be silly; I love spending time with you." She rose and walked into the kitchen. Kendrick heard her putting the dishes in the dishwasher, and after a few minutes, she returned carrying a stack of books.

"Do you want me to turn your shows on?"

"That'd be nice."

She picked up the remote and switched the television on. They sat in silence as he watched his shows and she studied from her books.

During a commercial break, Kendrick noticed that, at some point, the old man had stopped watching his shows and was watching the beautiful woman.

"You should have gone to college, met a fine young man, and had babies of your own by now," he said quietly.

She looked up, a surprised expression on her face. "I couldn't just leave you to take care of Mama on your own. Besides, I'm still going to college." She held up her nursing textbook.

"You'll be my age before you finish, taking one class at a time like you are. Sometimes, I wish I would hurry up and join my Lucy in heaven so you won't be tied to this house anymore."

The young woman flew off the sofa and dropped to her knees next to the old man's recliner. With tears in her eyes, she laid her head on his leg. "Don't say that! Don't leave me alone, Daddy; you're all I have."

The old man gently ran a gnarled hand over her soft blonde curls. "You're stronger than you think. My time is coming, girlie. When it's time to say goodbye, I want you to smile for me. I want you to be happy."

She shook her head. "I'm not strong."

"Yes, you are. You've sacrificed so much taking care of first your mother and then me; now, it's our turn to set you free. After I'm gone, sell everything–the house, the land, everything. Keep a few keepsakes, like your mother's jewelry, but sell the rest. Take the money, and you go to the best nursing school in the country, don't let anything tie you down."

The woman looked up, her eyes wide. Kendrick watched as she realized that her father was dying. He saw the exact moment the knowledge hit her.

"No!" She reached for the phone, and a wrinkled hand stopped her.

"Go to school... live your dream." The words were coming more slowly now.

"Daddy, please..." she begged.

"This isn't goodbye, not really. Your mother and I will be watching over you... so you won't be alone. Live every day to it's fullest so you have a lot to tell us when we see each other again." He smiled and took a deep breath. "You're the best thing I've ever done in life, girlie. I'm so proud of you." With a shaking hand, he brought her face close to his and kissed her forehead. When he slumped back against the recliner, Kendrick knew he was gone.

"No!" The woman buried her face in her hands and wept.

Darkness swept him away and carried him to another scene. The beautiful woman looked paler now, and her teal-colored eyes were rimmed red and she stared down at a headstone.

"I did it, Mama, Daddy. I graduated, and I'm a nurse now. I'm back home and working at the Duck In until I can find a permanent position." She blushed. "I've met a nice man, he's gentle and kind, I know you'd have liked him, Daddy. He's so easy to be around, I'm never awkward when I'm with him. It's nice to finally have a real friend." She knelt down and placed a bouquet of sunflowers on the double grave. "Maybe it's time to start thinking about having a family, I'm thirty-six already. It'd be nice to not be alone anymore." She stood and stepped back. "I'll visit more often now that I'm home. Please keep watching over me." She kissed her fingers and blew kisses to each name.

When the darkness returned, Kendrick fought against the pulling tide of inky blackness. He wanted to stay with her; he wanted to make sure she was okay. When the shadows disappeared, his heart began to hammer in his chest. A familiar nightmare began to take shape.

"No," he whispered harshly.

His younger brother Keelan lay broken, lifeless in the warrior's arms. Kendrick growled low. He knew these men; they were the Alpha Unit. The dream began to collapse around him.

"No! Why won't you let me see what happens to him? I can stop it if I know!" he screamed out.

But, like every other time he relived this nightmare, no one responded. He woke up with a start and sat upright in bed. He looked around, the musty scent of old books helped bring him back to the present. Breathing hard, he climbed out of bed and headed to the bathroom. He turned on the water and haphazardly splashed his face, heedless of where the water ended up. He wanted to wash away the image of his baby brother's lifeless body.

He looked up and stared at himself in the mirror.

"Keelan, please be safe."

CHAPTER ONE

Kendrick watched as the large shifter pushed the small woman behind him. From the name she had yelled, the man before him was apparently Aiden McKenzie, the Unit Commander.

"Where is my brother?" he repeated, locking eyes with the shifter.

Aiden stared at him for a moment then stepped back. "This way." He turned and started walking up the stairs.

Kendrick nodded at Amelia before following Aiden. Why was his brother's body being kept at the Alpha estate? Aiden stopped and opened the door.

"We brought him back to his own room." Aiden raised an arm, inviting Kendrick to step inside.

Kendrick shouldered past the massive commander and walked into the room. Lying serenely in the bed in the center of the room was his baby brother. Wires and tubes were everywhere, connecting him to the many beeping machines.

"He's alive?" Kendrick felt his legs give out. A strong arm kept his knees from slamming into the hardwood floor. When he looked up, a large fae supported him effortlessly.

"He's still breathing, but we don't know if he's alive," the fae admitted.

Kendrick shook his head, trying to make his exhausted mind work. He had researched his brother's unit decades before and kept close tabs on them, but for the life of him, he was having a hard time remembering the fae's name. Darian! The fae member of the Alpha Unit was named Darian Vi'Alina. "What in the hell is that supposed to mean?" He forced his legs to support him, and he stepped away from the men.

Darian spoke first. "Our enemy released a spell that strips a person's soul from their body. Keelan was protecting us from that spell when he fell victim to it. The enemy took his soul, for what reason, we don't know."

Kendrick froze in shock. What the fae described was forbidden. To separate a soul from a person's body was an affront to the Gods. No wonder the entire city was coated in black magic. He turned to find that the room was now filled with bleak-faced couples. The men he knew and, of course, his Amelia, but the other women, he did not know.

"What you're describing is forbidden." He met the eyes of each of the warriors.

"Well, there seems to be a lot of that shit going around lately, Keelan-From-the-Future." The small woman said sarcastically.

Kendrick blinked. "I'm not Keelan. My name is Kendrick Ashwood. Keelan is my younger brother," he explained.

The woman rolled her eyes. "Whatever, clone boy."

Kendrick stared. *Was this woman damaged?*

Amelia stepped away from Darian and wrapped her arms around his waist. Kendrick took a moment to enjoy a spurt of satisfaction as anger flashed in the fae's eyes. Who was he to keep his godsdaughter from him? Wait? Didn't Caiden say that Amelia had mated? So much had happened in the past couple of days. He returned the embrace and pulled back to pat her on the head like he always did. Her smile was wobbly, and her eyes were filled with tears.

"Can you help him?" she asked.

Kendrick forced a smile. "Of course, that's what big brothers do."

"We can get the guest room ready," Aiden offered.

Kendrick shook his head. "No. I'll stay in here with Keelan." He pointed to a sturdy looking recliner then turned back to them. "Who is in charge of those machines?"

A dark haired woman stepped forward. "I am. My name is Rheia Bradley. I'm a doctor. If there's anything you need, you have only to ask. We all want Keelan back."

Kendrick searched her face for deception and couldn't find a trace of it. She exuded sincerity and strength. She was a good doctor.

"We can leave him as he is tonight. I expended a lot of magic getting here so quickly, but tomorrow, I would like to know what each machine does. I may be able to cast spells to replace them depending on what they are doing."

The doctor stared. "There's healing magic like that?"

Kendrick was about to retort with sarcasm about humans meddling in the paranormal world when he noticed the looks of disbelief on the men's faces. It dawned on him that he wasn't in Storm Keep. Only younger witches were allowed to serve outside the city, and most of them weren't trained in healing.

He clenched his fists in frustration then forced himself to relax. There was no point in being rude to the woman who was caring for his brother, despite her lack of magical ability. He should be thankful, not judgmental. He knew from his own surly thoughts that the day was catching up to him.

"Yes, maybe in the next couple days I can show you different spells," he offered, trying to make his voice sound gentle.

"I would really appreciate that. The more I can do for the Keelan the better," Rheia said, wiping her eyes.

Kendrick felt like an ass. The poor woman obviously cared for his brother, and despite being pregnant, her focus was solely on Keelan.

"Thank you," he said simply.

Rheia sniffled then shook her head. "You're about to collapse. Get a good night's sleep, doctor's orders." She wagged a finger at him playfully.

He nodded. "I agree."

The couples waved goodnight and started to leave.

"Goodnight, Keelan-From-the-Future," the small woman said as she walked out the door.

Kendrick was about to reply then stopped himself; he was too tired. When he looked up, he noticed that only Darian remained.

"Can I help you?" he asked flatly.

"I have a message for you from Keelan," Darian said quietly.

Kendrick frowned.

Darian continued. "He knew. Somehow, he knew what was going to happen. Before the spell went off, he said, 'Tell my brother he was right, but this was the only way I saw where you all lived. Tell him I'm sorry for what I've done, but I'd do it again.' He created a shield that protected us from the spell; without him, we'd all be dead, or worse, feral."

Kendrick felt his stomach knot. Keelan had known all along what his fate would be if he joined the Alpha

Unit. Kendrick had told him of his premonition two hundred years ago. In fact, it had been the root of the argument that led to Keelan leaving home. That Keelan had had his own premonitions and thought of the others first, hurt. A part of him felt betrayed, as if Keelan didn't care that he was Kendrick's only family. However, that small, rebellious voice quieted when he looked up and saw the pain in Darian's eyes. For over two hundred years, Keelan had called the Alpha Unit home, and judging by the way the members of this house were acting, he had also called them family.

"I want to scream and curse him, you know," Kendrick finally admitted.

Darian nodded. "I called him an idiot and screamed in his face after it happened."

Kendrick looked into the large fae's face and recognized a look he had seen not only on his own face but on Caiden's as well, the expression of an older brother who had failed to protect his younger sibling.

"Do you think... was there..." Kendrick took a deep breath. "Was he in pain?"

Darian thought a moment and shook his head. "I don't think so. His face was peaceful and he was smiling." Darian visibly swallowed hard.

Kendrick snorted. "He would, the little shit. He has always been the most exasperating child. He always put others before himself, to the point where I would get angry with him for being so kind. What kind of bastard does that make me?"

Darian walked forward and placed a hand on his shoulder. "It makes you a brother. Trust me, I have an older brother, Oron, and he has said the exact same things to me. Sometimes, us kid brothers need to be reminded that we can't save everyone."

Kendrick ground his teeth together. "I didn't remind him enough." He looked over his shoulder at where Keelan lay, looking like he was simply sleeping.

"We'll get him back, I swear it to you," Darian vowed.

Kendrick stared him in the eye before he glanced down at the silver ring on Darian's finger. "I will hold you to that, Your Highness."

Darian flinched and removed his hand from Kendrick's shoulder to hide the ring. "There aren't many people outside the fae who recognize this ring. How do you know it?"

Kendrick shrugged. "I am an archivist. It is my job to study and to learn, and I have had a long, long time to do both."

Darian ran his hand over the back of his neck. "The others don't know. I would appreciate it if you didn't say anything."

Kendrick nodded; it was a reasonable request. "You have my word."

Darian looked relieved. "Thank you. Well, I'll let you get some rest. See you in the morning, breakfast is at eight, if you're up."

Kendrick inclined his head and Darian left.

Sighing, Kendrick walked over and sat down in the recliner next to his brother.

"From what I have seen, you have an amazing family here, Kee. I can see why you would want to protect them. What I can't understand is why you didn't call me for help? Did you think I was still angry with you for leaving? Did you think I wouldn't drop everything and move heaven and earth to get to you?" Kendrick rubbed his hands over his face. If only he could talk to his brother one more time.

He reached into the small leather pouch at his waist and pulled out his cell phone. He selected a number and dialed.

Caiden answered on the second ring. "Kendrick?"

"How much do you know?"

"Amelia called earlier to warn us. She said that the ones who'd kidnapped her were only interested in using her as a bargaining chip to get to me and my brothers, the Ironwoods and the Ashleighs. The enemy is harvesting powerful witches to steal their magic, and evidently, we're high on the list. I feel flattered." He chuckled dryly. "She also told me what happened to Keelan. I went to your place, but you had already left. Where are you?" Caiden asked.

"The Alpha estate."

"But that's across the country!" Caiden exhaled. "You know what? Never mind. I don't want to know what laws of physics you ignored. How is Keelan, really?"

"I've never seen worse. The only thing here is a shell–skin, bones, and hair. Nothing of my brother is here. The only reason he's in a bed and not in a grave is because this shell is breathing. They have him hooked up to so many machines I can't tell exactly what the body is doing and what help he is getting from the tubes and wires."

"Gods Kendrick!" He heard Caiden take a deep breath. "What do you need from us?"

Kendrick allowed himself one brief moment to contemplate calling his friend to his side, there was no family on this earth he trusted more than the Ironwoods and, through them, the Ashleigh brothers. But he knew that if he was selfish enough to call them to his side, he would only be putting them in danger. He would be doing exactly what their enemy wanted, getting the Ironwoods to leave the safety of Storm Keep.

"You stay there, it's not safe for you to come here. You'd be playing into whatever trap the enemy may have set for you."

"If it's that dangerous, then you need me more than ever. Don't forget, my baby sister has already been kidnapped once. You expect me to sit here and do nothing?" Caiden demanded angrily.

"Yes. Yes I do. There is a bigger picture here, Caiden, one that is so large I can't even see the edges yet. Leave Amelia to me. I won't let anything happen to my godsdaughter. In the meantime, I need you to tighten up patrols. Use your defunct Elder status to get the council to agree to lock down the city. If these monsters require magic, then Storm Keep represents a stockpile. I need you where you are," Kendrick replied evenly.

"Damn it all to hell, Kendrick! Why do you always make sense? If I had known that you would need me in my Elder hat, I would have told Father to stay home," Caiden complained.

Surprised, Kendrick asked, "You saw Marshall recently?" He hadn't heard that the Ironwood elder had returned.

"For all of about an hour before Amelia called. Evidently, Mother and Amelia are directly related to Commander McKenzie's mate. Once Mother heard that, she marched Father out the door to head to Lycaonia. They should be there soon." Caiden's voice held a smile.

"Godsdammit!" Kendrick swore.

Caiden laughed over the phone. "I know you get along with them so well."

Kendrick pulled the phone away from his ear and glared at it. *Wait. Amelia was related to the commander's mate?* He put the phone back to his ear.

"The commander's mate wouldn't be a short, deranged little human, would she?"

Caiden's laughter answered his question.

Wonderful.

"You mean to tell me my brother is lying here in a coma, every witch is in danger, my best friend and godsdaughter are at the top of the enemy's hit list, and I have two versions of Amelia to watch over, plus your flaky mother?" Kendrick bit off every word.

Caiden couldn't catch his breath, he was laughing so hard. "Serves you right. That's what you get for being a hermit for centuries."

"Bollocks!" Kendrick swore and hung up the phone.

Lily Camden, Amelia Ironwood and Meryn McKenzie in the same house at once. He looked over to his peaceful looking brother and shook his head.

"Lucky bastard." He sat back and reached down to the side of the recliner and pushed the seat back, took his brother's hand, and fell asleep.

CHAPTER TWO

Kendrick woke up and blinked. He heard the repetitive beeps of a machine and looked around. That's right; he was at the Alpha estate with Keelan. He stood and quickly looked over Keelan's body.

"He's the same as he was yesterday," a female said from across the room.

He turned and recognized Rheia. "I would say that no decline in health is actually an improvement." He was surprised he was able to string more than two words together before coffee.

She blinked and smiled. "I can agree to that. How did you sleep? Did I wake you?"

Kendrick rubbed his neck before he turned it sharply to the right, cracking it loudly. "I've actually slept on much worse."

Rheia walked over and took Keelan's hand. "Keelan always described you as some sort of powerful superman who slept in a cave of books like a dragon hoarding his gold."

Kendrick felt a small smile on his lips. "Well, he got the cave and books part right. I think that all older brothers seem powerful to younger brothers."

Rheia laughed. "I have five older brothers, and I always thought they could do anything."

"How did you explain moving to a town they could never visit?"

She shook her head. "My brothers are sort of adopted brothers. They are the Vanguard squadron that protects Jefferson."

Kendrick half closed his eyes and pulled out his mental file on Jefferson. "Radek Carson, bear, Marco Rodriguez, jaguar. Dax Vi'Eaereson, fae, Athan Durant, vampire and Levi Sorrel, witch."

Rheia's eyes widened. "You just did what Meryn does."

Kendrick didn't even try to hide his surprise. "What do you mean, exactly?" He had to be sure she meant what he thought she did.

Rheia pointed to his head. "You just pulled up some sort of mental file and read from it didn't you? Meryn can do that. She has what Aiden calls 'Meryn Moments' where she has to stop and allow things to process so she can store it correctly. If I hadn't done the physical on her myself, I would swear she was half computer."

Kendrick felt a spurt of hope flare. In all the centuries he had been alive, he'd never met anyone who thought like he did. That tiny, strange human could think like him? "She seemed a bit..." He didn't know how to describe her without being rude.

Rheia laughed. "Quirky, strange, immature, odd, manic? Take your pick. But the thing is, she's all that and brilliant. She sees things so much differently than we do that, honestly, it can be hard to keep up. We just let her do her own thing though; it would be a shame to force her to act normal, when she's so much more."

Her words triggered a memory of his mother. *'Kendrick why are you trying so hard to be ordinary when you are clearly extraordinary?'* The society in which he was raised didn't tolerate deviations from the norm, so he had left home to learn on his own. Yet here, in this house, they not only accepted Meryn as she was, they encouraged and nurtured her differences.

"I can't wait to get to know her better."

Rheia hesitated, took a deep breath, and met his eyes. "She hasn't had it easy, so please be patient with her. I don't think she has accepted what has happened to Keelan; it's why she was going to try to reach him with the Ouija board and why she calls you Keelan-From-the-Future. She has only recently experienced what it feels like to have a family, she hasn't learned how to process losing someone."

Kendrick felt a rare moment of shame. He had judged Meryn in the same fashion others had judged him in the past. "I promise to be both kind and patient with her."

Rheia's relief was written across her face. "Thank you." She looked down at her watch. "I'll let you get ready for breakfast." She turned and walked out of the room.

Kendrick removed the leather pouch at his belt and laid it on the bed next to Keelan. Next, he removed his clothes and folded them into a neat pile. He waited a moment for the spelled garments to reset and then put them back on thinking of the clothes he wanted to wear for the day. Instead of worn travel clothes, he now had on a pair of perfectly broken-in jeans, an undershirt, a black button-down, a thin black hoodie, and a black blazer to go on over it. Black boots covered his feet, and as usual, his magic washed his hair, teeth and body for him. He reattached his pouch and headed out the door.

He followed his nose to track down the source of the amazing, rich aroma of freshly ground coffee.

When he opened the dining room door, all conversation stopped.

"Keelan!" A child-like, female voice called out happily. Kendrick looked around the table and spotted the owner of the adorable, squeaky voice. Seated next to Rheia was one of the most adorable little girls he had ever seen–except for Amelia, of course.

Despite the lack of coffee, he found himself smiling gently at the child. "No, I'm afraid I'm not Keelan. My name is Kendrick, and Keelan is my little brother."

Her small face scrunched up in thought. "You make him better, like Momma?"

He nodded. "That's the plan."

She smiled brightly. "Good. Miss him."

"Me, too," he admitted before taking the open seat next to Amelia.

"That's Keelan's seat," Meryn grumbled.

Kendrick found that he actually liked the way she frowned at him. She didn't fear him one bit and didn't hesitate to let him know that he was sitting in Keelan's chair. Her honesty was actually refreshing.

"Why are you smiling?" she demanded.

"Was I smiling?"

"Yeah, it was kinda creepy."

"Meryn!" Amelia admonished.

"What? It was."

Amelia turned to him. "Yes, that is Keelan's chair, but I don't think he'd mind you sitting there. And yes you were smiling, but it wasn't creepy."

Kendrick ruffled her hair the way he always had when she was a child. She ducked from under his hand and narrowed her eyes at him. She hadn't liked it when she was a child, either, but it didn't stop him then, and it wouldn't stop him now.

Amelia was a born peacekeeper. Her empathy made her painfully aware of the feelings of those around her. She was happiest when those around her were happy, and she hated conflict and confrontation.

"You know I hate that." She swatted at his hand.

"Yes, I know," he admitted.

"Then why do you keep doing it?"

"Why would I stop simply because I know it annoys you?"

"Gods, that sounds like a Meryn question," Colton groaned.

Kendrick eyed the man. "Why did you make it sound as if being like Meryn was a problem?"

"Yeah Colton, why is being like me a problem?" Meryn challenged before throwing a roll at him.

He held up his hands in defense. "Sorry! I didn't mean to make it sound like an insult. Amelia acts like Meryn sometimes, but she doesn't really think like Meryn. Kendrick just processed the conversation like Meryn. I wasn't trying to be mean; I was just surprised."

Amelia clapped her hands together and smiled at everyone. "I know, let's do introductions."

"Amelia, I love you like a sister, but if you continue to act so damn chipper, I'll throat punch you," Meryn threatened.

Amelia stuck her tongue out at Meryn. "As if you could reach my throat."

"You're not that much taller than I am," Meryn protested loudly. Around the table, everyone laughed.

"Little peacemaker," he said softly, and Amelia blushed. "No need for introductions for everyone," he continued in a normal tone of voice, looking around the table. He let his mind bring forward his information on the Alpha Unit. "Unit Commander Aiden McKenzie, bear shifter. Born to Elder Byron and Adelaide McKenzie. Two older brothers, Adam and Adair, and one younger brother, Benjamin. Best friend, Colton Albright, wolf shifter, third in command in the Alpha Unit. Born to Robert and Alice Albright, no siblings. Gavriel Ambrosios, vampire, second in command in the Alpha Unit, parents, unknown. Age, unknown. Finally, Darian Vi'Alina, fae warrior in the Alpha Unit, recently mated to my godsdaughter, Amelia. I have met Rheia and spoken to her. I saw Meryn briefly last night; she left an impression. The others I haven't been introduced to yet."

Meryn's eyes were wide as she stared at him. In that instant, he knew she recognized herself in him. He winked at her, and her eyes widened even more, and her face broke out into an infectious grin. He would definitely have to keep an eye on this one.

"You seem to know quite a bit about us," Aiden commented dryly before taking a huge bite of his pancakes.

"Did you think I wouldn't? You serve with my brother; of course, I would investigate you all thoroughly." Kendrick looked down at his empty coffee cup then around the room for the coffee carafe. He was about to get up in search of one when he received the second surprise of his morning. A familiar Japanese man walked in through a set of double doors. He placed a plate of food in front of him seconds before setting down a cup of dark brown liquid next to it. Kendrick stared in wonder; the plate was a traditional Japanese breakfast. He hadn't had one like this in centuries.

He stood, and ignoring custom, pulled the man into his arms. "Sei! What on earth are you doing here? When did you leave Japan?" He pounded his back before pulling away.

Sei smiled and inclined his head. "*Heika*. After what happened to Keelan, I knew it wouldn't be long until you arrived. You were so intent on getting to your brother's side, you didn't even see me last night."

Kendrick shook his head. Was Fate rewarding him for keeping Caiden away by putting the only other man in the world he trusted at his side? "I never thought I'd see you again. What happened? Why are you here?"

Sei steered him back into his chair. "My old Master is gone, and I was banished by his family. I drifted for a long time before I found myself here in Lycaonia." Sei walked around the table until he was standing behind Meryn. "Fate brought me to this little one, and I serve her now. She calls me Ryuu."

Kendrick stared and couldn't stop the laughter if he tried. "Ryuu? How'd that happen?"

Sei turned his head but not before he caught the tinge of pink. "A simple mistake on my part. *Denka* was the first one to call me Ryuu, and I find that I prefer it."

Kendrick shook his head as he smiled. He knew he must look out of his mind to those around the table but didn't care. He had his oldest friend back, exactly when he needed him the most. "Then that's what I'll call you as well. Damn if it isn't good to see you! If only Keelan–" Kendrick stopped himself. Reality slapped him in the face. "Look at me, laughing, when my own brother is upstairs practically dead." He buried his face in his hands, elbows on the table.

"I don't think Keelan is the type of asshole that would begrudge you being happy because you have met up with an old friend," Meryn stated matter-of-factly.

Kendrick looked up and glanced around the table. Heads were nodding and he saw only smiles, not looks of disgust.

"*Heika*, your brother is simply sleeping. It is our duty to live our lives in such a way that we do not bring sadness to this home. When he wakes up, he will want to be told of glad tidings, not of how we blamed ourselves," Ryuu said kindly.

"So am I just supposed to pretend that nothing is wrong?"

"Be happy," the child responded.

"Exactly, Pumpkin Dumpling!" Rheia said, tickling the girl. She looked at him. "This is my daughter, Penny Carmichael. She's also no stranger to pain and loss. I became her mother after her parents were killed."

Kendrick looked at the small girl with her bright green eyes and brown curls. She reminded him of Amelia as a child. "So, just be happy?"

She nodded. "If I'm sad, Momma in heaven will be sad, too. So I'm happy."

Kendrick sat back and blinked. It was so simple, and because it was so simple, it was that profound. He couldn't change what had happened, and being sad wouldn't bring Keelan back. If he gave in to his anger and frustration and acted like a jerk, he would only end up hurting the ones that Keelan had given his life to protect.

"Okay little one, I'll try it your way, though I may need some help remembering to be happy," Kendrick said.

Penny nodded, her curls bouncing. "I'll help. I am a good helper; Papa says so. I even help train the men." She beamed proudly.

Kendrick raised an eyebrow at Aiden and then Colton. They just nodded and laughed.

Colton tickled his daughter until she squealed. "Though she cheats sometimes."

Kendrick turned to Amelia. "Reminds me of another little girl who used to torment unit warriors for fun."

She glared at him. "I didn't torment them."

Kendrick snorted. "If you didn't torment them, why did they nickname you the Little Terrorist?"

Darian turned quickly in his chair. "Ha! I didn't even have to call Caiden to figure out your nickname."

"*Athair*!" Amelia groaned.

Kendrick smirked and picked up his cup. He looked into it and turned to Ryuu.

"Cafe mocha, I remembered that you like sweet things," Ryuu replied.

Kendrick took a sip and practically shuddered. It was nectar in a cup disguised as coffee. "Gods in heaven!"

Meryn whimpered and pouted, her lower lip sticking out. "I want some."

"*Denka*, you know you can't have any caffeine," Ryuu gently reminded her.

"Can't she have chocolate?" Kendrick asked.

Ryuu shook his head. "No, she's off chocolate and coffee."

Kendrick winced in sympathy. He looked at Meryn. "I'm so very sorry."

"Finally someone who understands!" Meryn pointed in his direction.

Kendrick closed his eyes and took another sip and simply let it trickle down his throat. Sighing happily, he opened his eyes and looked at his old friend. "If I was slightly more attracted to men, I'd trade sexual favors for coffee like this every morning."

Around the table, the men began to choke. Kendrick hid a smile. He could tell a lot about a man in the moments when he reacted to discomfort. Kendrick looked around the table. Aiden and Colton, the two youngest, were blushing, yet their faces didn't show any judgement, just shock. Gavriel rolled his eyes and winked, acknowledging the test, and Darian grinned at him. Those two were the oldest among the four; of course they wouldn't be perturbed by casual references to homosexuality.

"What's sexual favors?" Penny asked.

Kendrick turned to the little girl. "Sexual favors are when–"

"Stop!" Amelia stood, her hands out in front of her. "No *Athair*. Just no. She's too young."

Kendrick frowned. Was she? "She can't be that much younger than you were when I explained human reproduction."

Amelia crossed her arms over her chest. "She isn't. And Caiden still hasn't forgiven you for telling me about the birds and the bees when I was seven."

"I don't understand; it's a natural part of life." Kendrick looked at Ryuu who shrugged. Okay, bad example of a person to look to in order to gauge normal human response. His eyes went to Meryn who looked equally confused. Yet another bad example of normal. Intrigued, he turned to Rheia. "Not appropriate?" he asked. Amelia sat down, shaking her head.

Rheia sighed and continued to thump Colton on the back as he choked on his breakfast. "She is a little young for that conversation, but I actually had been planning on explaining things soon anyway. She asked where the baby came from, and I refuse to tell her nonsense stories about a cabbage patch. She will learn the correct medical terms for our reproductive parts not silly baby names."

"No. She's too young," Colton protested when he could breathe.

Rheia eyed Colton. "Then you explain where our baby came from," she challenged.

"Challenge accepted," Colton growled. He turned to the small girl and lifted her into his lap. "Momma and Papa love each other very much. You know that right?"

Penny nodded.

"Well, one day, Papa couldn't hold in his love for Momma anymore, so he took her in his arms and kissed her so hard that his loved touched her heart and created a tiny seed. That seed floated down to Momma's tummy, and a baby started to grow in her belly."

Penny thought about it for a second. "So Papa loved Momma hard, gave her a seed, and made a baby?"

Beside Meryn, Gavriel choked on his coffee. Laughing, Meryn thumped him on the back.

Colton nodded. "Exactly."

"Oh Colton! You can't tell her that," Rheia said with a worried expression.

Penny turned to Colton. "Is that why you said you'd kill any boy who kisses me?"

"Yup. You're too little for kissing. You have to leave that to the grown-ups." Colton said nodding.

"When can I kiss boys?" she asked.

Colton thought about it for a long moment. He turned to Aiden, then Gavriel, then Darian. The men wore equally scary looking frowns. He looked down at his daughter. "When you find a boy who is stronger than your *Athair*." He pointed to Aiden. "Smarter than your Uncle Gavriel, more noble than your Uncle Darian, more loyal than your Papa, and kinder than your Uncle Keelan. When you find a boy like that, then you introduce him to us, and we'll let you know if it's okay to kiss him," Colton replied.

"Okay Papa. I think I know who." Penny kissed his cheek and hopped down. "I'm going to go color now before Grandma gets here." She skipped out of the room.

"Wait! Who?" Colton's eyes looked wild.

Rheia patted him on the arm. "She will grow up eventually."

Colton slumped backward. "No, she's not allowed. Ever."

Rheia rolled her eyes. "Cavemen, y'all are a bunch of cavemen."

Kendrick ignored Colton's brooding and smiled at the blonde next to Gavriel. "I don't think we've been introduced."

"I knew you'd get around to asking. My name is Elizabeth Monroe, I'm a *lepus curpaeums*..."

Kendrick smiled. "You're a bunny. There aren't too many bunny shifters left, I'd love to see you shift later."

Gavriel growled at him, his eyes turning red and Elizabeth laughed.

"What?" Kendrick asked.

"You will not see my mate naked."

"Who said anything about being naked? I just want to see the actual shift from human to bunny. Most shifters I meet weigh at least as much as their human selves in animal form. This is a rare situation where the human form weighs considerably more. I've been working on a hypothesis about where the extra mass goes," Kendrick explained.

Gavriel blinked, his eyes returning to their normal grey color. "You know, I never even thought about that."

"I don't mind shifting, but it will have to be much later. I'm in the middle of a nationwide multi-race census, so I don't have time to experiment," Beth offered.

Kendrick waved his hand. "Any time you have free."

Beth looked between him and Meryn. "Guess I'm Bunny for life." She sighed.

"What does she mean?" Kendrick asked.

Meryn grinned. "That's what I call her." She looked down at her phone. "On that note, I better head to the office. My minions await."

"Minions?"

"Jaxon Darrow and Noah Caraway. They're learning about programming languages and computer science to assist the units. We don't use nearly enough technology."

Kendrick held up a hand. "Before you go, I just have one question..." He took another sip of coffee. "How long has Lycaonia been covered with the stench of black magic?"

Everyone stared at him in shock. Aiden finally shook his head. "What do you mean, covered in black magic? The city is as it has always been. We don't deal in black magic in Lycaonia."

Kendrick sat back. "Someone has. There's a fine layer of black magic grime everywhere. I noticed it the second I entered the city's boundaries."

Aiden turned to Ryuu. "Is that true?"

Ryuu nodded slowly. "If *Heika* says that the city is coated in black magic, then it is coated in black magic. I am unable to tell the difference between white magic and black magic, so I can not see what he does."

"Great, just great! What next?" Aiden dropped his fork on his plate.

Kendrick, Meryn, and Ryuu winced. Asking a question like that invited more bad things to happen. Sometimes, higher powers had a twisted sense of humor.

Kendrick raised his chopsticks and took a bite of rice, then fish. "By the way, I'm joining the Alpha Unit." The men were silent as they each took him his announcement.

"You can't do that! That's not the way it works!" Aiden protested.

Kendrick just stared at him and took another bite.

"We have trainees. There is an order to this!" Aiden continued.

Kendrick stared.

"It doesn't work like that," Aiden grumbled.

"Give it up, Commander. I'll break it to Basil, I'm sure he'll understand, especially since Keelan and Kendrick are brothers," Colton said in a congenial manner.

"Wonderful. Now that we have that settled, do you have any of the necklaces that the ferals have been using?" Kendrick asked, continuing his breakfast.

Aiden frowned. "We had two; we broke one, and the council has the one that was given to Adam for study. After the last battle, Meryn and Rheia gathered the necklaces off the dead ferals in the courtyard. We kept five, and the rest were divided up and sent to the three other pillar cities for study."

"They are people!" Amelia said loudly. "They aren't just necklaces, they are people!"

Aiden turned to her, a sympathetic look on his face. "Amelia, we need to understand how these things are created."

Amelia shook her head. "It's inhumane not to set them free." Tears streamed down her cheeks.

Taking a deep breath, Kendrick laid a hand on her forearm. He let his magic gently seek out hers. As he had guessed, her empathy and earth magic were completely free. The box he had created for her magic when she was a child was now too small to keep it in check. Slowly, he began to construct the mental image of a hallway. On one side, he visualized a door etched with the symbol of mind magic; across the hall, he created another door with the symbol of earth magic emblazoned on it.

"Do you see the doors Amelia?" he asked.

"Yes, *Athair*."

"Good. Now very, very carefully start pulling your magic into those two rooms. Let them know that they won't be locked away forever, that you will come visit. Tell your magic that doors were created to be opened."

He monitored her progress, and when the last of her magic had been put behind the doors, he closed them firmly. As soon as the doors closed, she slumped against Darian.

Her mate looked at him, concern on his face. "Is she okay?"

Kendrick patted her on the arm gently. "She is now. Her magic, especially her empathy, was running unchecked; it can be draining. Whatever broke her bindings also allowed her magic to grow. I'll keep checking to make sure that all her new magic stays under control. Hopefully, we'll have everything settled in a week or so."

"Thank you, *Athair*. I didn't realize how out of control it was until you started to reel it in. I thought that my supply of magic would be exhausted after the battle, but there was so much of it. It's as if the battle never took place." Amelia leaned against Darian and yawned.

Kendrick kept a smile on his face. She was right. Her magic should have been nearly depleted, especially since his own anger had inadvertently channeled his magic through her. Yet when he looked inside her core, it was growing out of control like an untended garden. "You probably didn't use as much as you thought you did," he suggested smiling. There was no reason to share his concerns, especially when she couldn't do anything about it anyway.

She nodded and yawned again. "Does anyone need me for anything today? I'd like to go back to bed if I can."

Meryn and Rheia shook their heads. Elizabeth answered, "The only thing we had planned for today was to contact Anne. We have to tell her not only about our world, but also about what has happened to Keelan. Since she's a nurse, it makes sense that she would be the one to take care of him."

Kendrick looked at Elizabeth. "Why does it make sense that she would take care of him?"

Beth looked at him, then the other men. Gavriel cleared his throat. "Because Anne is Keelan's mate."

Kendrick felt his chopsticks slip from between his fingers. A mate! His brother had a mate! Smiling wide, he turned to Elizabeth. "I have a sister! Tell me about her."

Looking relieved at his reaction, Elizabeth smiled back. "I wasn't sure if you'd be upset, since Keelan hadn't told you."

Kendrick picked up his chopsticks. "Keelan always played his cards close to the vest, the more important something was to him, the closer he kept it."

Darian nodded. "He didn't tell anyone about the contents of his nightmares, either. The only thing he told Amelia was that he was having them, no details."

"Sounds like my little Kee."

Colton chuckled. "I can't wait to call him that."

Kendrick smiled at the wolf shifter. "You tease him, I'll break your legs." Still smiling, he took another bite of fish. Rheia was laughing as she consoled her mate. Kendrick ignored the pup and smiled at Elizabeth. "Tell me about my new sister."

Elizabeth smiled. "We don't know much. Keelan as you know, was very tight lipped about her. We do know that she's a nurse and she's just graduated."

"She's very pretty, like a doll. She and Keelan looked perfect together," Colton said.

"I remember that she was kind and did not judge us when she thought we put the diaper on Keelan for fetish play." Gavriel added.

"That sounds...wait...what? What about a diaper?" Kendrick demanded.

The men looked around the table, guilty expressions on their faces. Rheia cleared her throat. "The guys had to go to the store to get pull ups for Penny. They didn't know the size, so they used Keelan for comparison."

Everyone was silent. Kendrick gently placed his chopsticks down and looked around the table. He could almost see the tension in the air.

"Did you get any pictures?" he asked grinning.

The men around the table exhaled, and Colton began to laugh. "No, but I never felt worse in my life. What a way to meet your mate for the first time."

"She sounds perfect for my brother. When will you be bringing her here?"

Elizabeth looked at Meryn and Rheia. "What do you think? Right after breakfast? I called the Duck In yesterday. She works the morning shift today, we know where she'll be."

Rheia nodded. "The sooner the better, that way she'll be here for any health-related spells Kendrick explains."

"Wonderful." Kendrick turned to Aiden. "I'll need as many of the necklaces for study as you can get me."

Amelia turned to him, a sad expression on her face.

"I'm sorry, Amelia, but the best thing we can do for those poor souls is to determine how they were trapped. Once we figure that out, we can track down the ones responsible and prevent this from happening to any more people."

Amelia nodded and buried her face against Darian's arm. He gently ran a hand over her hair. Kendrick grudgingly admitted that Darian was a good match for her. He was strong enough to protect her, but gentle enough to understand her kind heart.

"I'll contact the Council and see what I can do about getting the necklaces," Aiden promised. Then a sly smile crossed his face. "After that, we have drills. I'd love to see what you can teach us." He smiled at Kendrick.

"Yes, about drills... I won't be doing those." Kendrick sipped his coffee.

Aiden's mouth dropped. "That's not how this works! Why join Alpha if you won't be part of the unit?" he demanded.

"It's quite simple really; it's because my brother gave up his life so that you all would live. He insisted on saving you, and after having breakfast with you, I can see why. He viewed you as family, and out of love, he kept you safe." Kendrick dropped his smile and let his power come just to the surface. The men reacted, and the predators inside of them tensed. "And I'll be damned to the deepest pit in hell before I let his sacrifice go to waste and stand by while you get yourselves killed." He put his smile back in place.

"Now, if you need me, I'll be in Keelan's room setting up a laboratory to study the necklaces you'll be procuring for me." He took one final sip of coffee and stood.

"Can I come see?" Meryn asked, completely unperturbed by his dual nature.

Kendrick nodded. "After I have everything set up. Some of the containment spells aren't safe to be cast around pregnant women."

"Okay Keelan-From-the-Future." Meryn chirped back happily.

Kendrick raised an eyebrow. "If you insist on calling me something other than Kendrick and wish to carry on this time travel facade, you can call me Time Lord." Kendrick hid his smile when her jaw dropped.

He turned to his friend. "Ryuu, a couple sandwiches later would be most appreciated."

Ryuu bowed. "Of course, *Heika*."

As he walked away, he heard Meryn whisper, "He is fucking awesome!"

CHAPTER THREE

Anne Bennett followed the three women through the house to a closed door. Without knocking, the smaller woman opened it and breezed through the doorway. Anne hesitated before stepping in. When she looked in the room, she recognized the men she had seen with Keelan the night she met him at work. In her many visits with Keelan since then, she'd heard so many wonderful stories about the men he called brothers. She looked around the room. The tall one built like a linebacker was Aiden McKenzie. He was married to the tiny woman named Meryn. She remembered that Keelan called her Menace. Anne thought the small woman was adorable, and from the way the large man melted when Meryn walked over to him, she knew Keelan had been right in calling the man a giant marshmallow.

The woman who had introduced herself as Rheia Bradley sat beside the one she knew to be Colton. He was the fun-loving one who was always playing pranks. It was for their daughter that the men had been in the store that night buying pull ups.

The third woman was Elizabeth Monroe. She was married to Gavriel Ambrosios, the handsome, dark haired man. She, Rheia, Meryn, and Colton, plus an

SUV full of men she didn't know had parked outside of her work this morning and turned her world upside down. She had run to her boss, Bart, and begged to leave early. Of course, the older man said yes; he hardly ever told her no. Like Aiden, he was a complete softie. Without a thought for her own safety, she had jumped into their SUV and returned with them to the place almost everyone in town knew existed but never dared to try and find.

Six small words had changed everything.

"Keelan is hurt and needs you."

Anne looked around the room. "Where is he? Where's Keelan? What's happened to him?"

Elizabeth, or as she liked to be called, Beth, pointed to the sofa. "It might be best if you sit down."

Anne looked around the room and saw their grave expressions. She sat down and folded her hands in her lap. "Well?"

Aiden began pacing. "You see, Anne, there are things in this world that not everyone knows about. Special things that can sometimes be scary but mostly aren't..." He rubbed his hand across the back of his neck.

Meryn looked at her husband. "You suck at this," she said flatly.

Aiden turned and glared at her. "The last person I tried to explain all this to knocked me unconscious."

"Big baby." Meryn rolled her eyes.

Anne looked at Aiden. "Are you okay? Concussions can be tricky."

Aiden exhaled and pointed at his tiny wife. "She did it with the deck of my toilet about four months ago. I'm fine now."

Meryn held up both arms and acted like she was flexing. "KO'd, first try."

Anne looked at her confused. "Congratulations?"

Aiden turned to Beth. "Maybe you should try."

Beth nodded and turned to her. "Anne, what do you know about the paranormal?"

"Do you mean like ghosts?"

Beth smiled gently. "Not exactly."

"Oh for crying out loud! Meryn two-point-oh will be here before you tell her." Meryn turned to her. "Shape shifters, witches, fae, and vampires are real."

Aiden buried his face in his hands, and the men groaned.

Anne looked around the room. "I know."

Everyone froze. Aiden looked up. "What?"

Anne smiled at him. "You don't remember me, do you?"

Meryn's eyes narrowed dangerously as she looked up at her husband. "What does she mean?"

Aiden, eyes wide, shook his head. "No idea."

Anne chuckled. "Not like that, Meryn. I was about six when I met Aiden the first time, though I didn't know his name then. I was in town riding the new bike my parents bought me, when a man tried to lure me into the alley with candy. Of course I knew better than to go with him. When he got desperate, he tried to pull me off the bike, pretending like he was my father." She smiled up at Aiden. "That's when you came along. You plucked me from his hands, and he tried to run. You simply picked up my bike and chucked it at him like a Frisbee. You made sure I was okay and left. The police came and arrested him. I remember my parents were mad at first about my bike being banged up, but when they found out what happened, you were in their prayers that night. A lot of people in town know something goes on out here."

"What do you mean, they know?" Gavriel asked, sitting forward.

Anne smiled around the room. "We're not dumb, you know. None of you age. The true locals, the ones who have been here for generations, know something is in these mountains, but we don't say anything, because you keep us safe."

"Wait. Bart knows?" Aiden asked.

She nodded. "I don't think he knows exactly what you are, just that you're something different. He was very disappointed today when he found out that the women wouldn't be staying for a chat. He wanted to talk to the 'feisty' one."

Meryn glared up at Aiden. "Why do I get the impression he was talking about me?"

Aiden kissed her forehead. "It's a compliment, baby."

Anne looked closely at the men and pointed to Gavriel. "Vampire?" He nodded. She turned and looked at Darian. "Fae?"

He smiled. "Good job."

Colton waved his hand. "What about me?"

Anne thought about it a moment. "Dog?"

Meryn burst into giggles.

Colton frowned at her. "I am *not* a dog." Pouting, he looked over at Anne. "Why did you guess that?"

Anne gave a half shrug. "Because you're so open and friendly. You were waving your hand so eagerly, it reminded me of my friend's dog wagging his tail."

Her response had all the men cracking up. Colton crossed his arms. "That's not fair. She guessed Gavriel and Darian right."

Meryn was giggling and pointed at him. "She got you right, too, admit it."

Colton sighed dramatically and winked at her, letting her know he wasn't really mad. "I'm a wolf shifter, so half right."

Meryn leaned in on her elbows. She pointed over her shoulder at her husband. "What about him?"

"Oh, he's easy. Bear."

Meryn's eyes widened. "How'd you know that?"

Anne looked Aiden up and down. "He's huge and kinda growly like a bear, but nice and gentle like a teddy bear. Plus, Bart always complains that Aiden eats all the honey buns as he walks through the store."

Aiden stared, his mouth wide open. He turned to Gavriel. "Did you know we were so easy to identify?"

Gavriel brought a hand up to cover his mouth. "I think you are a rare exception."

Anne remembered the reason why she was there. "That leaves witch. That's Keelan isn't it? What's happened to him?"

Colton was about to respond when Rheia held up her hand. "I'm sorry, but I have to ask. Are you sure you're okay? You're taking all of this extremely well."

Anne shrugged. "I'm a nurse; not much fazes me anymore. I've known since I was a child that something strange was in these mountains. Personally, I like the idea of vampires and shifter dogs as opposed to the alien invasion theory I heard at the feed and seed last week."

"I am *not* a dog!" Colton wagged a finger at her.

Rheia nodded. "You had me convinced at nurse."

"You're the doctor aren't you?" Anne asked, feeling a special kinship with the woman.

Rheia nodded and the twinkle in her eye told Anne she felt the same way.

Aiden cleared his throat. "Rheia said that nurses are like the human equivalent to military sergeants in the medical field."

Anne nodded. "That's about right."

"If that's the case, then I'm going to lay it out straight for you." Aiden took a deep breath. "Keelan is a witch. One of his gifts is premonition. In his dreams, he saw a scenario play out where all of us died. To prevent that from happening, he sacrificed himself to save us."

Anne sucked in a breath, and the room started to close in on her. "I thought you said he needed my help. I can't help him if he's dead!" She had finally found someone she cared about; she couldn't lose him, too!

Aiden was suddenly kneeling down in front of her, and he took her hands in his. There were tears in his eyes. "He's not dead, but he's not alive, either. The spell he protected us from stripped his soul from his body. My brother is also a doctor. He said we can keep Keelan's body alive for quite some time while we look for his soul, but it will be hard work. He'll need a lot of care."

Anne put the pieces together. "That's why you came to get me? Because I'm a nurse?" She shook her head. "There have to be hundreds of nurses out there who are better qualified. Why me?"

Aiden squeezed her hands. "Because, after meeting you, Keelan told us you were his mate, his destined partner."

Anne felt like all the air in the room was disappearing. She had recognized Keelan the second she saw him. She had been dreaming of him for weeks, but he had never said anything to her.

"You're telling me that the one man I am destined to be with has had his soul stolen and could possibly die?" she asked quietly, staring down at the floor.

"Yes," Aiden replied softly.

Anne had just enough time to turn to the one person in the room who could help her. Rheia's look of panic was the last thing she saw before she blacked out.

"It wasn't my revelation that made her pass out; it was yours," she heard Meryn say.

"She's coming to."

Anne tried to open her eyes, but something cold and wet was lying across her face. She reached up and removed the washcloth. She turned to Rheia who was sitting on the floor next to her.

"I guess I'm not as bulletproof as I thought," she admitted, feeling a bit embarrassed.

Rheia shook her head. "You are doing remarkably well. Don't sell yourself short."

She sat up and noticed the men around her flinched and reached out at the same time as if to steady her. She held up a hand. "I'm okay. I just need a moment. Tell me about mates while I remember how to breathe."

Colton began to speak and Meryn elbowed him aside. "She seems to be able to take my explanations."

Aiden brought a chair for Meryn, and Colton did the same for Rheia to get her off the floor.

Meryn tapped her lips. "Okay. Here it goes. Living in our world and being mated is like getting married to your dream prince, you're destined to be together like in a fairy tale, but more like *Grimm's Fairy Tales* and less Disney. Magic is real, and the fae kick ass. Vampires and shifters are kinda like what you see on TV except for the wolfman thing. The sex is off the charts, but you kinda have deal with some *Resident Evil* moments with some peeps called ferals, so it balances out. All in all, it's fun."

Anne blinked. "Oh, my God."

"Anne, Anne! Breathe." Rheia waved her hand in front of Anne's face.

"I'm okay; I'm okay." She stared at the floor again and concentrated on taking even breaths.

Resident Evil?

She whipped her head over to Aiden. "Please tell me there aren't any zombies! I can handle anything but zombies."

Aiden rubbed her back soothingly. "No zombies. We have ferals, but they are not zombies."

She began to calm down enough to process more of what Meryn said. "What are ferals?"

Rheia smiled at her. "Ferals are beings that used to be witches, fae, vampires, and shifters. But they chose to give up their souls by committing murder. They lose whatever made them good and they attack people."

Anne looked Rheia in the eye. "But not zombies, right? A scratch or bite won't turn you into a zombie like in *Night of the Living Dead*?"

Meryn shuddered. "That movie fucked me up for years." Anne nodded in agreement.

Colton winced. "Sort of."

Anne's eyes narrowed. "Define sort of."

Rheia glared at her husband. "What he means is, their bite can hurt you if you're a paranormal. Colton was bitten by a feral, and he began to decay from the bite but didn't turn into a zombie. Feral bites don't seem to affect humans, so you don't have to worry."

Anne stared in horror at the people around the room. "Is it safe here?"

When no one answered right away, she began to shake. If it weren't for Keelan, she'd head directly to her apartment, pack what little she owned, and disappear.

"I see you have discussed the somewhat scarier aspects of our world with her." A male voice said from the door. She looked up to see a beautiful Asian man approach while pushing a serving cart. His old fashioned butler's outfit seemed out of place, yet suited him perfectly.

"*Denka*, if you would excuse me?" he asked politely.

Meryn stood and nodded at the man before moving closer to Aiden.

He lifted Meryn's chair out of the way and rolled the cart closer. With elegant movements, he poured her a cup of fragrant tea.

"How do you take your tea?" he asked.

Anne blinked. "It depends on what type of tea it is."

He nodded. "This is jasmine green tea, a house favorite."

"I'll take it as it is please."

A look of approval crossed his face as he handed her the cup and saucer. When she was holding her cup, he bowed. "I am Ryuu. I am the squire of the house. If there is anything you need to make your transition any easier, please do not hesitate to ask."

"*Domo arigato gozaimasu*." Anne said softly, taking a sip of tea. The fragrance alone had helped to soothe her nerves enormously.

Ryuu's eyes widened in surprise. "*Do itashi mashite*."

Meryn looked at Anne. "You speak Japanese?"

Anne looked down at the floor. "A bit."

"If you wish to learn more, I would be honored to teach you. Kendrick is also fluent and can answer questions for you," Ryuu offered.

Anne looked up and smiled at the man. He looked like he had just walked out of one of her cosplay fantasies.

She turned to Ryuu. "Who's Kendrick?"

"*Heika* is Keelan's older brother," Ryuu explained.

"Oh my gosh, does he know I'm Keelan's mate?"

Everyone nodded. That would make him her brother-in-law. "Can I meet him? I'd also like to check on Keelan."

Aiden looked at Rheia. "I think that is an excellent idea. Rheia, if you would take her upstairs to meet with Kendrick, that would be appreciated. Alpha Unit has to report to the Council later this afternoon. I had just gotten off the phone with them when you all arrived. They have called us in for yet another meeting," Aiden sighed.

"Tell Dad I said hi," Meryn requested. She stood on her tiptoes for a kiss.

"Of course." Aiden kissed her and then rubbed noses with her.

Ryuu held out his hand. Anne took one last sip of tea and handed him her cup. "Thank you for the tea, it really helped calm me down."

"I'll bring up some more tea along with *Heika's* snack. I have a feeling you'll be up there a while." He winked at her, and she could feel herself blushing.

Rheia took her hand. "Come on, I can show you his chart and how we currently have things laid out." Rheia gave her hand a squeeze.

Anne felt relieved. She stood with a sense of purpose. Nursing she knew; she was good at it, and if they needed doctors like Rheia, then they needed someone like her, too. This was normal to her. Things couldn't be that scary if they were human enough to need doctors and nurses.

She took a deep breath. "Let's go see our patient." Anne said, feeling better now that she was on familiar ground.

Rheia knocked.

"Come in," a male voice called.

When Rheia opened the door and walked in, Anne followed. They immediately went to Keelan's bed.

She covered her mouth with her hands. "Oh, Keelan." Her heart was breaking. In her mind, she knew what a coma was; she was a nurse, after all. She knew what to expect. But this was Keelan, her closest friend since the death of her parents. She didn't want to see him hooked up to machines with IVs and other tubes running out of him. He should be sitting up and laughing, eyes sparkling as he teased her mercilessly.

Rheia wrapped and arm around her shoulders. "I know," she said simply.

Anne shook her head. "No, you don't understand. It's like whatever made Keelan Keelan is gone. I've seen coma patients before; this is different. I can't explain it."

"It's a shell," a male said from behind them.

When she turned, she felt her world tilt. "Keelan!" She turned to look at the man on the bed and then to the one behind her.

He shook his head. "I'm sorry; I know we look alike, so I understand your confusion. My name is Kendrick I..." He squinted at her. "Have we met before?"

Anne just stared. She had seen him before, every night for weeks. The longer, shaggy, auburn hair, the sexy stubbled chin. His defined jaw and angry expression only accentuated the power this man carried about him effortlessly. In her dreams, his eyes only softened when he spoke to her, and it was in his arms where she truly felt complete. He was also the only man to ever evoke any type of sexual response. Some of the dreams she'd had were downright pornographic, and she had enjoyed every second; in a wakeful reality however, he scared the living hell out of her.

She knew that if she loved him recklessly–the way she had in her dreams–and lost him, there would be no recovery. She would be destroyed. That was why she had been so relieved when she met Keelan. He made her feel comfortable, and he didn't threaten to steal her sanity with a dark look that promised the forbidden. Keelan ordered Chinese food and watched anime with her. He made her laugh with made-up fortunes from their fortune cookies. She didn't think twice about sleeping next to him on the sofa in her stained sweatpants. He was her best friend; he was safe.

She took a deep breath and told the biggest lie of her life. "No, sorry, I've never seen you before."

He blinked and his eyes narrowed. "Really?"

Double damn, he knew!

She turned her back to him and took Keelan's hand. "I would remember somebody like you."

"You would think," he replied flatly.

"Kendrick, can you tell us what type of magic you'll be using here?" Rheia asked. "I'd like to disconnect him from as many machines as possible. The more the body does for itself, the better."

Anne was thankful for the interruption. She had to concentrate on Keelan now. After all, they told her that Keelan had said she was *his* mate.

She turned around and looked Kendrick in the eye. "What can be done for my mate?"

He flinched, and the muscle along his jaw tensed.

"*Heika*, ladies, I have brought refreshments," Ryuu announced as he carried in a large tray.

"Impeccable timing, as usual, Ryuu," Kendrick muttered.

"Of course, *Heika*." Ryuu set the tray down on the round table in the middle of the room. "I took the time to make another of your favorites, but if you prefer, I can take them back downstairs..."

Kendrick peeked over at the tray, his eyes betraying him. "Is that *taiyaki*?"

Ryuu nodded. "I have red bean paste and cheese filled."

"*Anko*?" Anne and Kendrick asked at the same time.

Ryuu smiled. "It's so refreshing having the two of you here. Yes, *anko*."

Anne stepped forward. "I'd like one of those, please, and more of that green tea if you have any."

"I'd like two of the *anko* and one cheese filled, Ryuu," Kendrick said.

Ryuu turned to Rheia. "None for me thanks, my tummy is a bit on the wobbly side lately. Just some tea would be great."

Kendrick turned to her. "How do you know what *anko* is?"

"How do you?" she asked him in response.

"I have traveled all over the world, including a nice long stay in Japan. You?"

Anne looked down at the floor. There was no way in hell she was going to admit to being the biggest *otaku* in the state, especially not to him or Ryuu. "I must have seen it on the travel channel or something," she mumbled.

"She speaks with a perfect accent. She must have seen many programs with native speakers for her to speak so well," Ryuu volunteered.

Kendrick smiled at the squire. "Thank you for making another one of my favorites. I won't scandalize you again by offering sexual favors."

Anne felt her eyes nearly pop out of her head. Kendrick was flirting with him? Ryuu not only knew his favorite foods, but made them for him as well? Could they be mates? Maybe the dreams she saw was showed an older version of Keelan after all.

Rheia sipped her tea. "While you two snack, can you tell us what spells you'll cast?"

Kendrick had just taken a huge bite of one fish-shaped treat. He went to answer and nearly choked. Laughing, Anne handed him his tea. When their fingers touched, she felt a jolt of electricity run down her arm. He gulped down his tea, his eyes never leaving hers. Finally, she looked away and picked up her own snack.

Unfaithful hormones!

Kendrick cleared his throat. "I'll be casting a stasis spell, which will prevent muscle atrophy. I have material that can be used as a diaper that is self-cleaning and a set of garments that will not only become whatever type of clothing you require, but will also keep him clean."

Anne turned to Rheia. "That would eliminate the need for a catheter or rectal Foley, which can cause necrosis." She turned to Kendrick. "Your stasis spell, would that also prevent bed sores?"

Kendrick nodded. "Yes, it will preserve the body exactly how it is now. Considering the fact that there is no current physical damage, it will keep him in ultimate health."

Anne ran through the mental checklist for coma patients. If she didn't have to worry about bathing, turning or changing Keelan, then there was little need for most of their equipment. "How does that self-cleaning diaper work?"

"I'll put it on Keelan in the same way a mother would diaper her baby. Any form of elimination is immediately disposed of and the body cleansed. It requires no maintenance or monitoring," Kendrick explained.

"I can do that for you if you'd rather not," she offered.

Kendrick shook his head. "It wouldn't be the first time I've put a diaper on Keelan. I raised him after our parents died."

Rheia sucked in her breath. "Kendrick, I didn't know. I'm so sorry. It must be hitting you twice as hard since you had to be both a brother and a parent. I can't imagine Penny being..." She stopped and swallowed hard. Ryuu wrapped a comforting arm around her shoulders.

"Is he on any type of medications?" Anne asked Rheia gently.

Rheia shook her head. "As Kendrick said, he wasn't hurt physically so there was no reason for antibiotics or painkillers."

"So the only thing he'll need is a feeding tube and an IV for hydration?" Anne asked out loud.

Rheia thought for a moment and nodded. "Kendrick's spell and magic items will actually help Keelan tremendously."

Anne looked over at Keelan. "Kendrick, Rheia, whenever the two of you are ready, let's get our boy comfortable."

CHAPTER FOUR

Anne, Rheia, and Ryuu left the room while he stripped Keelan and got him into his new clothes and diaper. Anne was Keelan's mate? His mind was racing. Anne was the woman from *his* dreams. The one he was sure was his *own* mate. What kind of mind fuck was Fate trying on him now? The way Anne had looked at him, he was certain that she had recognized him, too, but she had made it a point to call Keelan her mate.

He carefully buttoned up the pajama top and pulled the blanket up the way Keelan had liked it as a child.

All the way to my chin Ken-nick, so the monsters won't get me.

Do you think that there are monsters out there dumb enough to hurt you with me watching over you?

No, but just in case there are real, real, real *dumb ones, tuck me in tight.*

Kendrick smiled at the memory and felt his eyes fill. Little did he know then, there were monsters out there that cared very little that he was Keelan's brother.

"You just sleep, little buddy. I'll figure out this clusterfuck before you wake up. Everything will be okay," he promised. He picked up a soft bristled brush and began brushing his brother's hair in place.

He heard a knock at the door. "Can we come in now?"

"Yes."

Rheia and Anne walked in as he was finishing up. "He looks so much better now." Anne said hurrying to Keelan's side.

Rheia nodded in agreement. "He really does. With only an IV and feeding tube, he looks almost normal. That stasis spell even preserved the flush in his cheeks. He's like a male version of Sleeping Beauty."

Anne turned to Kendrick. "Can you watch him for a couple hours? Colton and a gentleman named Sascha are running me into town before their council meeting. I need to pick up my things, break my lease, and let Bart know I quit. I hate leaving on such short notice, but he knew I could land a nursing job at any time."

Kendrick didn't want her in town alone with only two warriors for protection. Without confronting her about his dreams, he had no right to dictate her actions. "Maybe you should take a witch along as well, for safety," he suggested.

"I'm sure Colton and Sascha will be fine." Anne said.

"Actually, I agree with Kendrick. I'll suggest that they take Quinn along; he's in Sascha's unit." Rheia said.

Kendrick breathed in internal sigh of relief. "Foxglove?" She nodded.

Even better, he knew that Quinn was an exceptional witch when it came to protection, especially since he had personally sent the warrior some shielding spells from the archived grimoires. Technically, the older and more powerful spells were supposed to be studied and memorized in Storm Keep, which meant the younger witches serving in the units didn't have half the arsenal of spells they needed to keep them safe. Kendrick had been mailing copies of spells out to the warriors and the Vanguard for centuries in an effort to keep them all from getting killed.

"Quinn is an excellent witch; you'll be safer with him," Kendrick said, keeping his tone neutral.

"If you both think so," Anne hedged.

"We do." Rheia said firmly. Kendrick winked at Rheia; after all, it was her mate going into town as well.

"Okay, well, I'm heading to the clinic. A lot of the pregnant women will only stop in when I'm there, so I like to be there as much as possible." Rheia turned to Kendrick and surprised him when she gave him a hug. "Thank God you came when you did. I didn't know what else I could have done for him," she whispered.

Kendrick rubbed her back. "You just worry about yourself and leave Keelan to me. You have a brand new life growing inside of you; that takes a lot of work."

Rheia looked up at him, her confusion obvious. "You knew last night I was pregnant, yet I never said anything. How did you know?"

"What do you know about magic?" he asked.

"Absolutely nothing."

"Well, there are two main fields of magic, elemental and psycho/physical." Anne and Rheia just stared at him. "Earth, air, fire and water are elemental. Mind, body and spirit are psycho/physical."

Understanding lit up Anne's face. "I played an RPG where the magic was classified like that. Different classes were able to master different things. Like a Ranger could do earth magic and a cleric could heal."

"Exactly!" Kendrick paused his explanation. "Wait, there are human games like that out there?"

Anne nodded. "Yup. I always choose a paladin, a ranger, a knight and a cleric. I go for balance."

"Amazing. Paranormals think that humans know so little about the magical world, yet they invent games based on the very premise of our–"

Rheia cleared her throat.

Kendrick smiled ruefully. "Right, my explanation. Anyway. One of the types of magic I've studied is body magic. I could see the changes in your body. It's also how I knew that Keelan was an empty shell."

Rheia frowned. "If you have studied body magic, that must mean others have as well."

Kendrick nodded. "Some. It's not very popular since most paranormals heal quickly and rarely get ill."

"It's so frustrating. You can heal so much, and human doctors have to guess and try to figure things out by process of elimination." Rheia clenched her fists.

Kendrick walked over, took her hands, and gently bounced them until she relaxed. "There is another reason why body magic is so rarely studied. The body is constantly changing; every second, new cells are created and others die. Trying to treat something as simple as a virus can be life threatening to the caster. In that respect, your human science is the better method. In helping Keelan, my magic is keeping him exactly as he is, so the spell wasn't as taxing."

Rheia managed a smile and squeezed his hands. "You're not nearly as gruff as you pretend to be, are you?"

He dropped her hands and cleared his throat. "I don't know what you mean."

Rheia snorted. "Come on, Anne, the sooner you leave, the quicker you can get back. I know that Aiden wants everyone back before nightfall," Rheia said.

Anne looked at him. "I'll be back before he needs his IV bags changed."

"Take your time. I'll be in and out of this room setting up my lab anyway."

The women waved and left. For someone used to being on his own, Kendrick was shocked when the room suddenly felt empty.

Shaking his head, he walked past Keelan's antechamber. His brother had set it up to be his library and practice area; it was a sacred space for a witch. That was why Kendrick was setting up his lab in Keelan's bedroom. He cast a protective containment field around his work area and started unpacking his equipment. Grinning, he loosened his pouch from his belt. He opened it and began to pull books and test equipment from the bottomless bag. He looked back into the pouch and floated a long wooden table out and set it in the middle of the room. Now he had a place to work.

He loved his gifts from the fae. His clothes, which changed appearance and kept him clean, had been part of a set called Gentlemen Garments. He had gotten them during a visit to Éire Danu centuries ago. Keelan now wore one of the two pieces he received along with the washing towel which was now acting like a diaper. In addition to the garments, he had been given the infinitely useful Bag of Wishes; all were gifts from the fae queen herself.

The Bag of Wishes allowed him to store anything he wanted in his pouch, regardless of size and weight. He had tried to duplicate it's magic but could never get the mass equations correct. Shaking his head at the mysteriousness of fae magic, he never appreciated it more as his lab quickly began to take shape.

Once Aiden was able to provide him with the necklaces, he would be able to start testing the different types of magic that went into creating them, including tracking down the caster. When he did find the one responsible for his brother's condition, not even the Council would be able to keep the bastard alive for questioning. The second he knew a name, the witch was dead.

Anne watched as Colton looked down at the four boxes and blinked. "Seriously? This is all you own?"

"Yup. One for schoolbooks, one for clothes, one for keepsakes, and one for knickknacks. Right before my father died, he told me to get rid of anything that could tie me down and run after my dreams. Since I had to move across country for school, it made sense to get rid of anything that I absolutely didn't need. It just became a habit after that." She failed to mention that her most prized possessions, her massive anime and book collections, were kept safe in digital format in cloud storage. She didn't even want to contemplate moving her collections if they had been in hard copy. They'd be here for weeks!

"What'd your landlord say?" Sascha asked, picking up two of the boxes.

Anne smiled. "Mr. Clemson has known me since I was in second grade; he didn't give me any grief over the lease. Besides it's a downtown location–well, as downtown as Madison gets anyway. He won't have any problem renting this out."

Not to be outdone, Colton picked up the two remaining boxes. "How'd Bart take the news of you quitting?" he asked, balancing the boxes carefully.

Anne let out a huge sigh. "He's a stubborn old goat! I had to threaten to call his wife before he settled down. He knew I appreciated his concern though; he has daughters, after all."

Colton nodded. "Bart is a wise man when it comes to females."

Sascha looked at him intently. "Truly?"

Colton grinned. "He has lived through having six daughters and a wife."

Sascha's eyes rounded. "I need to meet this man."

Quinn came in through the door. "I moved the SUV to the building entrance so we can carry her stuff down." He blinked as he saw Colton and Sascha with the four boxes. "Is that it?"

"Y'all are too much. Come on, let's head back; I want to check on Keelan."

That got the men moving. Within minutes, the boxes were loaded, and they were back on the road. She rode with Colton while Sascha and Quinn followed in her Honda CRV; it had been her only splurge while in college.

"What?" Colton asked out of the blue.

"What?" she asked in return surprised at his question.

"You're frowning."

"Oh. It's just strange, I guess. I've driven down this road thousands of times over the years, ever since I was a kid. But now, it feels different since I know where we're going."

"How are you really? It's a lot to take in, especially with Keelan being..."–Colton struggled to find the right word–"unavailable."

"Unavailable?" She couldn't help the giggle that escaped. "You make him sound like a doctor busy with a patient."

"I don't like the other terms; they're too depressing."

"I wish I had been brought into your lives for a happier reason, but I don't regret being in your world. It's scary, and I wish Keelan was awake to explain things to me, but everyone has been so supportive, even Meryn in her own way."

Colton chuckled. "She may come across as a bit kooky, but she has a huge heart and is very protective of the ones she loves."

"She seems very heartbroken about Keelan. Were they close?"

Colton stared at the road for a moment. "Yes, but not in the way you'd think. They didn't hang out together, but I think, despite his fear of an uncaffeinated Meryn, Keelan was one of the few people that got her. He understood her sci-fi references and liked the same type of movies. To Meryn, that was priceless. Even now, amongst family, we all love the little menace, but not many people really understand her. "

"I know how Meryn feels. Keelan was the first person I was able to relax around since my parents passed away. It's why I miss him so much now," Anne admitted.

Colton reached over and patted her arm. "We'll get him back. His brother is supposed to be some kind of magical genius. If anyone can get Keelan's soul back, it's Kendrick."

At the mention of his name, Anne began to remember her dreams. It had to be Keelan, not Kendrick who appeared to her at night. Otherwise, why would Keelan say she was his mate? Even telling herself this over and over again, she couldn't ignore the burning attraction she felt for Kendrick.

"Hey Colton, did you dream of Rheia before you found each other?"

"Sure did. Most were nice, but they got scarier the closer I got to meeting her. Some nights, I went without sleep because I didn't want to see her get hurt in my nightmares."

"That's how you knew you were mates? Because you dreamt of her?"

Colton nodded. "She dreamt of me, too. It really helped her accept our mating. Why do you ask? Did you dream of Keelan before you met him?"

"Yes, I did; that's why I was so flustered that night in the store."

Colton laughed. "It didn't help that we had him in a pull up."

Anne smiled at the memory. "His face was the color of a tomato when he walked up to explain what was going on."

Colton groaned. "I still feel awful about that."

"Don't feel bad. It actually made talking to him much easier. There was no way I could be intimidated by him after that. In fact, I think that entire episode made it so that we could talk to each other."

Colton turned to her. "Really? You're not just saying that to make me feel better?" He turned his attention back to the road.

"Really. Normally, I get nervous around people. I was ten years older than my classmates in college, so I was on my own for a long time, but it was impossible to be nervous around Keelan with the image of him wearing a pull up burned into my mind."

"Thanks, Anne. I hated the idea that I might have ruined his mating."

"You're really very sweet. Rheia is a lucky woman."

The tips of Colton's ears turned pink. "I'm a lethal wolf shifter. I am not sweet."

"You keep telling yourself that."

Colton growled and laughed. She ended up laughing with him. Thanks to Keelan, she was making new friends. If only he could be awake to see.

Sascha and Colton carried her boxes up to the guest room closest to Keelan's bedroom. They said their goodbyes and headed downstairs to join up with Quinn before heading to some place called the Council Manor for their meeting. She stared at the boxes and felt no motivation whatsoever to unpack. So she decided to change into more comfortable clothes. She dug through her clothes box and picked out a pair of teal sweatpants, sherpa lined slippers, and her favorite sweatshirt that read, '*Anime...Crack would be cheaper*.' Wanting to be closer to Keelan, she grabbed her backpack and pulled out her laptop and charger.

She knocked on Keelan's door and waited. Getting no response, she exhaled in relief. She wasn't sure how to act around Kendrick and the feelings he evoked. She walked in and immediately went over to the bed. She checked Keelan's feeding tube and IV bag; both still looked great. She plugged in her laptop, sat down in the recliner, and made herself comfortable. With her laptop nestled in her lap she fired up her favorite boy's love anime. Boy's love anime was her favorite. What was better than one gorgeous guy going through the ups and downs of falling in love? Two gorgeous men. She was so engrossed in her latest episode, she didn't notice Kendrick's return until he was standing over her.

"Ahh!" She accidentally inhaled her own spit and began to cough. She set her laptop to one side as Kendrick hurried over to the table and brought back his cup of tea. She took small sips still trying to clear her airway.

"Were you trying to kill me?" she demanded.

Kendrick shook his head, an amused expression on his face. "You were so entranced by Tezuka-san and Yuri-kun, you didn't hear me call out to you."

Anne blinked as she realized he knew exactly what she had been watching.

Kendrick leaned down. "You forgot that I don't need subtitles to know what's going on."

"Oh, my goodness!" Anne buried her face in her hands.

"What?" Kendrick asked, walking back to the long table that hadn't been in the room before she left to get her things.

"You must think I'm the biggest nerd in the whole universe for getting caught up in an anime like this."

"Is that what that's called? I was enjoying listening to the story. In fact, if you don't mind, I'd like to find out if Tezuka-san will ever admit his feelings for Yuri." Kendrick picked up a large, ancient-looking, leather-bound book and began to read from it.

"You don't mind that it's two guys?"

"No, the story and dialogue are very well written, and the voice actors are superb. Not many of today's forms of entertainment hold my interest, this does."

Anne smiled. Of course he didn't mind that it was a love story between two guys. Not if he had a thing for Ryuu. "I can go back and start at the beginning. I'm only two episodes in," she offered hesitantly.

Kendrick turned to her, a smile on his face. "I'd very much like to hear how this entire debacle started."

Anne shook her head and double-clicked on the first episode. Within an hour, they were caught up and well into the next episode when Kendrick turned to her frowning. "I don't understand–why doesn't Yuri just tell Tezuka how he feels? They could avoid a lot of the confusion and trouble."

Anne rolled her eyes. "Because if he confessed his love and was rejected, it would destroy him. Right now, his dream of playing with Tezuka in nationals is the only thing keeping him going."

Kendrick shook his head. "I'm worried for Yuri."

"Me too. Should we keep going?"

Kendrick was about to answer when the door slammed open. An angry young man with blond hair stormed into the room. Anne jumped to her feet. "You can't be in here!" she said angrily, setting her laptop down in her chair.

The man walked up to Kendrick and poked him in the chest. "You! Who do you think you are changing the rules? When a member of a unit is killed, a trainee takes their place. You can't just waltz in here and do whatever you want, witch!" he hissed in Kendrick's face.

Anne stared in shock. Behind the angry intruder, four more young men appeared in the doorway, all of them looking equal parts mortified and apprehensive.

"Sterling, let it go! This was decided by the Unit Commander; you need to stand down." The dark haired man with blue eyes stepped forward acting as the leader of the group.

"Shut it, Lennox! By all rights, Basil should have been placed with Alpha when Keelan was killed," Sterling retorted.

Lennox ground his teeth together. "Keelan isn't dead, you jackass! Why do I get the feeling that you don't care the least bit about Basil? This is about you somehow isn't it?"

Sterling looked over at Lennox, a sneer on his face. "Aiden McKenzie has been changing too many rules lately. If he skips over advancing Basil, who's to say he won't skip over us?"

"I'll put money on the fact they skip over you, dickhead," the one with black hair muttered.

"Fuck you, Kai! You may like fawning over the warriors dreaming of the day for advancement, but I plan on advancing." Sterling swung his gaze back to Kendrick who remained seated. Kendrick licked his finger and turned the page, deliberately ignoring the man.

"I'm talking to you!" Sterling knocked the book out of Kendrick's hands.

Bad move dude.

Anne grinned openly as Kendrick stood to his full height. At six foot six, he towered over the young man.

Sterling's eyes widened as he took in Kendrick's muscled form. "B-b-but, you're a witch," he stammered.

Kendrick never said a word; he simply placed the tip of his finger on Sterling's chest. A second later, the man was convulsing on the ground.

"Kendrick!" Anne rushed over to kneel beside Sterling, who was now limp, as she reached for his wrist. She made sure he was still breathing and turned back to Kendrick. "What did you do?"

He shrugged. "A lesson in humility. I would move back if I were you."

Anne was about to ask what he meant when the smell hit her. Whatever Kendrick had done, it had caused Sterling to lose control of his bowels. She scooted back a bit and then stood. "But he's okay, right? Not a zombie or anything?"

Kendrick gave her a flat look. "No, not a zombie." He looked up at the group. "You and you, come here." He pointed to Lennox and Kai. The men straightened as if coming to attention and stepped forward.

"Yes, sir?" they said together.

Anne half expected them to salute at any moment.

"Take this child back down to where the other warriors are training, I'll let Aiden deal with him." Kendrick frowned down at the still form.

Lennox and Kai hesitated. Kendrick waved a hand over Sterling. "There, none of his filth will get on you now." He winked at the two men.

Both were visibly relieved. "Thank you, sir. We don't like touching Sterling to beat on him during drills, much less..." Lennox indicated Sterling's predicament.

"Perfectly understandable." Kendrick paused and looked over at the two other men at the door. His eyes landed on the smaller, youngest looking one with brown hair and eyes. "Basil, I presume?"

Basil nodded, went to step forward, and tripped over his own feet. If not for the quick reflexes of the man next to him, he would have ended up on the floor like Sterling.

"Sir?" he managed to squeak.

"Is it true that you would have been the one to take Keelan's place while he is... unavailable?" Kendrick asked.

Anne rolled her eyes. What was it with the men and that word?

"Yes, sir...I mean, no, sir."

Kendrick waited for a further explanation. "Well? Is it yes or no?"

"Yes, I am the witch trainee for Alpha, and in the event that Keelan is no longer able to serve in Alpha, I would take his place, but Keelan is still a part of Alpha, sir."

Kendrick smiled softly. "Excellent answer. Tell Aiden that you will be my assistant until further notice."

Basil's eyes got huge and a wide smile broke out over his face. "You really mean that sir?"

Kendrick nodded. "Normally, you wouldn't receive any further magical instruction until you have completed your responsibilities as a unit warrior; however, since I am here and will be working on magical theories while I study the necklaces, it would be a wasted opportunity not to train you further."

"Thank you, sir! If I can, I'd like to finish out my drills for the day and start tomorrow?" Basil asked hope in his eyes.

"I find that acceptable. Good of you to complete today's duties. I look forward to your assistance tomorrow."

Basil bowed and let the tall blond steer him out of the room since he seemed to be completely dazed. Lennox and Kai were teasing him about his good luck as they shut the door behind them.

Anne walked over to the table as Kendrick picked up his book and sat back in his chair.

"Why did those boys treat you like some sort of celebrity?"

Kendrick just shrugged. "I may or may not have a reputation amongst the warriors for disobeying council dictates in an effort to help warrior witches learn more, which may or may not have resulted in lives being saved."

"So basically, you're a badass?" She crossed her arms over her chest.

He looked up and winked. "Something like that. I don't like being told what to do, and I don't play well with others."

"If you don't play well with others, why did you volunteer to train Basil?"

"Because, despite his frothing at the mouth and self interest, Sterling was right. Basil should have moved up to Alpha. Since I have chosen to stay and act in my brother's stead, I can do the next best thing."

"What is that?"

Kendrick looked up and gave her a heart-stopping, boyish grin. "I can make him my minion. I can't wait to tell Meryn I have one, too," he said smugly.

Anne threw her arms up in the air. "Men!"

Kendrick ignored her outburst. "Put our anime back on."

Grinning, she ran back over to her chair and resumed their show.

CHAPTER FIVE

They had just wrapped up another episode when they heard a loud slam. Kendrick looked over at Anne and saw her startled expression. Anne checked Keelan's IV bag, and they headed downstairs. Kendrick could see the change in her already. When she first met him, she had been closed off, skittish. But after he expressed an interest in something she loved, she had opened up to him like a flower opening to the sun. Feeling self-congratulatory, Kendrick was sure he would be able to get her to admit that she had dreamt of him soon.

They walked down the stairs; he stopped at the bottom and pushed Anne behind him. Aiden McKenzie was two seconds away from losing his temper. Personally, Kendrick didn't mind if he trashed the place as long as Anne wasn't hurt in the process.

Meryn, Beth, Amelia, Jaxon, and Noah appeared from the downstairs hallway, and Rheia, Penny, and an older woman stuck their heads out of the front room.

"Aiden! What on earth is the matter?" Meryn rushed over to her mate.

Aiden growled and snarled, and Meryn's eyes narrowed. She pulled her foot back and kicked his shin. Aiden's growling stopped as he reached down to soothe the pain in his leg.

"Meryn! You have got to stop doing that," he complained, rubbing his shin.

"You were all snarly and spitting at me," Meryn said in an even tone of voice.

Kendrick was impressed. The Unit Commander had been an intimidating sight. Meryn seemed to think nothing of kicking him. It just proved that mates knew best how to handle each other.

Aiden took a deep breath and stood up straight. "I wasn't spitting."

"You were, but that's okay; I love you anyway. Kiss." Meryn lifted her arms.

Kendrick was confused for a moment until he realized that the only way the small woman could reach her mate's lips was if he lifted her to them.

Aiden's face transformed to a gentle smile as he easily lifted his mate and allowed her to kiss his face repeatedly.

"Better?" she asked.

"Much. Thank you, baby." He set her down but kept an arm wrapped around her shoulders.

Kendrick looked around the foyer to see that the other women had responded to their mates' anger as well. Elizabeth was rubbing her cheek over Gavriel's hand lovingly, Rheia and Penny were taking turns kissing either side of Colton's face, and Amelia was drawing hearts on Darian's chest and kissing the center.

"Would you gentlemen like to share what happened?" Kendrick asked.

Aiden's face tightened. "Family meeting in the dining room," he said shortly, and with his arm still around Meryn, they walked down the hallway.

The older woman plucked Penny from Colton's arms. "Ryuu brought Penny's dinner out a few minutes ago. We'll be in the family room watching a movie and later I'll get her up to bed."

Rheia kissed the older woman on the cheek. "Thank you, Mina. I don't know what we'd do without you. You're the best grandmother ever."

Anne pulled on his sleeve. "Does that mean us, too?"

Kendrick was thrilled that she had referred to them as 'us'. Being the two new people to the house apparently made them a team in her mind. Kendrick couldn't be happier.

Meryn stomped back down the hall toward them. "Yes, that means you two. Come on, people."

Anne casually looped her arm through his, and they walked together down the hall. When they entered the dining room, Kendrick sat in the same chair he had the night before, and Anne sat on his other side.

Once everyone was seated, Aiden looked around the table. "Alpha and Gamma Units were called in by the council today for a special hearing. Evidently, certain founding families have taken exception to the way I am running the units. They have called for an inquiry and review of my performance."

Colton growled. "I'd like to meet some of these unhappy founding family members. I'd love to introduce them to our new breed of ferals."

Elizabeth rested her chin on her laced fingers. "They can't do that. There is no governing body that can dictate to the Unit Commander."

Gavriel ground his teeth together. "There has not been, until now."

Kendrick sat forward. "What?"

Aiden turned to him. "A group of founding family members from the Elder Generation has come together to create what they are calling the Committee. It consists of seven men from founding families representing the four pillar cities. I'll give you two guesses as to which city only has one representative."

Kendrick sat back and rubbed his chin. "Let me guess...Lycaonia."

Aiden nodded.

Darian gave a harsh laugh. "It gets even better. René Evreux is Lycaonia's representative."

"That douchebag?" Meryn exclaimed.

Anne looked up at him. "I know nothing about your world or how things are normally run. But when a group is formed like this, it's usually done with a purpose in mind, and I don't think it has anything to do with Aiden's performance."

Kendrick looked down the table. Anne's words rang true. "So what are they really after?" she asked.

Aiden hesitated and looked around. "Ryuu?"

Ryuu appeared in the doorway. "Sir?"

"Could you step into the room please?" Aiden asked.

Ryuu stepped inside completely, and when Aiden turned back to Kendrick, their eyes met. Without having to be asked, Kendrick closed his eyes and cast a soundproofing spell.

He opened his eyes. "Done."

Aiden relaxed back in his chair. "Thank you."

Ryuu walked over until he was standing behind Meryn. "I take it from my requested presence that my input is also welcome?"

Aiden turned his head and looked up at the squire. "Yes. I'm not too proud to ask for opinions and help. Except for the women, with Keelan laid up, Colton and I are the two youngest paranormals in the room. I have a feeling that whatever is bubbling to the surface, started brewing a long time ago."

Gavriel turned to Aiden. "The Elder Generation has never been satisfied with the division of power after the Great War. Many of them held seats of great influence before the four pillar cities were created and we became more diverse. With the exception of Evreux, all of the Committee members I saw today have much to gain if they garner the people's favor by uncovering nefarious deeds performed by everyone's most trusted Unit Commander."

"So, it's a witch hunt?" Anne asked then gasped. She looked up at him. "Sorry."

He smiled at her. "No offense taken, the term is used correctly. What grievances have they brought forward?"

Aiden sat back, his eyes closed. He looked too exhausted to answer. Knowing how most bureaucratic bodies worked, Kendrick guessed that he had probably been raked over the coals all afternoon.

Colton spoke for his friend. "Offenses include, but are not limited to: allowing Meryn to command the units; being responsible for Amelia destroying the town square; being responsible for damages caused by Meryn's flour spell that made the invisible ferals visible; Aiden leaving Lycaonia while it was under attack; Aiden taking units away from Lycaonia while the city was under attack; unilateral decisions regarding technology; unilateral decisions regarding warrior training; placing unit warriors in positions of power to gain more influence; allowing a unit witch to cast the perimeter spell over the whole city, and finally, allowing a unit warrior to be compromised by the enemy."

Meryn paled. "Holy shit balls, that's mostly crap I've done," she declared.

Amelia's cheeks were flushed with anger as her eyes flashed dangerously. "They are daring to complain about the square and Meryn's flour spell? We saved lives! Or does that not matter anymore?"

Rheia's voice trembled. "I can't believe they are using what happened to Keelan as a grievance, and we have no idea who cast the perimeter spell."

Elizabeth turned to Aiden. "Who are they talking about when they said you put a warrior is a position to gain more influence?"

Aiden sat up and sighed heavily. "Caiden. He's been performing two roles since Amelia was born. When his father, the witch elder, decided to travel with his mate, Caiden picked up the duties since it didn't require a lot of attention. He's been acting as Storm Keep's witch elder and unit leader for decades. I don't see why it's such a big deal now."

Elizabeth pursed her lips together. "I'll bet you my favorite day planner they use that as a platform to put someone else of their choosing in that role– 'temporarily', of course. Aiden, you have to be prepared to lose him as a unit leader; he's too valuable as an elder to lose that seat due to positional jockeying."

Gavriel agreed. "Beth is correct. We need every ally we can get at the council level."

Aiden nodded. "I'll start looking at rosters."

Anne frowned and looked around the room. "So, basically, what you're saying is that the charges are technically accurate?" Her question was met with silence. She continued. "Then what you need is a good, old fashioned, spin doctor."

Colton blinked. "A what?"

Amelia clapped her hands excitedly. "She's right! This so-called Committee is trying to launch a smear campaign, so what we need to do to counter that is share all the great things that Aiden and Meryn have been doing."

Darian didn't look convinced. "Do you think that will work?"

Elizabeth nodded slowly. "If done correctly, yes, it could definitely work. But we need to avoid giving them new ammunition against us."

Everyone at the table turned as one to look at Meryn.

"What?" she demanded.

Amelia wagged a finger at her. "You know what. Be good."

"Why does everyone always say that to me? I'm never really bad." Meryn pouted dramatically.

Aiden chuckled. "My little angel."

Meryn grinned devilishly up at her mate before looking around the table. "On to the next order of business, ferals." Meryn pulled her legs up until she was sitting cross-legged in her chair. "Okay, so what do we know? I'm not sure how much information Kendrick had available to him. There's no telling what was released by the officials at Storm Keep, and I know Anne is clueless, so let's lay it all out for them."

Amelia wrapped her arms around herself. "We now know that the necklaces are made from souls."

Darian wrapped an arm around her and pulled her close. "We know that the necklaces are being created for the express purpose of giving the wearer shifter abilities, halt physical and mental degradation, and they can sometimes render the user invisible."

Elizabeth turned to Gavriel. "We know they are actively trying to recruit warriors by any means necessary."

"We know that the necklaces glow bright green when you break them." Aiden grimaced. "We've already broken a few–one by accident and the others because they were hurting Amelia."

Meryn tapped her fingers on the table as if she was typing on an imaginary keyboard. "We also know they have been organizing for a long time; this shit didn't happen overnight."

Anne leaned forward. "Not to sound like a five-year-old, but why? What are they after?"

Kendrick looked up. "The number one reason for every cause of misery in the paranormal world since the dawn of time."

Everyone looked at him expectantly.

Kendrick looked around the table. "Power."

Meryn scrunched up her face. "That's stupid. Power to do what?" She curled her fingers in air quotes. "Rule the world?"

Kendrick remained silent. He had been around a long time; he had seen what the taste of power could do to people.

Meryn's mouth dropped. "Seriously? We're dealing with a paranormal version of *Pinky and the Brain*?"

Kendrick blinked at her. He couldn't help himself; he started to laugh. How did she do it? How did she manage to reduce the most serious threat to their world since the Great War down to a cartoon?

"Meryn, I love you," he said and wiped his eyes. Around the table, everywhere he looked, he was met with confused expressions. Only Rheia and Anne were smiling.

Kendrick scowled at the men. "Don't any of you watch television?"

Darian shook his head. "Not really, though I'm surprised that you understand Meryn's references."

Kendrick sighed. "I don't get out much. Television is a welcome change of pace when I need a break from my studies."

Anne giggled at his side. "And he doesn't play well with others."

Aiden frowned. "Why does that sound familiar?" He glanced down at Meryn.

Gavriel cleared his throat. "So we have the Committee using our current crisis with the ferals to gain political leverage to change our current power structure..."–he laid his head back with a sigh–"all while we are scrambling to deal with the destruction and chaos the super ferals are creating."

Meryn reached under the table and pulled out her laptop. "Are we going with the term 'super feral' as the official name?"

Gavriel raised his head and stared at her. "You know, you are right. We have not come up with a name for them as of yet."

Colton shook his head. "I don't like it. It makes them sound more impressive than they really are."

"What about reapers?" Anne asked softly. "They're responsible for taking people's souls right?"

Meryn smiled at her. "That's perfect! So the rambling, brainless monsters that y'all are used to are ferals. The ones that wear the soul necklaces and lead armies of ferals are now called reapers." Meryn tapped away on her laptop.

Kendrick noticed that Anne had turned white. He leaned down. "What's the matter?"

She looked up at him, her blue eyes wide. "She said rambling, brainless monsters. That sounds a whole hell of a lot like zombies to me!"

Meryn looked at her. "They are not zombies because they don't go after people's brains; they kinda eat all the body parts."

Kendrick watched as Anne started to sway in her seat. "Just breathe. Nothing can get to you here, I promise."

Meryn shook her head. "Actually we've been attacked here twice."

"Meryn! Remember what I told you about being more observant to social cues?" Elizabeth hissed.

Meryn looked over at Anne, and her eyes got wide. "Sorry!"

Kendrick wrapped and arm around Anne and pulled her close. "That was before I was here. Nothing can attack this house and survive."

Anne looked up. "Promise? I swear, I normally have nerves of steel, but I just can't do zombies. When I was a kid I stayed up after my parents went to bed and watched *Night of the Living Dead*, I've been having nightmares ever since."

Kendrick took one more moment to enjoy the feel of her tucked in close before he gave her a final squeeze and let her go. "Promise. An army of those things could attack and they wouldn't make it to the first step of the porch."

Aiden snorted. "Don't make promises you can't keep. Those things are strong and ruthless. They think and they learn. They aren't like normal ferals."

"Reapers, call them reapers," Meryn interjected.

Kendrick looked across the table. "I never make promises I can't keep."

Colton laughed. "Come on Kendrick, you versus an army?"

Kendrick just stared at him.

Colton quieted. "Seriously?"

Kendrick decided that it was time to give the men a reality check. "Gentlemen, I have more than enough power to handle these so-called reapers and not break a sweat. You're used to working with witches that are under five hundred years old. Storm Keep will only allow young witches to serve in the units outside of Storm Keep. Once they hit five hundred years old, they have to return to the city where they continue their studies and are assessed. If they are deemed too weak to serve the city as a witch, they can resume their positions amongst the units; however, most do fairly well and go on to master their chosen field of magic."

Aiden stood, his face a mask of anger. "Why? Why are we struggling and losing good men when Storm Keep could turn the tide easily by sending out older witches?"

Kendrick shrugged lazily. "Why doesn't Noctem Falls send out their older vampires, those capable of mind control and illusions? Why doesn't Éire Danu let warriors use their portals? No, race is willing to give up their best and brightest; nor are they willing to share valuable secrets. These terms were agreed to when the pillar cities were formed and the units created. Besides, I don't think it's a simple case of throwing magic at something. Even if you had the power of the older witches at your command, it wouldn't do you much good. Most of them specialize in only one form of magic. I know men who have dedicated centuries to perfecting a single spell. You might get one or two spells out of them, and then they would be cannon fodder. You're actually better off with younger witches who can take orders and cast multiple types of spells repeatedly."

Aiden sat back down his brows pulled together. "What about you? I doubt you would end up cannon fodder."

Behind Aiden, Ryuu began to chuckle. "*Heika* is an exception to the general rule when it comes to the witches."

"So we kinda lucked out that he's Keelan's brother?" Meryn asked.

Kendrick smiled at her. "Pretty much."

Aiden scowled up at the squire. "Any other words of wisdom?"

Ryuu nodded. "You remember the old saying about these types of tricky situations?"

"Follow the money?" Meryn quipped.

Ryuu shook his head. "No. Keep your friends close, but your enemies closer."

"I don't want to be closer to that douchebag," Meryn complained.

Kendrick snapped his fingers. "Meryn, you've given me a great idea."

"You're going to follow the money?" she asked.

"No, but if I can get ahold of enough necklaces, I may be able to trace the magic back to the caster. It all depends on how they were created."

"What do you mean?" Anne asked.

Kendrick wondered how he could explain higher magic in terms they would understand. "For everyday magic, the caster relies on his own power; it's like a well stored inside of them. But for higher, more complicated magic, a caster has two options: gain the power of a higher being or offer the universe something in exchange for what you are asking."

Anne's eyes lit up. "I know what you're talking about!"

Kendrick stared at her in shock. "You do?"

She nodded. "I saw this in *Fullmetal Alchemist*. I think it goes something like, 'Humankind cannot obtain anything without first giving up something in return. To obtain or create something, something of equal value must be lost; that is alchemy's First Law Of Equivalent Exchange.' In the show, two brothers try to resurrect their dead mother, but the price was too great. Just making the attempt cost one brother an arm and a leg and the other his entire body. His soul had to be attached to a suit of armor."

Kendrick fumed. "Between video games and anime, any teenager can learn the sacred arts; it isn't right."

"What video game? If it teaches magic, I'm so in." Meryn declared.

"It's an RPG; I can show you later," Anne promised.

Aiden, looking a bit pale, turned to Kendrick. "It's just a game right? They can't really learn magic, can they?"

Kendrick growled and thumped his fingers on the table. "I have no idea. Then again, I didn't know they were teaching the masses alchemy via anime either. Knowledge gained with no effort is like handing a child a loaded weapon."

Gavriel cleared his throat. "Your idea? I believe you were going to explain how you could discover the identity of the necklace creator."

Kendrick shook his head. He would have Anne show him this anime about alchemy later. "Right, my idea. So basically, exactly what Anne said. If the person who created the necklaces could not contract help with a higher being, then they would be subject to the laws of equal exchange. If that's the case, I can easily trace it back to the spell caster."

"How?" Elizabeth asked.

"Oh! Because the caster would have had to offer up something of equal value, something they themselves owned. I bet it was their own soul," Anne suggested.

Kendrick stared down at her in amazement. "Are you sure you're human? So far, you have understood every aspect of magic I have discussed."

Anne nodded. "Of course I am, but I have always loved reading books about fantasy, playing RPGs, and watching anime." She smiled up at him.

"That is so cool! You know way more than I do about this stuff, and I've been living here for months. I bet you like *Doctor Who*, too." Meryn grinned.

Anne shook her head. "Sorry, no."

Meryn's smile disappeared.

Elizabeth chuckled. "It was bound to happen sooner or later."

"Wait!" Meryn stood. "You mean you don't watch *Doctor Who*? Like, at all?"

Anne shook her head again. "Nope."

"Does not compute! Does not compute!" Meryn waved her hands in the air.

"*Denka,* calm down. We need to start your meditation lessons sooner than I anticipated." Ryuu clucked as he gently pushed her back down into her chair.

Meryn took a deep breath and turned her gaze back to Anne. "You have to be in-Doctor-nated. Clear your schedule. Besides taking care of Keelan, you will be learning about the Doctor."

Anne crossed her arms over her chest. "Fine, only if you agree to watch my favorite anime shows with me."

Meryn nodded. "Deal."

Anne nodded. "Deal."

Colton shuddered. "Why do I feel like I just watched an unholy union?"

Rheia bumped shoulders with him. "Goof! I'd like to watch some of the anime shows, too."

Elizabeth looked at Amelia who nodded. "Count us in, too."

Anne's smile lit up her whole face. "I've never had anyone else interested enough to watch with me before, just Keelan and Kendrick."

Colton looked at Kendrick. "Really?"

Kendrick grinned at him. "It had a great story. You should watch the one Anne introduced me to earlier."

Anne giggled.

Colton smiled at his mate. "Why not? I watch *Digimon* with Penny, and that's not too bad."

"You'll love it," Kendrick promised wickedly.

"If most of the serious discussions have concluded, I need to finish preparing dinner." Ryuu looked at his watch.

Aiden stood, rubbing his stomach. "Food sounds like an excellent idea. After a day like today, I'm looking forward to dinner."

"By the way Aiden, how did your father take the news about the Committee?" Elizabeth asked.

Aiden shook his head. "Mother will probably be making him his favorite Honey Bun cake for weeks." Aiden looked down at Meryn. "I wish you would learn how to make that cake; it is perfect for stressful days."

Meryn looked up at him confused. "You don't want blow jobs anymore?"

Aiden turned bright red. "Meryn!"

"What? Cake or blowjobs? You're not getting both," Meryn insisted.

Around the table the men turned their faces to hide their laughter.

Aiden got a calculating look on his face. "Let's go upstairs and discuss it."

Meryn giggled and jumped to her feet. Aiden swept her up and dashed from the room.

Once the couple was out of sight, everyone gave up on being dignified and laughed.

"He needed that levity; I've never seen Aiden so stressed," Elizabeth commented as everyone stood to leave the room.

"What Aiden forgot to mention is that the Committee will be stopping by sometime tomorrow to meet with you ladies. I am sure he is upstairs laying ground rules with Meryn now. Be prepared," Gavriel advised them.

Anne looked nervous. "Does that include me?"

Darian smiled at her in sympathy. "I'm afraid so. However, since you haven't been here long, they probably won't ask you any questions besides your name."

"Gods above, give me strength to help Meryn tomorrow," Elizabeth murmured in prayer.

"So mote it be," the men echoed together.

Kendrick had a feeling it would take every God listening to keep that spitfire under control. Smiling, he escorted Anne back upstairs to check on Keelan. He knew no matter what, Meryn was going to be Meryn. Without a doubt, he would be sitting in on those introductions with the Committee; he wouldn't miss it for the world.

CHAPTER SIX

Later that evening, after dinner, Anne found herself back in Keelan's room with Kendrick. Throughout the day, Kendrick had been attentive and supportive. He hadn't judged her for watching anime and even began watching it along with her, despite it being a boy's love series.

She peeked out at him from behind her iPad. She had tried to dive into a new book, but found that, for once, reality was better than fiction. Every time she started a sentence, her mind wandered back to Kendrick. Every time they touched, she could feel a jolt of raw need race through her body. When she had been scared at the thought of killer zombies, he comforted her. His arm had been warm, and the second he pulled her close, she realized she had never felt safer in her life.

But Keelan was her mate, wasn't he? She shook her head. He had to be; he had told his family that she was.

"Kendrick?"

"Hmmm?" Kendrick's eyes stayed glued to the massive book he had been reading earlier.

"Has anyone ever made a mistake claiming their mate?" she asked.

He closed the heavy tome and turned in his chair to face her. "There have been a few documented cases, mostly amongst witches, where a mistake was made. Why?"

"Why witches? Why not the others?"

"Because witches are the only race that finds its mates by having dreams; we rely on sight alone. Vampires and shifters can smell their mates, although with vampires, it's their mate's blood they scent, not their bodies. The fae can see the aura of their mates, but witches have only their dreams," he explained.

"But Colton said that he had dreamt of Rheia, and he's a shifter, right?"

Kendrick set the book down on the long table in front of him. "Sometime last year, the matriarchs of Lycaonia went to Elder Airgead with concerns that their sons' mates were out in the world and dying. So, the elder cast a spell that would bring their mates to them. Aiden was the first to dream of his mate, which was Meryn."

"All of the warriors are dreaming of their mates, even if they aren't witches?"

He nodded. "I believe that, since it was a witch who cast the spell, it influenced how the men would find their mates."

"And the women dreamt too?" Anne hugged her iPad to her chest.

Kendrick looked at her with a serious expression. "So I've been told. Why? Did you have dreams as well?"

Anne looked away. "Yes."

"Dreams are tricky. People usually remember what they see but not how they felt, and that can change the dream dramatically. Personally, I think they are the worst way to find one's mate, but who am I to judge?"

She heard him turn, and when she looked back, he had picked up his book again and was reading. Wasn't he going to ask her who she had dreamt of? Did he not ask because he knew she was Keelan's? This was so confusing!

She stood. "Keelan is all set for the night, I think I'll turn in. It's been the longest day of my life."

Kendrick stood, which made her smile. All of the men had courtly manners; the simple gesture made her feel special.

"Despite the outrageous changes in your life, I have to say you handled yourself with grace and intelligence. I know of much older individuals who would have broken down today, yet you came through the day shining brightly."

Anne felt her cheeks begin to burn. "I did faint when they first told me about Keelan."

Kendrick inclined his head. "As any normal person would do after finding out the dire circumstances of someone they care about."

Anne felt her eyes fill at his praise. "I don't think I could have done so well without you. Thank you, Kendrick."

"You are most welcome. Sweet dreams, Anne." Kendrick gave a slight bow.

Unsure whether she should curtsey in response, she did the next best thing. " 'Night," she mumbled and ran from the room.

She didn't stop running until she was leaning against the closed door to her own guest room. Drat that man for affecting her so much.

Mindlessly, she changed out of her clothes and into a sleep shirt. A quick trip to the bathroom left her with a clean face and freshly brushed teeth. She pulled back the covers and slid between icy sheets.

I bet Kendrick could warm these for me.

I mean with magic! Ahhh! Stupid hormones!

Anne pulled the covers over her head.

I wish I knew what to do!

Slowly her own body heat began to warm the bed and she drifted off to sleep.

"Hurry up! Kendrick and the boys are waiting!" Keelan pulled her hand as they ran through the woods.

"Keelan, slow down!" Anne laughed. Keelan looked back at her, his usual smile shining brightly.

"I'm sorry for the confusion, it's my fault." Keelan navigated them through branches and low hanging limbs.

She was about to ask him what he was talking about when they ran out into a clearing. In front of them, a large picnic was laid out in the afternoon sun. Kendrick was laughing and wrestling with three auburn haired little boys who looked to be about three.

"Come on." Keelan tugged at her hand, but she couldn't move forward.

She knew without a shadow of doubt that the boys were hers. Tears filled her eyes; the children were so beautiful.

A cloud moved overhead, casting a long shadow. She looked at Kendrick then at Keelan. Who was the father of her sons? She looked back at Kendrick. He was sitting up, watching the boys as they started eating their lunches. He was waiting patiently, a gentle smile on his face.

"Who is my mate?" she whispered.

Keelan leaned in and kissed her on the forehead. "Ask Darian."

She turned to ask him what he meant, but the dream began to fade. She screamed, reaching for the boys to protect them from the darkness.

"Anne!" She heard Kendrick calling out to her.

She opened her eyes and sat up, gasping for air.

"Anne! Are you okay?" Kendrick sat at the edge of her bed, a worried look on his face.

Remembering the happy dream with Keelan and her sons made the darkness of reality that much harder to face. She buried her face in her hands and wept. There was no happy family for her. Keelan still lay in a coma in the next room, and the boys' laughter was a fading memory.

Warm arms enveloped her in a tight embrace. She held on to Kendrick's solid frame and laid her head against his chest. She let the rhythmic thudding of his heartbeat soothe her. For the first time since her parents had passed away, she didn't feel like she was all alone. Everyday in school, she had passed by people, never receiving more than a second glance or a nod as they walked by. At the hospital where she had trained, the only physical contact she had was when she reached out to help a patient. Did he know how intoxicating the very warmth of his skin was to her?

After a few minutes, he broke the silence. "Do you want to talk about it?"

She sniffled. "How did you know I was dreaming?"

"I heard you call out."

"Oh, no! Do you think I woke anyone?" She didn't think she could face anyone else if they came to see if she was okay.

She felt him shake his head. "I don't think so. The only reason I heard you was because I had just awakened from a dream myself and was reading."

"What did you dream?"

"It was a warm dream. It was bittersweet because it was wonderful but had to end."

"It was almost like because it was so wonderful the act of waking made it a nightmare," she whispered.

He pulled back and cupped her face with both hands. "Did you see Keelan?"

She nodded.

He dropped his hands to rest on either side of her body. "I did as well. He looked healthy and happy. He was smiling."

"It was like the sun was shining because he was smiling." She felt the dream starting to slip away.

"Did he say anything to you?"

She nodded again. "He told me to 'ask Darian'."

Kendrick frowned. "Ask him about what?"

Anne stared down at the bedding. "I asked Keelan about matings; that's when he told me to ask Darian."

Kendrick put a finger under her chin and gently tilted her head up. "This is important. Did he say anything else?"

"That all the confusion was his fault."

Kendrick leaned forward and kissed her on the forehead exactly as Keelan had. "Get some rest, I'll speak with Darian in the morning."

Anne was too afraid to ask him about the children; she nodded and lay back down. "Keelan? He's out there somewhere, isn't he?"

Kendrick's expression was sad as he nodded. "Yes, but don't worry. I'll find him, I swear it." He stood and quietly left the room, leaving her with more questions and mixed emotions. Did she want it to be Kendrick because he was here and able to comfort her?

"Dammit it all!" she muttered, turning on her side. She hugged a pillow close and closed her eyes. When she slept this time, there were no dreams to haunt her.

Anne lingered in the hallway upstairs. She heard the other couples walk by on their way downstairs and had waited until they had gone before she left her room to wait by Kendrick's door. She didn't feel quite like an outsider; it was more like she and Kendrick were a team, and it felt wrong to go downstairs without him.

When Kendrick opened the door and stepped into the hall, she felt a wave of relief. He saw her expression and frowned. "Were you waiting for me?"

"Yeah."

"Kendrick!" a male voice called.

They turned to see a blond young man jogging toward them with a package in his hands.

"Yes?" Kendrick asked, stepping forward.

"My name is Noah Caraway. I work with Meryn. This package just arrived for you from a vampire courier." Noah held out a small box wrapped in brown paper.

"Thank you, Noah."

"No problem. Well, I better get back to work. Meryn will be finished with breakfast soon, and she'll want to look over my coding." Noah crossed his eyes and made a face.

Anne laughed. "Good luck."

"Thanks!" He waved and ran back the way he came.

Anne looked down at the package. "What do you think it is?"

"Only one way to find out." He held his door open, and they walked inside. Kendrick immediately went to his table. Carefully, he cut the twine that held the wrapping in place. When he opened the box, his eyebrows shot up. "I must have done something right." He reached into the box and pulled out six black necklaces. The faint stench of death made Anne take a step back.

Eager and smiling like a child, Kendrick began placing the necklaces onto individual stone crystal plates. As each necklace touched the respective plates, it began to glow in different colors.

Kendrick stood back, a satisfied look on his face. "We should get preliminary results by tomorrow."

They walked back out into the hallway and Kendrick closed the door behind them. He whispered a spell then turned to Anne. "Place your hand on the doorknob."

She reached forward and grasped the metal knob. "What am I doing?"

"These necklaces are probably the most important things in the city. If I had a separate room for study I would lock them in there. Since they are in the same room as my unconscious little brother, I'm not taking any chances. I've bespelled the door so that only you and I can enter."

"What would happen if someone other than you or I tried to enter the room?" she asked curiously.

He gave her a wolfish grin. "It would not be pleasant."

He straightened beside her and offered her his arm. She blinked at his elbow and looked up at him. Smiling, he reached down, took her hand, and placed it on his arm.

"It would be an honor to escort you downstairs." He turned and walked them down the stairs and into the dining room. When they walked in, the other men stood, and Kendrick pulled her chair out for her. She smiled at him and sat down. The men took their seats, and Ryuu began going around the table with his serving cart handing out cups of coffee.

"Ryuu! Come back here and let me sniff Kendrick's drink some more," Meryn pleaded.

Ryuu sighed and looked at his charge. "Why torture yourself?"

Meryn dropped her head to the table. "I want coffee." She sounded so pitiful, Anne thought for a moment Ryuu would relent; instead, he reached down to the second shelf of the cart and pulled out a small bowl of coffee beans. He walked over and set this in front of Meryn "You can smell these to your heart's content."

Meryn scowled at the squire fiercely. Anne realized that the small woman had been planning to sneak sips all along.

Ryuu rounded the table and passed Kendrick a cup that smelled faintly of chocolate before turning to her. "I wasn't sure what would be to your taste, so I waited to see what you might like this morning."

Anne turned to Kendrick. "May I try some?"

He nodded and carefully handed her his hot cup. She blew on the liquid and took a tentative sip. The mixture of chocolate and coffee was perfect.

"Oh my goodness."

When she went to hand the cup back to Kendrick, he smiled and shook his head. "You keep that one. Ryuu, one more please."

Ryuu bowed. "Of course."

Kendrick raised a hand. "Ryuu, before you go, since everyone is here, I have a small announcement. I received the necklaces from the council this morning for testing. To keep them and my brother safe, I've placed a warding spell on the door, if anyone other than myself or Anne tries to enter the room, they will be severely injured."

"Understood." Ryuu said and went into the kitchen.

Rheia stood. "I'll let Penny, Noah, Jaxon, and Mina know." She hurried out of the dining room.

Colton scowled. "Do you really think something so dangerous is necessary in the house?"

"I wouldn't have done it if I didn't." Kendrick said casually as he eyed the pastries in the basket at the center of the table.

Darian slumped back in his chair. "First Keelan, then the Committee, now we're reduced to warding spells in our own home. What have our lives come to?"

Colton cut his roll in half and smeared a layer of thick jam on each side. "At least we have the perimeter. No matter who cast it, it's keeping those damn ferals out of the city."

Rheia came back in and sat down next to her mate. She eyed his gooey roll and shuddered. He had lathered it on so thick, it was almost as if he was eating jam with a bit of roll.

Ryuu reentered the room carrying a cup of steaming coffee. He placed it beside Kendrick and went to Meryn. "*Denka*, you have to eat something." The squire had a worried look on his face.

"Not hungry," Meryn muttered, her face still on the table.

Everyone stopped what they were doing to stare at Meryn. Anne wondered why that was so surprising.

Aiden turned in his chair and scooped Meryn into his lap. "What's wrong, baby? You've been eating three breakfasts lately; why aren't you hungry?"

Meryn didn't answer, she just turned her head into his chest. "I'm tired."

Aiden looked at Ryuu and Ryuu nodded. "*Denka*, how about a very small cup of coffee, with chocolate in it. Just like what *Heika* is drinking."

Meryn turned her head slowly to look up at her squire and nodded. "Please."

At first, Anne thought Meryn was just playing to get some coffee, but the worried expressions on the faces around the table told her that this was a severe deviation from Meryn's normal behavior.

In less time than it took him to make Kendrick's drink, Ryuu returned with a cup for Meryn. Anne thought that she would gulp down the sweet beverage, but when Meryn only took a single sip and set the cup down, she knew that this was serious.

Ryuu took Meryn's wrist between his fingers and closed his eyes. When they opened, he turned to Kendrick. "*Heika,* could you please?"

Kendrick stood immediately and hurried around the table. He eyed the blue tattoo and raised a brow at Ryuu, who shrugged. Turning his attention back to Meryn, he gently held her hand between both of his.

Anne found herself holding her breath as she waited to see what Kendrick would find. When his eyes popped open, she almost fell out of her chair. She was surprised at how quickly she had come to care for the odd woman.

Kendrick's astonished expression turned to Amelia and then back to Meryn. "Extraordinary."

"What?" Aiden growled.

Kendrick smiled. "Fate is a mischievous female. I am constantly amazed by her woven designs." He began to whisper, and when he was done, he placed Meryn's hand back in her lap.

She blinked and looked around the table. "I feel much better." Before anyone could tell her not to, she snatched up the mocha and began to down it's contents. When she was done, she exhaled loudly and set the cup back on the table. "That was fucking awesome!"

Kendrick watched Meryn, a bemused expression on his face. Beside him, Ryuu sighed. Kendrick clapped him on the back. "She deserved a little pick-me-up."

Meryn wiggled until Aiden set her back in her chair. "I think that coffee made me hungry." She turned and looked up at Ryuu. "Do we have any pancakes? And bacon? And hash browns?"

Ryuu's smile was indulgent. "That's what you requested for breakfast yesterday."

Meryn smiled. "Does that mean I can't have it again today?"

Ryuu shook his head. "You can have whatever you want. It's a good thing I froze the leftover pancakes yesterday." He bowed to Kendrick and headed into the kitchen.

Kendrick patted Meryn on the head as if she were a puppy and walked back to his chair.

"Wait a damn minute. What happened there?" Aiden demanded.

Kendrick sipped his coffee. "What do you mean?"

"What I mean is what was wrong with my mate?" Aiden growled.

"I'm not quite sure, but I have an idea."

"An idea? Care to share?"

"No."

"No! What do you mean, no?" Aiden glared at Kendrick from across the table.

Anne had had enough. Kendrick didn't deserve any of this. She stood and slammed both hands down on the table. "That's enough!"

Aiden sat back his eyes wide. "I didn't mean to upset you, but I have to know what happened to my mate."

"Then you should ask politely like a normal person!" She crossed her arms over her chest. "I've known Kendrick just as long as the rest of you. Magic abilities not withstanding, I know that he isn't the type of person who would withhold information to hurt someone. If he says he doesn't know, that means he needs to look into it further before he makes a diagnosis. If he announces it's one thing and it turns out to be another you'd blame him for that, too.

"I know I'm the new kid around here, but the unwarranted hostility you have shown him is obvious. For Keelan's sake, I'll only say this once: Stow your shit!" Anne was breathing heavily, and her emotions were spiraling out of control. She hated it that, every time she got upset about something, she cried. People always assumed it was because she was weak when, in truth, she was trying really hard not to kill people.

Rheia stood. "She's absolutely right. I was going to let Kendrick's actions dictate my own, but you all are upsetting Anne, and she has enough to deal with right now. I see this type of behavior all the time as a doctor. People expect us to have all the answers; sometimes, we don't. Sometimes, it's better not to say anything at all without having all the facts. I know you men miss Keelan; I do, too. Nevertheless, that is no excuse to treat his brother so poorly."

Elizabeth rose to her feet elegantly. "We are a family, every single one of us in the house. Look at Anne and Amelia." The men looked at Anne who was still fighting back tears and to Amelia whose face buried in Darian's chest. "We have enough challenges from those outside this house attacking us; we don't need conflict in the house as well."

Meryn reached for a roll. "He's not Keelan," she declared. "He looks like Keelan, but he isn't him. I know that each one of you feel like shit because you think you should have been able to save Keelan, but don't take that out on Kendrick. He hasn't blamed us once, and he has every right to."

Anne looked around the table and met the eyes of the other women. She'd never had close friends before, and their support and gentle smiles were her undoing. She covered her face with her hands and started to bawl like a baby.

She felt Kendrick move beside her, and before she knew it, she was safe in his arms. "Shush now. Us poor men have our marching orders; cut us some slack okay?" He rubbed her back.

She sniffed and opened her eyes. "I'm sorry!"

Aiden stood, a concerned look on his face. "You have no reason to be sorry, Anne. I'm the one who should apologize. Thank you for having the courage to stand up for Kendrick." Aiden turned to the rest of the men. "They're right, all of our ladies. I do feel guilty. I think I kept expecting Kendrick to lash out, so I was always on the defensive." He looked straight at Kendrick. "I am sorry."

Kendrick shook his head. "I'm pretty thick skinned, Aiden. It will take more than your baby bear growls to shake me."

Aiden looked down at the table. "No. I'm sorry I couldn't save him. He was my responsibility, and I failed him."

Colton and Gavriel stood quickly. "It was not your fault. We are the ones who had to drag you out of that building; we are the ones who abandoned him." Gavriel's face was a mask of pain.

Darian turned his head away from Kendrick to stare at the floor. "I was the one who walked away. He was right in front of me, and I left him there."

Under her hands, Anne could feel the effect the men's words were having on Kendrick. His entire body tensed and his breathing became more rapid in what seemed to be an effort to stay in control. She did the only thing she could in that moment. She wrapped her arms around him and held him close.

Kendrick drew a shuddering breath. "Thank you." Everyone turned and stared at him. Anne looked up and was shocked to see a steady stream of tears coursing down his cheeks. "Thank you," he repeated. He looked up and the men flinched at the stark grief on his face. "Thank you for loving my brother as if he were your own flesh and blood. If I had any doubts about your loyalties, they have been washed away by your confessions. If anyone is to blame, it is I. I knew over two hundred years ago he would die as a member of the Alpha Unit.

"I could have done so many things to turn him from the path he chose, but to do so would have crushed Keelan's kindness. I would have turned him into something he would have hated. So, I let him live his own life knowing what would happen. I was so confident in my own power, I was sure I could see any impending doom and swoop in and save the day." He gave a hollow laugh. "I guess I wasn't as all-seeing and powerful as I thought I was, and my brother paid the price."

Anne shook her head. "I don't know what happened to him, but I like to think I know Keelan pretty well." She looked around the table. "His face would light up when he spoke of you all. He called you his brothers, and I don't think he could have been more proud to call you family. If he made the decision to protect you, then that is exactly what he wanted, because if any of you had been hurt–or worse, killed–and he lived knowing he could have saved you, it would have destroyed him." She turned to look at Kendrick. "The way he described you, I was half expecting you to have a cape. There was no one he looked up to more."

Beside them, Amelia wiped her face. "It's true, *Athair*. He told me that he fully intended to call you and my brothers if things got too dangerous. I think everything happened so fast, there wasn't time."

Gavriel wrapped an arm around his mate, and she slumped against him. "So what do we do now?"

She felt Kendrick straighten. "We're going to listen to a very wise little girl and be happy."

Anne watched as slow smiles began to appear around the table. Everyone sat down and kept smiling. Anne reached under the table and took Kendrick's hand. He didn't change expression or give any outward indication that he noticed her gesture, yet his long, warm fingers squeezed her hand and didn't let go.

Anne took a deep breath and looked around. She realized everyone needed this to begin moving past their own guilt.

As she was looking around, she caught Meryn's eye and Meryn winked. "You're officially family now; you've cussed at the breakfast table."

Anne made a face and Meryn laughed in response.

"Then you were officially family in the first thirty seconds after you sat at the breakfast table for the first time. I distinctly remember you threatening to castrate Colton." Gavriel teased.

Colton groaned. "Don't remind me."

Anne kept her left hand wrapped around Kendrick's and picked up her coffee with her right. For the first time in a very long time, she felt like she had a family again, cussing, jokes, and all.

CHAPTER SEVEN

After breakfast, everyone lingered over coffee. Anne suspected that no one wanted to leave each other's company just yet.

Meryn was tackling her second stack of pancakes when she turned to Kendrick. "By the way, Keelan-From-the-Future, you keep showing up wearing different clothes, but you didn't have any luggage. You've set up a lab, but didn't have anything delivered, how did you get all your stuff?"

Kendrick smiled and detached a small pouch from his belt. He held it up swinging from his fingers. "It's bigger on the inside."

Meryn dropped her fork and stared. "Can I see?"

Kendrick nodded, and Meryn ran around the table. He set the pouch in her hands and watched as she opened it.

A look a disappointment bloomed on her face. "It's empty."

Kendrick winked and cupped his hands around hers and whispered a word.

Meryn's eyes widened. "Holy shit balls! It's like a whole castle in here. Wait! Go back! Was that a library?"

Kendrick nodded. "It's called the Bag of Wishes. I can place anything I want inside, regardless of shape, size, or weight."

Meryn looked at his clothes. "So you have a closet in here too?"

He shook his head. "No, these" he plucked at his blazer, "are the Gentlemen's Garments. I received them as a present from the queen of the fae."

She smiled. "Like my dress."

Kendrick tilted his head. "You're the new owner of the Gown of Éire Danu?"

She bopped her head yes and kept tilting the pouch side to side.

"Interesting," he murmured.

Elizabeth snorted. "You have no idea."

Meryn placed the bag in his hands and turned to Aiden. "I want one."

Aiden's mouth dropped. "Baby, I can't just go out and buy you one. Enchanted fae items are extremely rare."

Meryn walked back to her chair and sat down. "I need it in my life."

Aiden turned to Darian who was chuckling. Darian nodded at Aiden. "I'll see what I can do."

Meryn smiled brightly at Darian. "Thank you big brother-cousin."

Darian looked around the table. "We never really stood a chance, did we?"

The men all shook their heads. Kendrick laughed. "Never has a truer statement been spoken. Women always have the upper hand, always."

Meryn pumped her fist in the air. "Because we kick ass!"

Kendrick smiled slyly. "It's because you have the magic bean."

Meryn frowned as Aiden choked on his coffee. "What magic bean?"

Elizabeth blushed. "Oh, dear."

Anne had to suppress a giggle.

"I only know of two magic beans: the cocoa bean and the coffee bean," Meryn insisted.

Kendrick clucked his tongue. "Commander, you have been remiss in your duties."

Around the table, the other men were trying not to laugh and failing horribly.

Finally, Gavriel took pity on the confused Meryn and leaned in to whisper what the third magic bean was. Meryn's reaction caught Anne by surprise when she erupted into giggles.

"Ha, ha, ha, magic bean! Hey baby, want to swallow my magic bean later?" Meryn leered up at her mate.

Aiden smirked and shook his head before leaning down to nip Meryn on the neck. "Only if you're very, very good," he promised.

Meryn reached over her head and traced a halo before folding her hands in front of her as if in prayer. "I'm always good."

Colton chuckled. "Hey Meryn, did you have to get a custom-made halo to fit between those devil horns?" he teased.

Anne lifted her hand and tapped her lips. "What do you think Meryn? We could sew his lips shut in his sleep."

Meryn's eyes brightened, and she turned to Rheia. "You don't need to kiss him for a while do you?"

Rheia shrugged. "I could go without."

Colton's mouth dropped as he cuddled his mate. "Darlin', you wouldn't let them do that to me, would you?"

Rheia just winked at Meryn and Anne.

Meryn leaned back in her chair. "Face it gentlemen, you're no longer the baddest motherfuckers in the room anymore."

Aiden kissed the side of Meryn's head. "Don't let the other warriors find out."

Anne smiled. "Don't worry, your secret is safe with us," she promised, and the other women laughed. Anne finally felt like she belonged in this house with these people.

Kendrick cleared his throat. "Not to put a damper on things but..."

Colton smiled ruefully. "But we still have some pretty serious allegations against us."

Kendrick set his empty cup down. "Thanks to Anne's suggestion, I may have a plan for that. But that wasn't what I was talking about. I was talking about the perimeter."

Aiden blinked. "But the perimeter is the one good thing that came from this whole mess. The ferals haven't been able to breach it since it went up; we're safe."

Kendrick twisted the cup in his hands. "Maybe I'm being pessimistic, but when something looks too good to be true, it usually is."

Amelia turned to him. "How can the perimeter be a bad thing?"

Kendrick stopped turning the cup. "What if the perimeter wasn't designed to keep you safe by keeping the ferals out. What if it was designed to keep the ferals out to keep *them* safe?"

Aiden frowned. "I don't like where this is going."

Kendrick looked at the men. "Over the centuries, I've seen many different types of magic, but I've never seen anything like this perimeter. No one in the city is stepping forward to lay claim to it, and if any of the warriors had done it, they would have told you right away. So, if no one in the city cast the spell, who did?"

Colton swallowed, looking ill. "The enemy."

Kendrick nodded. "What if the perimeter is keeping the ferals out because when the perimeter goes down it will shrink into the center of the city, stripping people's souls as the magic collapses? If ferals are in the city when that happens, their precious necklaces could be destroyed."

Aiden thumped his fingers on the table. "Do you have any proof?"

Kendrick shook his head. "No, but I thought it would be irresponsible if I didn't put the theory forward. You're included in more high-level meetings than I am. If you hear something that may explain a portion of my theory, at least you could make the connection."

Aiden stood and stretched his arms up over his head. "I'll keep an ear out. In the meantime, we have drills, gentlemen."

Kendrick stood beside her. "I may join you."

Aiden looked pleased. "I thought you didn't do drills."

"I don't, but I need to speak to a few of your men."

Aiden laughed. "I'll get you on the course eventually."

Amelia shook her head vehemently. "You really don't want that, Aiden."

Aiden's brows snapped together. "Why?"

Amelia squirmed in her chair. "Do you remember that time Caiden had to request that the council approve renovations to the Storm Keep obstacle course?"

Aiden nodded. "He said that the men had gotten used to the..." he looked over at Kendrick.

Kendrick smirked back at the commander.

Aiden turned toward the door. "Never mind. Come on men." He leaned down, kissed Meryn on the top of her head, and walked toward the door.

Anne watched as the other men around the table said goodbye to their mates. Kendrick stood and looked down at her. "When you check on Keelan, stay away from the table. If you see anything glowing bright red, evacuate the house and come get me."

"I heard that!" Aiden yelled from the foyer.

Kendrick winked at her then turned to Meryn. "Tell your little friend that he has access to Keelan's room. The warding doesn't apply to sprites."

Meryn reached up and laid a hand on her shoulder. "Thanks Kendrick. Felix has been spending a lot of time with Keelan."

Anne looked at Meryn but didn't see anything. "Sprite?"

One second there was nothing, the next, a tiny fairy sat on Meryn's shoulder, fluttering his wings. He waved and she waved back. When she blinked, he was gone again.

She turned to Kendrick. He leaned down, and their eyes met. She was surprised at their intensity. She thought he was about to kiss her, but at the last moment, he moved his head so that he whispered in her ear, "Thank you for sticking up for me. No one has done such a thing in a very long time. I'll give you a treat later. Have fun with the girls." He ruffled her hair and walked out behind Darian.

Once the men were gone, the room was silent. Meryn gulped down the last of her orange juice. "So, I don't feel like adulting today. Let's watch anime and eat snacks."

Rheia, Elizabeth, and Amelia looked at each other and grinned.

Amelia nodded. "That sounds like a great idea." She turned and looked at Anne. "In this you'll be our Yoda."

Anne frowned. "He was the green one right?"

Across the table, Meryn began making sounds as if she was having an epileptic fit.

Amelia wrapped an arm around her. "Ignore her. Beth usually handles Meryn when she's like this. Let's hit the kitchen and get some post-breakfast snack foods."

Anne looked over her shoulder to cast a worried glance at Meryn. She figured if Rheia wasn't concerned, she wouldn't be either. Maybe she was getting used to the dynamics of this house.

"Why am I here again?" the dark haired young man asked. After checking on Keelan, Anne was formally introduced to Jaxon and Noah when the women invaded command central to take over the sixty-five inch television.

"Because I'd miss you if you weren't here," Meryn answered.

"You do realize this isn't in English right?" Jaxon asked.

"Yup, now hush. I think Tezuka is about to confess to Yuri." Meryn threw popcorn at Jaxon who laughed.

Noah sat on the couch with his legs drawn up, a look of enthrallment on his face. He had been immediately sucked into the story line and had teared up a time or two already at Yuri's plight. Anne had to admit, Noah had to be the prettiest boy she had ever met. If he was drawn to be in an anime, he would be a *bishōnen*, or beautiful boy.

Anne had already watched nearly half of this season with Kendrick so her attention was solely on the tiny sprite who had made himself visible after some coaxing from Meryn. He now sat on Anne's shoulder, watching the anime along with them. Anne thought Felix was absolutely adorable. When he saw that her hands were shaking as she went to hold him, he smiled up at her shyly, and she was lost.

Meryn laughed and kept tapping away on her phone. Anne had no clue how Meryn was keeping up with the subtitles while on her phone, but every comment she made about the story had been right, so she must be paying more attention than Anne realized.

Rheia pointed to the screen. "What are those?"

Anne looked up and smiled. "Those are *takoyaki*. They are round, made from a flour-based batter filled with minced octopus, pickled ginger, green onions and sometimes tempura scraps. The *takoyaki* dressing is to die for; it's like a mix between Worcestershire sauce and mayo. I haven't had any since moving back to Madison."

"Ryuu!" The women yelled at the same time Meryn paused the anime.

A moment later, Ryuu appeared in the doorway. "*Denka*? Is everything okay?"

Meryn turned around on her knees to peer over the back of the sofa. "Can you make those?" She pointed behind her at the screen.

Ryuu looked up and a look of pleasant surprise crossed his face. "Of course."

"Oh, and ramen?" Rheia asked licking her lips.

"I would love to try the *yakisoba*." Amelia rubbed her stomach.

Ryuu's mouth twitched in a smile. "How about I plan a night where you can try multiple dishes from my homeland?"

Meryn threw her fist in the air. "Yes!"

Ryuu bowed. "I have a friend back home I can contact. He should be able to send the necessary supplies via a fae trade portal. Now, if you ladies will excuse me, I will bring in mid-morning tea in just a moment." He closed the door behind him.

Amelia stared at the closed door for a second. "You know, I bet he gets homesick. Maybe we should have Japanese food once a week."

Meryn turned and sat back down. "That's a great idea. I want to try those octopus balls."

Anne and Amelia cringed. "*Takoyaki*." They both corrected Meryn at the same time.

Meryn shrugged and smiled at her phone. "This is great, I'm getting so many friend requests." She paused and looked at them. "Do octopi have balls?"

Elizabeth shook her head. "Oh, Meryn."

Meryn grinned evilly and turned back to her phone.

Everyone's attention turned back to the anime. After a few minutes, Elizabeth's phone began to ring. She took it out of her pocket, looked down, and frowned. "Uncle? Hello, Uncle. What! No! No. Never mind. Stop laughing! Goodbye!" Elizabeth wheeled on Meryn. "Why did you put that you and I were in a relationship on Facebook? All of Noctem Falls is buzzing that I am in a lesbian relationship with the Unit Commander's mate!"

Meryn looked puzzled. "We are in a relationship, you're my sister."

Elizabeth simply fell over onto her side and buried her face in the pillows. Rheia, Jaxon, and Noah had their hands over their mouths trying not to laugh. Amelia was at Elizabeth's side rubbing her back. "There, there. It can't be that bad."

Elizabeth sat back up. "Take it down now."

Meryn shook her head. "I think it's too late. I have eight hundred and seven comments and three thousand shares."

"Give me that!" Elizabeth snatched Meryn's phone and began to scroll. Her face went pale for a moment and she looked up. "You can*not* refer to your shifter friends as your 'furries'!"

"Man down! Man down!" Jaxon laughed, pointing at Rheia who was wheezing on the floor. Noah was beet-red and having trouble drawing breath.

Amelia swallowed hard and looked like she was fighting not to smile. "She did what?"

Meryn went to get her phone back, but Beth stood and held it over her head. Meryn put her hands on her hips. "Why is that wrong?"

Anne cleared her throat. "Meryn the term 'furry' refers to a subculture that is interested in anthropomorphic animal characters with human personalities. It's also a type of sexual fetish where people take the interest into the bedroom."

Meryn blinked. "So, technically, I'm still right."

"I give up! I'm deleting your account." Elizabeth tapped on Meryn's phone.

Meryn shrugged. "I can always post on Aiden's account."

Amelia sighed. "I always wanted to be a shifter. Becoming an animal must be liberating."

Defeated, Elizabeth paused and handed the phone back to Meryn. "It gets old after a while." She sat down, looking a bit shell-shocked. "Let's resume our anime watching. I don't feel like adulting anymore, either; the rest of the paranormal world can just get along without me today."

"Sounds like I brought tea just in time," Ryuu said as he pushed his serving cart into the room.

Noah paused the anime and turned to them, his eyes bright. "I didn't know they had anime where two boys fall in love."

Elizabeth perked up. "It doesn't hurt that they are so pretty."

Noah blushed and turned to Anne. "Can you recommend some more?"

Anne nodded eagerly. "Of course."

Noah sighed, a dreamy look on his face. "Too bad you don't see that sort of thing in real life."

Jaxon bumped shoulders with his friend. "What about Sydney and Justice?"

Noah thought about it for a moment. "They are the exception."

Meryn looked up at her squire, a mischievous look on her face. "What about Kendrick and Ryuu?"

Rheia spit out the tea she had just sipped. Amelia offered her a towel and looked at Meryn. "You can't keep doing this to Rheia," she said sternly.

Meryn looked over at her friend. "Sorry, Rheia." Instantly, her attention was back to her squire. "So?"

Ryuu didn't bat an eye. He continued to pour their tea. "A man or woman would be very lucky indeed to find themselves with *Heika*."

Meryn rubbed her hands together. "Sounds promising. Kendrick did offer sexual favors for coffee."

Noah was wide-eyed and stared up at the squire. "They would make an amazing couple."

Elizabeth sipped her tea. "You may be on to something, Meryn."

Anne accepted her cup of tea from Ryuu. His eyes met hers, and he winked. Anne turned away, her cheeks on fire. Was it evident to the others how she felt? That the mention of Kendrick with anyone else was enough to make her feel ill? Ryuu laid a hand on her shoulder briefly before turning back to the teacart to resume serving.

She thought of Kendrick and the dream she'd had the night before. Was that the reason why he joined the men today? So he could ask Darian about her dream? She sipped her unsweetened green tea and hoped Kendrick found an answer, one way or another.

Kendrick felt a chill run down his spine. He stopped mid-step and shuddered.

Darian gave him a funny look from where he hung doing inverted sit-ups. "Are you well?"

Kendrick rubbed his arms. "Someone must be talking about me." He walked over to Darian and leaned against the workout station.

"Did I just see you talking to my brother?" Darian asked.

"Yes, I needed to ask a favor of him."

Darian sat up and hopped off the bench. "But that wasn't why you joined us today was it?"

Kendrick glanced back at the house. "No, I need to talk to you about something."

"Of course. What's on your mind?"

"Keelan," Kendrick said shortly.

Darian exhaled slowly. "What can I tell you?"

"Did he say anything about Anne?"

Darian's eyes narrowed. "How do you mean?"

Kendrick looked up at Darian, giving him the full weight of his stare. "Did Keelan say anything about them being mates?"

Darian ran a hand through his hair. "Maybe." He looked around to see if anyone was listening. "Right before he... it happened, Keelan confessed to me that he wasn't attracted to Anne at all."

Kendrick's heart began to pound against his breastbone. "What did you tell him?"

"I asked him if he had tried being attracted to her, he said, yes, of course, but there was nothing between them. He said they got along great, but he was not drawn to her at all."

Kendrick shook his head. "But he dreamt of her." It all came back to this. If Keelan had had a mating dream of Anne, then she wasn't his.

Darian nodded. "And a good thing he did, too; otherwise, she might be dead."

Kendrick grabbed Darian's upper arms and shook him. "What do you mean?"

Darian took a step back to dislodge himself from Kendrick's grasp. "Calm down; she's unharmed. Keelan dreamt that there was something wrong with her car and she died when it went off the road and slammed into a tree. When she took the car in at his insistence, they found that there was something wrong with her brakes."

Kendrick stared at the large fae. "Gods!" he whispered harshly. "It wasn't mating dreams at all; he was having premonitions to keep her safe."

Darian blinked, then blinked again. "You know, I think you may be right. The dream he had about her car wasn't the first premonition that he had about Anne."

"He had dreamt of her before?"

Darian nodded. "Though I don't think he remembered. The only reason I remembered is because of what Anne told us when we met her. She recalled the first time she met Aiden. He saved her from being kidnapped, but we wouldn't have been in town that day if not for Keelan's insistence that we had to be there." Darian frowned. "But why Anne? Why was Keelan getting so many premonitions about Anne if she wasn't his mate."

Darian's question had Kendrick reeling, because the answer was too unfair to be true. "Because he was protecting his brother's mate," he whispered, staring down at the ground. Around him, the day went as usual, but Kendrick was trapped in this moment of realization.

He heard Darian suck in his breath. "Oh, Gods, she's your mate!"

Kendrick looked up and laughed harshly at Darian's expression. "You don't get it."

Darian stepped forward and laid a hand on his shoulder. "Talk to me Kendrick; your eyes are flashing silver. I'm not a witch, but I know that can't be good."

Kendrick pulled all of emotions into his core. He took a deep breath and began channeling the anger and hopelessness down through his legs and into the ground. Only when the urge to destroy everything around him receded did he open his eyes to look at his brother's friend. "Two hundred years ago, I had a premonition that Keelan would die as a member of the Alpha Unit. When he told me he had volunteered to come to Lycaonia, I forbade him to come. For the first time in his life, he defied me. He said that he had his own reasons for coming to Lycaonia. I always believed that he had put your wellbeing as his fellow warriors above mine as his brother, and I was angry. I didn't understand until this morning how much you care for each other. What if Fate had to use Keelan to save my mate because I couldn't leave Storm Keep? What if it's my fault he was hurt?"

Kendrick stared at the fae's feet, unable to risk the look of condemnation that he was sure was in Darian's eyes.

"Kendrick?"

Kendrick looked up just in time to see a large fist flying toward his head. When the punch connected, he flew backward and ended up staring up at the sky. Darian walked to where he lay and leaned over him. "Feeling better?"

Kendrick blinked. His jaw was killing him but his head was clear. "Yes, actually, I am feeling much better, thank you. Hand up?"

Darian reached down and pulled Kendrick up. "You know the only reason you're not buried up to your neck is because I really did need someone to put me in my place?"

Darian nodded. "It's what brothers do for each other."

Kendrick stopped brushing off his clothes and looked up. "Brothers?"

"That's how this works, Kendrick." Darian waved his arm and pointed to where the unit members were laughing, teasing, and playfully knocking each other senseless. "Meryn was right; we're family, and family looks after each other. I think you've been alone too long, my friend."

Kendrick didn't know what to say. "So we're brothers and friends?"

Darian laughed. "Would you let anyone else get away with sucker punching you to knock some sense into you?"

Kendrick smiled ruefully. "I can honestly say that has never happened before. Usually, I am the one doing the punching."

Darian leaned against the bench. "Under normal circumstances, you are probably the one best suited for dealing with these types of situations. But this is about Keelan and Anne, so you're not really thinking clearly. Nevertheless, I am discovering that not thinking clearly is the norm when dealing with mates." Darian's eyes flicked back to the house. "They drive you insane. They don't listen; the very thought of them hurt makes you want to kill, but life without them would be no life at all."

"I've only had Keelan for so long. I could get used to having more brothers," Kendrick admitted.

Darian's look became devious. "Then as a brother, could you do me a favor?"

Kendrick grinned. "Depends, what do you have in mind?"

Darian pointed across the training yard where a white haired warrior was sparring with his unit. "That's Sascha. He and Keelan would go back and forth with pranks. Sascha liked turning Keelan purple and Keelan liked electrocuting Sascha. Maybe we should zap him for Keelan."

"I like the way you think. How about this?" Kendrick brought up his power hand and twirled his finger in the air. The air around Sascha began to move, picking up rock and dirt. Sascha looked around wildly and saw Kendrick and Darian laughing.

"That's not funny, assholes!" Sascha went to walk through the seemingly harmless breeze and stopped short when a spark flew. "Hey!"

The men were laughing uproariously as they walked over to Sascha. "I heard you liked playing pranks on my baby brother, so I decided to join in the fun so you don't miss him too much."

Sascha growled as the air calmed down. Tentatively, he tested the area around him and breathed a sigh of relief when he wasn't shocked again. "Ha, ha, very funny. I do miss Keelan though, the little guy always gave as good as he got." He glared at Kendrick. "No more sparks, I'm getting zapped enough on patrol; the damn perimeter gets me every time." The men laughed at Sascha's bad luck.

Kendrick chuckled. "I'll add that to my list of things to investigate about the perimeter." He turned and shook hands with Darian. "Thank you again. I know what I have to do now." He looked back at the house. "Can you watch over them while I'm away?" Kendrick looked around and spotted a timid-looking Basil standing on the sidelines. He waved the young man over.

Darian released his hand and nodded. "Of course, where are you going?"

"Into the city, there are some errands I need to run. I'll be back in about an hour or so. Oh, and tell Aiden I'll be using Basil as an apprentice for a while. I forgot to mention it at breakfast." He turned to Basil. "You're coming with me. We'll hit the magic supply stores in town to pick up what's needed for you to conduct your own experiments."

Basil stared. "My wallet is in the barracks."

Kendrick raised an eyebrow. "What kind of master would I be if I didn't provide my apprentice with the basics he needed to learn?"

Basil beamed up at him, and in that moment, reminded him so much of Keelan his heart ached. He cleared his throat and laid a hand on the young witch's shoulder.

Darian nodded at them then looked around frowning. "Wait. Where's your car?"

Kendrick smirked. "Who said anything about driving?"

Kendrick took a deep breath and began moving. With each step they took, his magic condensed long distances into short, manageable ones. To Darian and the others, he and Basil would have simply disappeared. He would make his way into town to meet with some of the residents, pick up supplies for Basil, and then he would return to the Alpha estate to claim his mate.

CHAPTER EIGHT

It was late afternoon, almost evening. After Anne changed Keelan's IV bag they had switched from Tezuka's story to another anime when she said she wanted to watch the rest of it with Kendrick. She was just about to press *play* and start a new series when they heard car doors slam outside. Elizabeth stood and pulled the curtain back. "Gods above, it's the committee members." She whirled around to face Meryn. "Remember what we talked about. You are a shy mute."

Meryn crossed her arms over her chest and pouted. "You're not being nice."

Elizabeth went to the mirror and fixed her hair. "I don't have to be nice; I'm your Yoda. You're nowhere near ready to tangle with these sharks, maybe in another couple years, but not now."

Meryn sat up. "I don't see what the big deal is."

Elizabeth turned. "Because you won't be able to win them over by being blunt and funny. They only respect one thing and that's power. Frankly, you haven't built up enough of a reputation for them to take you seriously. These men were around before the pillar cities, Meryn; they live and breathe etiquette and deportment. Please, just this once, listen to me on this," Elizabeth begged.

Meryn sighed and nodded. She took pinched fingers and dragged them across her mouth. "I'll be mute."

Anne exchanged glances with Rheia who was looking equally as nervous. Anne turned to Elizabeth. "What do we do?"

Elizabeth smiled. "If asked, just introduce yourselves. Keep it short and polite, either Amelia or I will do most of the talking."

Amelia stood and straightened her sweater. "I'm used to these types of men. I sit in for Caiden all the time at home for council meetings. I may carry some clout since I'm an Ironwood and can trace my line back to the royal palace."

There was a knock on the door and Ryuu stepped in. Anne could see that he did not look happy. "Ladies, you have visitors in the front room." Penny and her grandmother walked in. They had been displaced by the visitors.

Elizabeth turned to Noah and Jaxon. "You two stay here, I don't think they're here to question you." Both Noah and Jaxon looked relieved. She turned to the room. "Come on ladies, let's not keep them waiting."

Rheia kissed Penny on the cheek and ruffled her hair.

"They can die of old age for all I care," Meryn muttered.

Elizabeth shot her a dirty look. Meryn rolled her eyes, took a deep breath, and right in front of Anne, it was as if she transformed. Gone was the quirky, vibrant woman and in her place was a wide-eyed, scared looking creature.

Elizabeth patted Meryn on the head. "Good girl." Meryn held on to the hem of Elizabeth's sweater and they walked out of the room.

"Freaky," Amelia and Anne said at the same time.

Rheia shook her head. "I think that transformation will give me more nightmares than the ferals."

They left command central and headed to the front room. Ryuu had brought in more seating to accommodate so many people. In addition to the seven-man council, there were also the three Lycaonian council members seated before them. The men rose as they entered the room. There were only enough empty seats left for the five women to sit down. Anne looked around the room, trying to spot Kendrick. Darian stepped forward from where he had been standing next to the wall with the other Alpha and Gamma Unit members and leaned down to her ear. "He had to run to the city to do some errands; he should be back any minute now."

Anne nodded and turned back to face the imposing men in front of her. To the left, an older version of Aiden smiled at them. Beside him, a blond fae man was nodding encouragingly. Elizabeth and Meryn both smiled back at him. Next to him was a man in emerald green robes. There was a small coffee table between those three and the seven committee members. The dark haired, oily-looking man bowed and remained standing when the other men sat back down.

"Ladies, thank you for joining us. Allow me to introduce everyone. To my far right, the Lycaonian Shifter representative, Elder Byron McKenzie. Then we have the Lycaonian fae representative, Elder Celyn Vi'Ailean, and then our esteemed Lycaonian witch representative, Elder Rowan Airgead." He pointed to his chest. "I am Daggart Hemlock, a witch representative of Storm Keep and head of the newly formed Committee. To my left is my colleague, Adalwin Dulse, another witch representative of Storm Keep."

Anne thought both men looked like they belonged in a dungeon as torturers. She couldn't shake the feeling that they were up to no good. Adalwin looked like he had been up for days. Since being introduced to paranormals, she had never seen any of them looking so tired and haggard. He looked like he should be in bed, not out causing trouble.

"On the other side of Adalwin are the fae representatives of Éire Danu, Brion Li'Aereil and Varis Vi'Eilendis."

Anne noticed that Elder Celyn flinched at Varis's name, which made her like Varis even less. If Elizabeth and Meryn liked Elder Vi'Ailean, then she would trust his opinion, and judging by the way he was looking at Varis, there was bad blood between them. Of the two fae introduced, Varis was the more arrogant one. Brion twitched nervously and kept looking around the room.

"Beside Brion, we have our vampire representatives, Edmond Devan and Jourdain Régis." Daggart continued.

Anne thought that Edmond looked like every version of vampire she had ever seen on television. He wasn't handsome like Gavriel; he was very ordinary, from his stereotypical dark hair to his Victorian style dress. Jourdain, on the other hand, was handsome, and he knew it. His lip seemed to be stuck to the tip of his nose in a permanent sneer. Anne instantly hated him.

"And last, but certainly not least, our Lycaonian representative, Réne Evreux." Daggart sat once he concluded the introductions.

Anne thought that Réne looked sullen, as though he wanted to be anywhere but here. If she didn't know better, she would have said he looked angry with the other committee members.

Anne looked over as Elizabeth stood gracefully. "Thank you for such a thorough introduction. Allow me to do the same. I am Elizabeth Monroe. My uncle is Magnus Rioux of Noctem Falls, and I am mated to Gavriel Ambrosios. To my right, we have Meryn McKenzie, the mate to our esteemed Unit Commander and future Elder, Aiden McKenzie. Next, we have Rheia Bradley, a much-respected doctor and mate to Colton Albright. Beside her, we have Amelia Ironwood, daughter to Elder Ironwood of Storm Keep and mate to Darian Vi'Alina. And this is our newest family member, Anne Bennett. She has just completed arduous schooling to become a nurse, and she has been taking care of Keelan Ashwood, the warrior who sacrificed his life so that the Alpha Unit would live." Elizabeth sat back down and took Meryn's hand in a gesture of support.

The men nodded at the women as they were introduced. Mostly, all eyes were on Meryn, but Anne noticed that vampire Jourdain stared at Elizabeth.

"Now that we know each other, let us move on to the topics at hand–" Daggart began.

"Don't you mean allegations?" Elizabeth interrupted.

Daggart smiled at her. "Allegation is such a harsh word." He smiled at her in a condescending manner. Anne fought the urge to smack him.

"So you simply wish to discuss certain topics, with no intention for any actions to transpire after the fact?" Elizabeth asked.

Daggart shook his head. "There have been some extremely reckless decisions made by some of you ladies that have resulted in damages to public property."

Elizabeth raised an eyebrow. "I disagree. Everything that was done was in response to unusual and dire circumstances. I can't believe that the Committee would value property over the lives of our people."

Adalwin shook his head. "Had things been done the way we have always done them, we wouldn't have had any damages."

Elizabeth smiled sweetly. "In that case, can you please go to the super ferals–"

"Reapers," Meryn whispered.

Elizabeth glanced down at Meryn and continued. "Please go to the reapers and convince them to go back where they came from and to stop killing people. That way, we can go back to doing things the way we always have."

Adalwin's face flushed at her response.

"We don't need her introducing human technology; it isn't needed," Edmond protested.

To Anne's surprise, it was a white-haired man leaning against the wall who responded. "I'm Sascha Baberiov, Gamma Unit leader. We..."–he pointed to the rest of the warriors–"the units disagree. Since the introduction of updated technology, we have been able to save lives without losing warriors. I know of several instances where Noah and Jaxon were able to direct units away from pockets of ferals in the last battle using the city's surveillance cameras. They were able to avoid being outnumbered and were able to escort civilians to safety."

"Who the devil are Noah and Jaxon?" Edmond demanded.

Elizabeth smiled. "Noah Caraway and Jaxon Darrow are the first students in Meryn's technology learning program. As the Gamma Unit leader has pointed out, it's already a huge success."

Daggart pointed to Elizabeth. "That brings me to my next point. We have methods of teaching our young people so that they can be closely monitored. How do you explain your out of control witch unit warrior who cast the perimeter spell?"

Aiden stepped forward and Anne could tell it was taking every ounce of his will not to yell at the accusing committee members. "As previously reported, no unit member witch is responsible for casting the spell that created the perimeter."

Elizabeth leaned back in her chair, looking smug. "Maybe you should reevaluate your teaching methods, witch representative of Storm Keep. It looks like one of your witches has been naughty."

Anne could hear the wood crack under Daggart's hands as he grasped the arms of the chair. "Our methods are perfectly sound."

Jourdain locked eyes with Elizabeth until she shuddered and looked away. Gavriel was behind her in an instant, his eyes glowed bright red as he hissed at the other vampire.

Jourdain smiled mockingly and spread is hands. "Forgive me, but I haven't seen little Bethy in quite some time; old habits die hard."

Elizabeth held onto Gavriel's hand so tight Anne could see her knuckles turning white. "I'm fine." She took a deep breath and sat up straighter. "If you gentleman have nothing more substantial to discuss, frankly, I find your allegations groundless and insulting." Her voice held an edge that hadn't been there before Jourdain's stare.

Jourdain leered at her. "We're just getting started. We haven't even discussed how the Alpha Unit let one of their own warriors be compromised and fall into the hands of the enemy."

Anne felt him before he even walked into the room. She turned to the doorway to see Aiden and Colton parting to allow Kendrick to enter. The committee members turned to look at the new arrival. Daggart and Adalwin were staring with mouths open at Kendrick. Suddenly, the room felt smaller, as if it couldn't contain Kendrick's very presence.

"I will not allow you to turn my brother into a political stepping stone." His deep voice resonated through the room.

Jourdain turned back to Elizabeth, ignoring Kendrick's entrance. "You may have a pretty answer for our reasonable concerns, but you cannot deny that... that *human* is incapable of leading our units." His long finger pointed directly at Meryn.

Byron stood, growling lowly. "First, be very careful how you address my daughter, Jourdain. Second, I follow her lead, as do the men. Are you trying to tell us that, with our combined thousands of years of training, we don't know what *we* are doing?"

Jourdain scowled. "Of course not."

Kendrick walked behind the chairs of the committee members slowly, causing each one of them to flinch. He stopped at end of the row. "I believe she is doing exceptionally well."

Daggart looked up, his eyes dark. "And why would the opinion of an archivist who has yet to receive a Mastery level matter to anyone?"

Kendrick nodded while smiling. "You're absolutely right, I'm just a poor scribe from the Lower City."

Daggart smirked at Kendrick's admission.

"However, Lady Fairfax isn't, and neither are many of her other highborn friends, or many of the Lycaonian citizens I spoke with today." Kendrick kept walking until he was behind the women's chairs. "You see, they trust Meryn implicitly. Because, when it mattered, this pregnant *human* female took up arms and protected not only her mate's unit warriors, but also the people of the city. Unlike certain elders who show up after the fact, pointing fingers."

Daggart raised a hand to interrupt, but Kendrick kept going, ignoring him.

"They love her so much, in fact, the editor of the *Lycaonian Herald*–an old friend of mine, by the way–will be doing a multi-page article about Meryn and how she is changing the lives of the Lycaonian people for the better. The paper will, of course, be distributed to the other three pillar cities, where interest in Meryn's technology programs is growing every day."

Brion spoke up. "What about the charges for having a unit leader acting as Elder to gain even more influence?"

Kendrick stopped mid-step and faced the fae. "Are they charges now?"

Brion flushed. "I misspoke. We have *concerns* regarding this matter."

Kendrick shrugged lazily. Anne had to turn her head. She was starting to understand his body language. Whenever Kendrick made it look like he couldn't care less, that was when he was the most agitated.

"This sort of thing happens from time to time doesn't it? Especially with hereditary seats. Caiden has done such an amazing job performing both roles over the past thirty years that no one noticed until very recently that he had been doing both."

Elizabeth let a snicker escape and coughed as if she was trying to cover up her slip. But Anne was learning; Elizabeth never did anything without reason. The woman wanted to let the men know that their concern was a laughable matter.

Daggart glared at Kendrick, his affable personality fading. "That doesn't change the fact that Unit Commander, Aiden McKenzie not only left the city while it was under attack, but also took valuable units with him."

Kendrick held up a hand to Aiden who had stepped forward growling. Aiden nodded and stepped back glaring at Daggart. Kendrick looked at the witch representative. "That is very true, but it isn't as if he left the city defenseless. All I heard today from the people was how *safe* they felt after seeing so many of their neighbors step up during the battle as inactive or retired warriors. To quote one shopkeeper: 'It's as if there is a warrior on every corner keeping us safe.' She didn't seem upset at all."

Kendrick walked until he was behind Amelia's chair. He laid a hand on her shoulder. "Let us not forget that the person they went to save is right in front of you. And that by leaving the city and saving her life, the Alpha Unit not only learned more about the enemy's intentions, but was able to destroy one of their facilities." Kendrick's hard glare pinned the committee members to their chairs. Some looked away, embarrassed. They *had* forgotten that Amelia was the one who'd been taken.

Adalwin broke the ensuing silence. "What about the damages?" he asked weakly.

Kendrick smiled. "I thought you'd never ask." He looked over at Oron who nodded at him from where he stood against the wall with Sascha. "Queen Aleksandra herself has gifted the city of Lycaonia with the services of her very best fae craftsmen to clean up and rebuild the square as a personal gift to Meryn."

Daggart gasped. "Impossible! It takes weeks to get an audience with the queen!"

Oron stepped forward, grinning. "Not when you're close to the throne." He turned to Meryn. "The queen is very excited to see another female in a position of authority, and she says she can't wait for you to visit."

Daggart's jaw dropped as Meryn gave Oron a thumbs up sign.

Elizabeth turned to the men. "Gentlemen, did you have any other concerns for us to address?" she asked sweetly.

Daggart was about to respond when he was interrupted by a faint buzzing sound; everyone looked around to try and locate the source of the noise. Ruefully, Aiden pulled his phone from his pocket. "Aiden here. What? How many? Position? They what? Roger that. I'll call back with orders."

The men closest to Aiden who had heard both sides of the conversation looked sick.

Daggart looked at Aiden. "Well?"

"Reapers and ferals have taken a large refugee group coming from Jefferson hostage just south of here. They are demanding that we lower the perimeter in exchange for the refugees' lives."

Everyone began talking at once. Colton brought two fingers up and whistled sharply. Aiden smiled at him. "Thank you." He looked over at Kendrick then at his father. "Suggestions?"

Anne watched as Byron glanced up at Kendrick and flicked his eyes over to Meryn. Kendrick nodded and went to stand behind Meryn. "What do you think we should do, Meryn?"

Meryn looked over at Elizabeth who nodded. Anne smiled; Meryn was getting the okay from her Yoda to talk.

"How many ferals?" Meryn asked.

Edmond snorted. "Shouldn't you be asking how many hostages?"

Meryn glared at him "No. I know what I meant to ask."

Daggart stood. "This is preposterous! This woman has no right to be included on important decisions."

Aiden stared down at the officious man. "She has more of a right than you do."

As arguments broke out, Anne could see Kendrick's patience running out. He simply held up his hand and released a spell causing everyone to freeze. It was instantly quiet. He opened his hand and everyone was able to move again. "Let me try to clear this matter up for you gentlemen once and for all. Then we can concentrate on the hostages that need us." He moved to the middle of the row.

"Amelia represents a normal woman, she's warm, caring and intelligent. All wonderful qualities, and as much as I love my godsdaughter, because of these qualities, I would never put her in the position to make such a hard decision. Meryn on the other hand, is...different. She thinks the way I do, the way a trained leader would, and I trust her implicitly to make hard choices because of this."

Adalwin looked confused. "How can you possibly show us that?"

Kendrick held up a finger. "Amelia, Meryn, I am going to describe an emergency situation. You will be able to ask me one question before deciding on your course of action; however, once you hear my answer, you must reply immediately." Both women nodded.

"You are the captain of a ship that is sinking. For argument sake, let's just say that there is only one way to save the ship. You have to seal off the lower levels. However, there are fifty people down there who, no matter what you do, won't be able to be make it to the upper levels in time to be saved. What is your question? Amelia?"

Amelia swallowed hard. "How many children are there?"

"Twenty-five. Half of the trapped passengers are children. Your answer?" Kendrick asked sharply.

Amelia flinched. "I'd try to save them."

Kendrick looked at the men around the room; nearly all of them were nodding in agreement. He turned to Meryn. "Your question?"

Meryn shrugged. "How many people are on the boat?"

"Three thousand. Your answer?"

Meryn responded instantly. "I'd seal off the lower decks."

The room was silent. "As you can see gentlemen, Meryn knew what question to ask and chose the best course of action."

Kendrick turned to Aiden. "I believe she asked how many ferals there were."

Aiden nodded. "Epsilon reported anywhere from thirty to fifty ferals and approximately one hundred hostages."

"Are they willing to accept anything else?" Adalwin suggested.

Aiden picked up his phone and dialed. "Hey Santa, can you let the bastards know that we can't lower the perimeter, ask if they would settle for something else in return."

Everyone waited silently as the Epsilon leader communicated with the ferals.

Aiden nodded. "Okay, stand by. I'll call back." He put his phone back in his pocket.

"Santiago said that the reaper leader is willing to accept our necklaces in exchange."

Rowan stood and inclined his head to Aiden. "Personally, I don't think it would be a loss taking the perimeter down. I have complete faith in our unit warriors, they have protected us for centuries without a perimeter, and I feel that they can continue to do so. But, since we don't know who cast the perimeter, being able to take it down as requested is off the table."

"It looks like the necklaces are our only choice," Réne confirmed.

Rowan shook his head. "Unfortunately, someone has already given them to Kendrick here for study." Réne scowled at Rowan, who ignored him.

Rowan turned to Kendrick. "Well, son, do you think you can give up on your tests to save the lives of our people?"

Anne watched as Kendrick looked at Réne. An odd look appeared on his face and disappeared just as quickly. He shook his head at Rowan's question and turned to Meryn. "Well?"

Meryn looked up at him. "Maybe I am human; maybe I'm too young and too American, but in a situation like this, I refuse to negotiate with terrorists. I would send out every unit we have plus any volunteers to exterminate this threat. If we start giving in to them now, we'll be opening ourselves up for more hostage situations down the road."

Anne looked over at Aiden and Byron who were both already on their cell phones. Aiden was coordinating the units to meet at the Alpha estate, and Byron was calling the older warriors to see if any would volunteer to assist.

Rheia stood and walked over to Anne, a cell phone to her ear as well. "Adam we have a situation where we could be facing a lot of casualties. Bring anything that isn't nailed down to the Alpha estate. Oh, by the way, we have another nurse now." She paused. "I don't want to hear you complaining about not having any supplies after the last battle. I don't care if you have to shit bandages, get out here on the double."

The committee members were staring at Rheia in shock. Rheia didn't even give them a second glance. "Anne, you're with me. We're setting up triage on the front lawn. Normally, I would have everyone sent to the clinic, but we're closer." Rheia left the room yelling for Ryuu. Ryuu appeared and she began giving him a list of hot beverages and blankets she would need to help treat shock victims.

Elizabeth was on the phone with her uncle, asking that he send any spare medical supplies via portal to the Lycaonia clinic, the sooner the better.

Anne watched as Amelia coordinated with Kendrick and Sascha to use her magic to level the ground making it easier to care for the wounded. Meryn was on a handheld walkie-talkie talking with unit warriors. "I miss you, too, Adonis. After this is all over, you have to swing by to meet my new peep, over and out."

Anne blinked. "Who is Adonis? Sounds sexy," she teased. Meryn grinned, and before Anne knew it, Aiden and Kendrick were heading in their direction.

Aiden growled at Meryn and nipped her neck, and Kendrick scowled at her. "Never mind any Adonis." He looked out the window. "I'm going out with the men to try and minimize the number of casualties, but it will be difficult doing this in the dark. I need to be able to see to cast. Unfortunately, my form of light is fire, so unless we want to burn the forest down, I'll be relying on flood lights from the warriors."

Colton clapped him on the back. "Not as easy as you thought, is it?"

Kendrick shook his head. "No, but I'll do whatever I can to keep you all safe."

Colton didn't say anything, just clapped him on the back again, and walked to Aiden.

Anne grabbed his arm. "You have to be safe, too." It was sinking in that the men were about to head out to battle; they could be killed.

Kendrick looked down at her, and she was confused by the frustration in his eyes. Suddenly, he leaned down and kissed her forehead. He kept his lips to her skin and whispered. "I'll be back. You and I have unfinished business."

When he pulled away, she felt as if he'd pulled a piece of her heart out of her chest with him.

"Be careful!" She called after him. He nodded and ran to catch up with the men who were already filing out the door.

Rheia walked up and wrapped her arm around Anne's shoulder. "It doesn't get any easier no matter how many times I do this. It helps to stay busy."

Anne nodded. "Point me where you need me doctor."

Rheia smiled. "That's what I wanted to hear."

Anne quickly began to notice that they were receiving more injured than just she and Rheia could handle on their own. When two more shifters showed up with bullet wounds, Anne made the decision to send all critical patients to the clinic.

She ran up to one of the warriors carrying a stretcher. "No. Get him in a vehicle and send him to the clinic."

The man frowned. "But Dr. Bradley said that we were to bring all the patients here."

Anne put her hands on her hips. "That was before we realized how many injured were on the way. This man needs surgery; that cannot happen on the front lawn."

Rheia raced up to them. "She's absolutely right."

Anne looked around the lawn. "Noah!"

The blond turned to them and quickly jogged over. "What do you need?"

"Follow behind me. Get a pen and paper, and tag each patient for transfer that I point to." She turned to Rheia. "You need to call the clinic doctor and tell him to stay there and expect incoming."

Rheia nodded and pulled out her phone. She was giving orders when a new batch arrived in an SUV. She cut the call short as they both ran over. The new arrivals were two children who had a death grip on Sascha. He handled them very gently, one perched on each hip. When he saw Rheia and Anne approaching, he practically sagged in relief. "Thank the Gods! Can you look these two over? I don't think anything is wrong, but they are so little," he fretted, looking with worried glances between the two.

When Rheia reached for the little boy, he turned and buried his face in Sascha's chest. Sascha looked up at Rheia, a frantic look on his face.

"Doc! We need you over here!" another warrior yelled. He was straddling a man's body on a stretcher holding blood-soaked bandages. Rheia immediately ran over to assist.

Anne looked at Sascha. "They seem to be okay. I don't see any broken bones or open wounds. Keep them calm and warm." She turned and ran back over to where the wounded where being laid out in rows.

"How do I do that?" Sascha yelled.

"Blankets and hot chocolate!" she shouted.

Noah caught up to her, and they quickly worked their way through the wounded. Out of the one hundred hostages over thirty of them had been hurt. When they were done prioritizing the care of the seriously wounded, Anne and Noah looked for Rheia.

Rheia's face looked pinched as she worked on a patient too critical for transport. She looked panicked when she called out for items she needed only to realize there was no one to assist. Anne ran forward. "I'm here, keep going."

"Noah! I need you and four warriors to grab blankets, tarps, whatever you can and create a makeshift operating room. We need as much coverage as possible!" Anne yelled.

Noah took off like a bullet. Anne turned her attention back to Rheia and calmly handed her the instruments she needed to remove the deeply lodged bullet. She hardly noticed when the wind stopped blowing her hair in her eyes due to Noah's superb efforts to keep them protected.

Anne ran through the list of steps in her mind and was determined to stay two steps ahead of Rheia, anticipating her every need. She was never so grateful for her mentor's suggestion to volunteer as an ER nurse. In the ER, one needed to know a little bit of everything. It had been equal parts exhilarating and frustrating. She had been determined to learn as much as possible, and it was paying off.

An hour later, the man was stable and most of the patients were wrapped in blankets and ready to be sent to the city.

She was washing her hands for what seemed like the thousandth time that night when Rheia walked over. "You have to be one of the best nurses I have ever seen. Are you sure you aren't psychic?"

Anne smiled and shook her head. "No. I just hated it in nursing school when a patient suffered because I didn't know something. So I studied everything."

"You are exactly what we need here in Lycaonia. I don't think I could have handled this on my own. You and Noah were invaluable at getting the patients lined up with the correct care. You thought clearly and adapted well. Good job." Rheia nodded at her in admiration, and Anne's breath caught.

"Thank you, Dr. Bradley."

"You're very welcome, nurse." Rheia stretched and rubbed her back. "How do you think Sascha faired with the kids?"

Anne grinned and nodded her head to the edge of the treatment area. Sascha had spread blankets on the ground and sat leaning against his SUV. Both children were sound asleep with their heads in his lap.

Rheia shook her head. "Big softies, every single one of them."

Anne couldn't help but agree. "We wouldn't want them any other way."

"You can say that again!" Rheia exclaimed and looped her arm through Anne's.

They inspected the area together, making sure that everyone who needed treatment had received it.

CHAPTER NINE

Kendrick sat on the front porch steps and watched as people milled around him. The battle had been surprisingly short. When the reapers realized they weren't going to get what they wanted, they turned on the hostages, wounding many and killing five before the warriors were able to get between them and their attackers. At the end of the skirmish, Kendrick ended up with more necklaces for testing.

This is what Keelan had been doing for two hundred years? How did he do it? Feeling useless, Kendrick stood and decided he had to find a way to help. He had more magic than he knew what to do with; surely he could accomplish something useful.

He was walking around trying to find Anne when he spotted Amelia. She stood in the middle of the training yard, a blank look on her face. He hurried over to her, grabbing a blanket from a nearby pile on his way. He wrapped her up and held her close.

"Shush, it's going to be okay Amelia." She began shaking under the blanket.

Looking around, he caught Darian's eye and nodded to Amelia. Darian almost plowed people over in an effort to get to her side.

"What's wrong with her?" he asked.

"Let's get her inside and away from these people. Then I want to look at her magic." Darian swept Amelia up in his arms.

Kendrick looked around and spotted Meryn. She was scowling fiercely at everyone, breathing heavily, and snapping at anyone who got close enough. He ran over and scooped her up. "You're coming, too."

"What gives? Put me down!" Meryn screeched.

Aiden's head whipped around at the sound of Meryn's yells. He charged over. "Kendrick, you wanna tell me why I shouldn't kill you?"

Kendrick jerked his head toward the door. "Inside."

Kendrick didn't wait for Aiden. He hurried toward the house where Ryuu met them at the door, a relieved look on his face. "Thank the Gods, I was about to come find her. How did you know, *Heika*?"

Kendrick kept walking. "I had a feeling she'd be upset." Ryuu and Aiden followed him until they were in Aiden's office. It was the quietest room downstairs and where Darian had chosen to go with Amelia.

Kendrick set Meryn down next to Amelia. He reached out with both hands, grasping Meryn with his left and Amelia with his right. Gently, he sent his magic through them, searching. As he had suspected, Meryn had a touch of magic. He carefully corralled their magic and secured it behind the mental doors he created. It was easy for Amelia, she had been raised thinking this way and he had done this with her once before, but Meryn's magic was completely wild. He took his time and coaxed it behind the thick door before closing it for her.

He sat back on his heels. "Well, I know where you got your empathy from Amelia."

Amelia shook her head as if trying to clear it. "Wait, what?"

Aiden collapsed into a chair. "What?"

Kendrick moved so that he could lean his back against the coffee table. These two would be the death of him. Getting their empathy under control was exhausting.

"Is everything okay in here? We saw you carry Meryn and Amelia in and we were worried," a soft voice asked.

Kendrick looked up and smiled. Anne, Rheia, Elizabeth, and the rest of the Alpha Unit were walking through the door.

"Evidently, *denka* has magic," Ryuu replied.

"No, I don't. I would know if I had magic," Meryn protested.

Kendrick raised an eyebrow at the stubborn female.

"I don't!"

"Meryn, I was told that you didn't have it easy growing up, is that correct?"

Meryn quieted immediately.

Kendrick kept going. "You have magic, but it's a very small amount, just enough to be bothersome. You have empathy, the same gift as your cousin."

"No, she doesn't." The sentiment was echoed throughout the room.

Kendrick shook his head at their denials and continued to look at Meryn. "It's just enough so that you would know someone's true feelings, just enough so that you would know when they were lying. Amelia was raised in a warm and loving home, where people said what they felt, didn't lie, and were very kind." Kendrick gently held Meryn's hands. "Now, this is just a guess, but I bet that wasn't true for you."

Meryn shook her head.

Kendrick continued. "I bet the people you grew up around were petty and hurtful."

Meryn nodded silently.

Kendrick looked around the room. "If you have the gift of empathy and were raised in such an environment, what do you think would happen?"

Amelia hugged Meryn close. "She would turn away from people and keep to herself, because if she's alone, she can't be hurt."

Aiden got up and sat beside Meryn. He pulled her into his lap and rubbed his chin on the top of her head. "My poor baby."

Meryn settled in against her mate. "It wasn't all bad, and it brought me to you." She tilted her head back, and he placed kisses all over her face.

"It could also explain why she can see sprites," Gavriel theorized.

There was a knock at the door and then it swung open. A blond man Kendrick hadn't met walked in. "Aiden, we have just about everyone sorted. The units are escorting the people into the city and your committee members just left."

Aiden sighed. "Thanks Ben, I had forgotten about them." He turned to Kendrick. "Will there really be an article about Meryn in the paper?"

Kendrick nodded. "Yes. The committee should be well behaved little kittens after I pulled their fangs and claws." He turned to Elizabeth. "Though I must say, it was a much easier task thanks to you."

Elizabeth smiled. "One of the benefits growing up in a noble household."

Rheia clapped her hands together. "It's been a long evening, everyone should wash up and grab some dinner."

Ryuu stepped forward. "Tonight's meal is a variety of different soups. They have been simmering all day. If you leave me your choices I can have your dinner waiting for you when you come down."

Colton grabbed a pen and piece paper off of Aiden's desk and began organizing their selections. Anne shocked Kendrick when she chose the beef stew, he had pegged her for a vegetable kind of girl. He chose the lentil soup and made his way over to Anne. Smiling, he held out his hand. "Let's go check on our boy." Anne's face lit up and she grasped his hand. He took a moment to enjoy the simple act of walking hand-in-hand with her up the stairs. It was time to tell her the truth.

Anne walked into the bathroom, her heart in her mouth. The walk up to her room had been too short. She wanted to enjoy holding Kendrick's hand a bit longer. Looking in the mirror, she had to face the realization that she was already half in love with Kendrick. She didn't know what she was going to do if they found out she was truly Keelan's mate. She took a deep breath and smiled at herself. This was something her mother taught her to do as a child. When things get difficult, smile at yourself in the mirror. Your body is tricked into thinking that it's happy, and your smiling face mentally bolsters you. Today, she bared her teeth then stuck her tongue out for good measure.

She took the world's quickest shower and dried off with one of the softest towels she had ever used. She looked at the clothes she had chosen and sighed. What she really wanted to wear was her anime sweatshirt, but the only other person who dressed like that for dinner was Meryn, and she had a feeling Meryn could get away with just about anything. She compromised with herself and wore her favorite jeans, but picked out a dressier shirt. The bright coral color set off her teal eyes, but the buttons on her shirt pulled slightly across her chest. She sighed and accepted the fact that she wouldn't be comfortable again until bedtime.

She towel-dried her hair one last time before walking out into the room with her brush and a hair tie in hand. Kendrick was sitting on the edge of her bed, presumably waiting for her. Seeing him sitting there wreaked havoc with her body. She needed to stay away from him, especially him and any sort of flat surface, like the bed. Images of throwing the man backward and straddling him had her pulling a throw off a nearby chair and settling on the floor to do her hair.

Slowly she began to brush and finger-comb her hair.

"I spoke with Darian," he said quietly.

She froze. "And what did he say?"

Kendrick stood and walked over to sit down behind her. He extended his legs out on either side of her. Before he answered, he took the brush from her hand and began sliding it through her hair. Carefully he began to twist the hair into a braid.

"He said that Keelan admitted to him that he wasn't attracted to you." She felt him secure the hair tie around the braid.

The words stung. Not because she had to face the fact that Keelan hadn't been attracted to her, but because now Kendrick knew how his brother felt. Would that sway his mind?

"I wasn't really attracted to him either. I was too comfortable around him to be attracted. He was more like a best friend than boyfriend," she confessed.

"Anne, I don't think that you and Keelan are mates."

Anne stood and began to pace the length of the room. "Then why did he say he dreamt of me?"

"Because he did, but those were premonitions, not mating dreams," Kendrick explained. "Anne, who did you dream of?" His voice deepened, and she turned to face him. When she took in the scene at her feet, she gasped. Just like in her dream, he was sitting on a blanket waiting for her with a patient smile. She felt tears fill her eyes and then drip down her cheeks. "You. I so wanted it to be you." She closed her eyes and covered her face with her hands.

Seconds later, she felt him pull her close. "I dreamt of you, too, my love."

She pulled back and looked up at him. "What did you see?"

"The day your father died."

"Oh."

He held her close and started to sway back and forth. "You've always lived for others. First, your parents, then your patients, and now Keelan. Will you allow me to put you first? I've waited a very, very long time to meet you."

She wrapped her arms around his waist. "How old are you anyway?"

"Older than anyone believes."

"Older than Aiden?" Kendrick nodded.

"Older than Darian?" Kendrick chuckled and Anne looked up. He was looking down at her with such a sad look on his face. She reached up and soothed the area between his brows with her thumb.

He smiled. "There you go, taking care of me again."

"I don't mind as long as it's you."

He leaned in very slowly, giving her every opportunity to turn away. When he was about to kiss her, she couldn't help it and began to giggle.

Looking confused, he smiled at her. "What brought that on?"

She waved a hand at him. "You. Being so careful. If you're going to kiss me, kiss me, and be sure you do a damn fine job of it."

He took her at her word and took possession of her mouth. He gently ran his tongue along her lips until she opened for him. She gave him an inch and he took a mile. His tongue teased the roof of her mouth before he began to nibble on her lips. He explored and dominated every part of her mouth.

When there was a knock on the door, they broke apart, both breathing heavily.

"Dinner is ready, peeps," Meryn announced.

"Be right down," Anne croaked.

She looked up and felt a bit of satisfaction that Kendrick was just as affected as she was. "That was amazing."

Kendrick nodded then glanced back at the bed.

She swatted his arm, laughing. "Hold your horses Romeo, I don't even know your middle name."

Kendrick blinked. "I don't have one. Is that going to be a problem?"

Anne laughed. "No, of course not. Why don't you have a middle name?"

He shrugged. "We didn't use them back then."

She put her hands on her hips. "How old are you?"

Kendrick's teasing gaze made her knees go weak. "Kiss me again and I'll tell you."

She took a step back at his devilish expression. "Hmmm. Nope." She turned on her heel and marched toward the door.

He caught up to her immediately and wrapped his arms around her. He began to kiss the back of her neck, sending chills throughout her body. "Stop that!"

Kendrick spun her in his arms. "You seem different."

Anne thought about it for a moment. "I do?"

"You seem more sure of yourself."

She nodded. "I think I am. Before, when there was confusion about Keelan, I wasn't sure where I belonged. Guilt at my attraction to you made me doubt who I was, but now..."–she wrapped her arms around his neck–"...now I know that's it's okay to be in love with you."

His eyes widened.

Oops!

She smiled brightly and bolted for the door. "Dinner smells great!"

She was halfway down the stairs when she heard him running. She squealed, and laughing hard, she ran for the dinning room. She burst into the room and everyone looked up in surprise. Grinning, she braced herself against the closed door. Seconds later, she was jolted by the impact of Kendrick hitting the door.

"Sonofabitch!"

Laughing, she ran for her chair. Everyone around the table was grinning.

Kendrick swung the door open and stepped through slowly, his eyes narrowed dangerously. "I know that Anne wouldn't block the door against me, causing me to bump my nose." He glared at her.

Anne shook her head. "You're right. It was Colton." She pointed at the blond whose mouth dropped open at the accusation.

Kendrick crossed his arms over his chest and began to tap his finger against his elbow. "I see. So Colton, why would you want to keep me from my mate?"

At his question, there were gasps around the table. Anne scowled at him. "You could have told them in a better way."

Kendrick shrugged and walked over to stand beside her chair. He looked around the table. "This isn't going to be a problem, is it gentlemen?"

Darian shook his head and looked around at the other men. "Keelan admitted to me that he wasn't attracted to Anne. Kendrick and I worked out that the dreams he had been having were premonitions to keep her safe, not mating dreams." He looked up at Kendrick. "I'm assuming that you both have been dreaming about each other?"

Anne nodded and looked up at Kendrick; he winked at her and sat down.

"Have you claimed each other yet?" Meryn asked.

"Meryn!" Elizabeth exclaimed.

"What?" Meryn looked at Anne and Kendrick. "Too personal?"

Kendrick shrugged, and Anne just smiled at Meryn; the odd woman had grown on her. "I don't mind telling you when he claims me, but I'm not going into detail. Something tells me it will be too scandalous to share." She leered up at her mate. He just nodded and picked up his water glass.

Meryn giggled and held up her fist. Anne lifted her hand and gave the woman her imaginary fist bump. Meryn sighed happily. "I knew you'd fit in."

Colton watched her with a careful look. "She was hiding her crazy," he accused.

Rheia laughed and shook her head. "She was probably very conflicted about how she felt about Kendrick, especially considering what we told her about Keelan. Now that she's settled, I bet we see more of the real Anne Bennett."

Anne nodded. "She's right. Before, I knew I wasn't attracted to Keelan in that way, but everyone was calling me his mate. Then I met Kendrick, and I was drawn to my supposed mate's brother. I felt like utter shit."

Amelia reached around Kendrick to pat her on the shoulder. "Don't feel bad, that's five for five for relationships starting on the wrong foot in this house." All the women were nodding.

"At least you didn't beat Kendrick with any plumbing fixtures." Aiden commented.

Meryn threw her hands in the air. "Still?" She looked over at Anne. "At least he didn't lock you in his trunk." She turned and stuck her tongue out at her mate.

Laughing, Elizabeth chimed in. "I almost bled to death a couple of times."

Rheia hugged Colton's arm to her. "I surprised Colton with a daughter the day we met."

Amelia turned and held up her hand. "Don't even get me started about feeling guilty. Darian and I have you beat hands down."

Anne's face hurt from smiling so much. Everyone was trying so hard to make this less awkward for her and to help her feel like part of the family. "You'll have to tell me your stories later; they sound amazing."

"There's never a dull moment around here, that's for certain," Ryuu said, pushing the serving tray into the room. He had ladled out everyone's soup of choice and began serving as he made his way around the table.

"Sorry I stole your man, Ryuu," Anne joked.

Ryuu smiled down at her as he placed her dinner in front of her. "How shall I go on?"

Amelia clapped her hands together. "I know! Let's find a mate for Noah!"

Anne nodded enthusiastically. "I'm in. He's so beautiful; he deserves an amazing man."

Meryn began to bounce in her chair too. "Smart like the Doctor."

Anne nodded. "Handsome like Tezuka."

"Faithful like Rory." Meryn sighed.

"Considerate like Yuri." Anne added.

They looked at each other and Anne grinned. "I think our geekdoms overlapped."

Meryn threw her arm in the air. "Score!"

Elizabeth unfolded her napkin. "I don't think I have a geekdom, but I do like to organize things."

"I love make-up," Amelia confessed.

Anne turned to Rheia for her interests. Rheia shook her head and laughed. "I have a four-year-old; I can barely see straight at the end of the day, much less do make-up or keep to any organized plan."

Meryn picked up her spoon. "Yeah, I've pretty much given up on the smokey eye; my new nemesis is liquid lipsticks. They make me look like I've been kissing clowns." Grinning, she looked over at Aiden.

"Hey!" he laughed.

Anne thought about it for a moment. "I don't really have a lot of hobbies besides anime and cosplay when I had the odd weekend off." She paused. "Does baking count?"

Elizabeth nodded. "Absolutely. What is your favorite thing to make?"

Anne shrugged. "Anything really. I like cakes more than cookies though. When you make cookies, you roll everything out into one-inch balls. It takes forever to roll out two hundred and forty one-inch balls." She shuddered at the memory of last Christmas.

"That is a lot of cookies," Gavriel said.

"I donate to the women's shelters around the holidays. They hardly get anything homemade like that," Anne confessed.

"What a wonderful idea! How did you manage to do that and go to school?" Elizabeth asked.

Anne smiled. "It's not like I go out much. I'm pretty content staying at home watching television and making cookies. The sugar helped around exam time."

Colton exhaled in relief. "She's normal crazy, not like that one." He pointed to Meryn.

Meryn didn't even look in his direction. "I enjoy my crazy, thank you very much. I noticed a long time ago that those who value normalcy to the point of making someone else feel like shit for being different were assholes. I stopped caring about what people thought of me after that."

"We enjoy your crazy, too, Menace," Colton teased.

Anne laughed. "Why do they call you Menace?"

"Because that's what she is," Darian answered. "She likes to mess with us poor, hard-working unit warriors."

Amelia bumped shoulders with her mate. "She does not."

Darian gave Amelia a look. "Then answer me this: Why did Meryn have binoculars to give you right after you first arrived?"

Amelia opened her mouth then closed it. She looked over at Meryn. "Why did you have binoculars?"

"She likes to bird watch," Aiden answered.

Anne looked around the table to see if she was the only one who didn't believe that. She leaned forward in her chair to see Rheia's expression. Okay, that would be a big, fat no.

Meryn grinned. "Yup, I like to watch."

"Oh, Meryn." Elizabeth hid her face against Gavriel's upper arm. Gavriel's lips twitched as he tried not to laugh, but every once in a while, a snicker would escape.

Colton and Darian were exchanging looks. Colton nodded toward Aiden. Darian shook his head and pointed to Colton.

And the winner is? Anne wondered who would be brave enough to tell Aiden the truth.

Colton cleared his throat. "You know, Aiden, I don't really think Meryn is bird watching."

Aiden frowned. "What else would she be doing with binoculars?"

Kendrick raised his spoon and sipped his soup. "I assume you have a ranking system?"

Meryn laughed and nodded. "I even created a database."

Kendrick nodded in approval. "You'll have to show me how it works. I'd love to get some of the reference materials I've accumulated over the years into an easier to search format."

"Ranking system?" Aiden frowned.

Meryn ignored Aiden's question. "Sure, swing by the office any time," Meryn offered.

"Excellent," Kendrick agreed. "By the way, where did I rank?"

Meryn shook her head. "We haven't placed you yet since you haven't worked out with your shirt off."

Realization dawned on Aiden's face. "Meryn!" he bellowed.

"What? It gets boring around here," she complained.

"To whom is she referring, when she says 'we'?" Gavriel asked, his lips dancing along Elizabeth's neck as he spoke.

Elizabeth laughed, her cheeks flushed. "Noah. They only have me judge in the event of a tie."

Colton turned to Rheia. "Did you know about this?"

Rheia nodded. "I helped supply the chest measurements they needed for some of the more closely contested ranks."

Colton became thoughtful then turned to Meryn. "Am I at least in the top ten?"

Meryn nodded. "Your smile saved you."

Colton beamed a bright smile around the table. "Yes!"

Anne looked at Kendrick then at Meryn. "Can I help judge when Kendrick is shirtless?"

Meryn nodded enthusiastically. "If we have three judges we won't have ties anymore."

Kendrick looked at her. "What makes you think I'm going to train shirtless with these lunatics?"

Anne flashed him a sultry look to show him how she felt about the thought of seeing him bare chested. Kendrick's amber eyes darkened before he turned to Aiden. "What time do you muscle heads start in the morning?"

Anne winked at Meryn who was all smiles.

"Between never and never thirty," Aiden replied sourly.

Kendrick shrugged. "I guess I can walk around shirtless in the house."

Gavriel growled. "We start right after breakfast. Keep your clothes on in the house when you are around my mate."

Kendrick turned to Elizabeth. "No offense, but I'm attracted to teal-eyed nurses who like to introduce me to anime shows and then don't let me watch the endings."

Anne smiled wide. "I didn't know you liked the show that much."

Kendrick groaned. "Was that all you heard?"

Anne blinked. "Huh?"

"Nothing." Kendrick shook his head.

"I can't wait to tell my minion we have someone else to help us," Meryn said, swirling her soup with her spoon.

Kendrick smacked his forehead with the palm of his hand. "Minion! I completely forgot about Basil! After we got back, I told him to inventory his new supplies along with what he already had. I promised to show him the crystal spells today. I hadn't anticipated helping in pitched battles with ferals this evening."

"You got a minion too?" Meryn asked excitedly.

Kendrick nodded. "Basil Barberry. I felt horrible about taking his spot on Alpha so I decided to show him some higher-level magic while I'm here. I can't believe I forgot about him."

Darian chuckled. "Don't worry about that one. He's sharp as a tack and a hard worker. As soon as he saw everyone mobilizing, he volunteered to help escort the hostages. He and the other trainees helped to get them settled in the city. I bet you anything he'll be here first thing after breakfast and ready to go."

Kendrick slumped back in his seat, looking relieved. "Thank the Gods. I'm glad he wasn't upset."

Colton laughed. "Our trainees are great, well, except for Sterling. But you've already handled him."

Aiden laughed loudly. "It made my morning coming back from that council meeting to find Sterling stewing in his own shit. I'm going to talk to my father. There has to be something that can be done about him, he's not cut out to be a warrior. He's too rank-conscious."

Colton was about to respond when they heard a knock at the door.

Meryn jumped up and ran out of the room toward the door.

Everyone stood and hurried after the small woman.

"Don't answer it, Meryn!" Aiden yelled.

Meryn froze mid-step, hand extended toward the doorknob. She straightened. "I told you, bad guys don't knock."

Aiden strode past her. "Only in your own little world."

Meryn rolled her eyes and pointed to the door.

Aiden opened it. "Can I help you?"

Anne stayed back with Kendrick. They couldn't see the visitors past Aiden's large body.

"Is Meryn or Amelia here?" A female voice asked. Aiden opened the door further. Anne could see a man and woman standing on the porch.

"Mother!" Amelia cried and flew past Aiden into the arms of a dark haired woman and tall, silver-eyed man.

"Amelia! It's so good to see you! Let me look at you." The woman turned Amelia around taking in every inch. "I've been so worried! We got reports on the road that ferals attacked the city. Of course, I told your father to drive faster so we could get here to help."

"Lily and Marshall Ironwood, I presume," Aiden said, opening the door completely to allow the couple to walk in, Amelia wedged between them.

Marshall stopped and offered Aiden his hand, and they clasped forearms in greeting. "It's great to finally be able to meet you, Commander. I have heard nothing but wonderful things from my sons."

"They are a credit to your line. I trust them implicitly with running the units in Storm Keep," Aiden said, smiling at the older man.

Anne's attention wasn't on Aiden or Marshall; she was watching Meryn who had quietly walked behind the men and closed the door. She was hunched in on herself, trying to appear as small as possible. It was clear, at least to Anne, that she was scared to death to meet her relatives.

Finally, Amelia's head popped up and she looked around. She spotted Meryn off to one side, went to her, and had to practically drag her by the arm to stand in front of her parents.

"Mother, Father, this is Meryn. She's my baby sister-cousin."

Lily pulled Meryn into her arms. "My dear, sweet child." She pulled back and looked at Meryn carefully. "You look just like your mother."

Meryn looked like she was about to bolt at any second. Anne was about to go to her when Ryuu appeared at Meryn's side. "*Denka*, perhaps everyone would be more comfortable if we returned to the dining room?" he suggested.

Wordlessly, Meryn nodded and led the way.

Anne didn't know a lot about Meryn's past, but when boisterous people got quiet, it was never for a good reason.

CHAPTER TEN

Anne noticed that Kendrick's entire body had become tense. He kept his head down, concentrating on his soup.

She leaned closer to him. "Dinner can't be that fascinating," she whispered.

Kendrick's mouth moved, and Anne had to assume it was his attempt at a smile. Amelia was practically vibrating in her chair as she made introductions, and Meryn looked like she was two seconds away from sliding under the table.

She and Kendrick had chosen to scoot down to open up seats for Lily and Marshall next to Amelia and Darian. This put Kendrick at the end of the table opposite Aiden with Amelia sitting to his left. He didn't look like he was happy with his new seat.

Lily had her arms around Amelia and was brushing away tears. "Thank the Gods that you're safe! Caiden waited until we called to tell him we had arrived in Lycaonia to tell us about your kidnapping. It's all our fault!"

"Lily." Marshall called her name sharply.

Meryn sat up, bristling. "She can say whatever the hell she wants to."

Anne grinned. There was the pint-sized whirlwind she had come to know. Beside her, Kendrick snorted.

Marshall turned to Meryn, a look of shock on his face. "Of course, she can," He stopped and raised his right hand. He began to whisper, and the air seemed to shimmer. "There, I've soundproofed the room. I was simply warning her that we could be overheard, sweetheart. I wasn't trying to censure what she was saying. Once you get to know your aunt, you will realize that would be an impossible task."

Lily beamed at Meryn. "You don't act a thing like your mother," she said laughing.

Meryn shrugged. "I wouldn't know; she died when I was little," she mumbled.

Lily sobered instantly. "I wish you could have known her. She was sweet and kind. She never had a bad word to say about anyone, much like my Amelia here."

Meryn stared down at her plate. "I'm not like her at all."

Lily smiled. "No dear, you're not." Meryn winced. Lily continued. "You're just like me."

Meryn looked up, eyes wide. "Really?"

Marshall chuckled. "Gods help us all, but I think she's right. Lily would have put me in my place exactly as you did just now. She's very fierce about the ones she loves."

Amelia stared at her mother in shock. "She is?"

Lily cuddled Amelia closer. "It's time we told you the truth about what is happening. You and your brothers are already being targeted, there's no reason to hide what we're doing anymore."

"Mother?" Confused, Amelia looked from one parent to the other.

"Yes, Lily, Marshall, please share what you mean." Kendrick sat back and crossed his arms.

Marshall glared at her mate. "I don't have to answer to you Kendrick Ashwood, despite you being my daughter's *athair.*"

Kendrick laced his fingers behind his head. "I think we're all very curious as to what you meant by your statements, that's all."

Lily pulled back and took Amelia's hands in hers. "Your father and I haven't been traveling around communing with nature all these years."

"What have you been doing?" Amelia asked.

Lily looked over at Marshall who nodded encouragingly. She took a deep breath. "Right before you were born, we were tasked with a very important mission. We've been tracking down Storm Keep's missing royal couple."

Beside her, Kendrick exhaled slowly. Anne looked up and saw that his jaw was clenched and the muscles in his neck were strained. She reached out, took his hand, and slowly began massaging the center of his palm. She was satisfied when he relaxed a fraction.

"I thought you were eating alfalfa sprouts and learning yoga!" Amelia exploded.

Lily shook her head. "It has taken us decades, but we're close to finding our king and queen."

Gavriel leaned forward. "Kiran and Celeste disappeared over five thousand years ago, just after the Great War and the creation of the four pillar cities. Their castle had just been finished when they were attacked and forced to flee."

Marshall nodded. "That was when the council rose to power. The royal house fell, and the heads of the two noble houses were murdered." He looked over at Amelia. "That would be your great-grandparents and the Ashleighs' great-grandparents. The two noble families wouldn't be able to return to Storm Keep for nearly one hundred years, and even then, they weren't allowed to move back into the royal palace. So, the surviving family members slowly bought up most of the land around the castle and built the two enormous estates that still stand today, the left and right sides that create the gate tower for the upper city.

"To this day, we have carried out our sworn duties to protect the royal family. We, the Ironwoods, act as the royal shield; the Ashleighs act as the royal sword. We protect the royal family from harm and they destroy their enemies."

"Well, obviously y'all did a real bang-up job, seeing as how they were kicked out of their own castle and have been missing for five thousand years," Meryn said sarcastically.

Marshall winced. "I have spoken with Thane's father and compared the journals that we have from our parents. There is more to the story than we know. Despite actually being there and witnessing everything firsthand, their accounts of the events of that night are sketchy. Even our covert interviews with the few remaining witches who were alive at the time revealed the same exact vague details. Whatever happened was so subtle and so precisely done that the entire kingdom failed to realize something huge had taken place. It was only after I compared my notes with Thane's that we even saw the pattern. When asked certain questions, everyone gave the exact same response. It was as if one day we had a king, and the next, we had a council, and no one marked the change."

"That's impossible! The people must have turned on the king, there's no spell that can affect so many different people all at once," Kendrick insisted.

Marshall nodded. "You're right, which is what led Thane and me to Noctem Falls."

Kendrick sucked in his breath. "The vampires?"

Gavriel shook his head, his eyes flashing dangerously. "Wait a moment, what you are suggesting could be grounds for the next Great War; be very careful what you say."

Anne gripped Kendrick's hand tightly. He squeezed her fingers and covered their joined hands with his right hand. He turned to her, and she watched his lips move silently. She felt the pressure in her ears build.

He turned to her. "We don't have much time before Marshall notices that I cast a soundproof bubble."

"What do you need me to do?" Anne asked. Whatever was happening, she knew she would do anything he asked.

"My levelheaded nurse." He smiled tightly. "I will have to reveal some things that may change our lives forever. But if you tell me right now that you don't want any part of this mess, I won't say anything. We can remain an archivist and a nurse and probably live a fairly normal life."

Anne searched his face for a clue to what he was talking about; all she saw was sadness. "If you say whatever you were going to say, could it save lives?"

He nodded once.

"If you don't say anything, could good people die?"

He nodded again.

She brought his hand up to her lips and kissed his hand. "Then I think you already know what we should do."

He turned their hands over and kissed hers in return. "I love you, Anne Bennett. I wanted you to know that before everything changes. I loved you from the moment I saw you in my dreams. I loved the way you wept for my brother because you saw your friend was hurt. I love how you can watch a love story and be swept away. I love how, in a crisis, you remain a rock in the storm. Fate could not have chosen better for me."

"And I love you, too, Kendrick Ashwood. I love how you can tease one moment and be serious the next. I love how protective you are of the ones you care about. I love how patient you were with me, how you weren't pushy or angry about our situation. I love that you are probably the most powerful one at this table, but you're also the kindest."

"I have to collapse the bubble now." He leaned forward and kissed her lightly.

She smiled. "Remind me to tell you about our sons later."

"What!" Kendrick exclaimed.

All eyes turned to them. Aiden looked around as if evaluating possible threats. "Everything okay, Kendrick?"

Anne looked up at her mate and smiled. She reached up and patted his cheek. "He'll be okay," she said casually.

Kendrick blinked, then blinked again. He turned, looked at everyone, and blinked again.

Anne, super nurse, one. Almighty Kendrick, zero. This will probably be one of the best moments of our relationship. I should take a picture!

Anne reached into her pocket and pulled out her phone. "Kendrick, look this way."

He turned, still looking shocked. She clicked the picture and put her phone away.

"You are a very, very evil woman," he croaked.

"Don't be silly." She looked at Marshall. "I'm sorry, what were you saying? We may have missed a bit."

Marshall had an amused expression on his face as he looked between them. "Kendrick, welcome to being mated." He tuned back to Gavriel. "As I was saying, we don't believe that the entire vampire race is plotting against the witches. Hell, we're not even saying a large faction even knows what happened, but the only explanation for that many people suddenly being perfectly fine with losing their beloved king is if they were manipulated by either a very powerful vampire or a small group of vampires working together."

Amelia looked at her parents. "Why? Why didn't you tell me? Why did you let me think that you just didn't want me?"

Lily covered her face, and Marshall reached past his mate to run a hand over Amelia's hair. Anne could tell Amelia had been hurt by her parents' revelations.

Marshall smiled at his daughter. "Because my darling, it was the only way to keep you safe. There wasn't a day that went by that we didn't think of you."

Amelia wiped at her eyes. "What about that day when I was little, in the forest, when you tried to teach me to commune with nature, and I ended up covered in bug bites? Was that just an act to make me believe your story?"

Lily shook her head. "We were being tracked and monitored. It was the only way I could think of to make you sit still. We didn't come home for a long time after that."

Darian held Amelia close. "Why now? After all these millennia, why did you have to leave right after Amelia was born?" His voice was stern. It was clear he didn't like anything upsetting his mate, even her own parents.

Marshall responded. "Thane Ashleigh had a vision that our king would return. So, we started searching for him while he and his brothers tried to uncover the truth about what happened five thousand years ago. We're supposed to find our king and queen and protect them, and they are to eliminate any remaining threat to them."

Marshall looked at Amelia with tears in his eyes. "The safety of our king and the future of our kingdom are the only things that could have taken us from you."

Beside her, Kendrick took a deep breath. "What if I asked you to abandon your search? What if I reached out to Thane, Justice, and Law and called them in? What would you do?"

Marshall frowned. "Why would we give up now when we're so close? Why should we abandon our missions? For decades we have sacrificed so much to see our kingdom restored. You may not see it Kendrick, but I do. Every day, witches are moving away from who we are as a people. They are abandoning the old ways, and the only thing that matters to them are their assessment scores. Storm Keep has become a corporation where the council is practically selling the services of our people to the highest bidder. King Kiran would never stand for this. He believes in the connection to nature and our Gods. King Kiran–"

"Is dead," Kendrick said softly.

Marshall stared at him. "You lie," he choked out.

Kendrick shook his head. "I wish I were. I buried them both, with my own hands, three hundred years ago."

Lily began to shake. "But we found a cabin; we found King Kiran's signet ring."

Kendrick looked at her, pity in his eyes. "Do you think that the king would leave something so important behind?"

Marshall took a deep breath. "They have to be alive, or everything was for nothing."

"They are buried about a half mile behind the cabin, in a small clearing at the edge of the forest, under a large oak tree." Kendrick's voice was calm, even gentle.

Marshall slammed his hands on the table. "How could you keep something like this a secret?" he demanded.

Kendrick looked him in the eye. "Who was I to tell? Their enemies knew they were dead, and their people had long since forgotten them."

Lily eyed him with suspicion. "Why you? Why did you know where they were? Did they contact you? Why couldn't you save them?" Her voice was filled with emotion.

Beside her, Kendrick clenched both fists. "You think I didn't want to save them? That I wouldn't trade places with them in an instant if I could?" He threw his head back and laughed.

Anne's eyes filled with tears. The laughter she heard wasn't born of mirth; it was dredged from the darkest places of his soul, through pain and a sorrow so deep she couldn't imagine ever smiling again after laughing like that.

Kendrick's macabre laughter echoed through the room. When he was done, his eyes looked empty. He smiled, but it was hollow. "Forget about your grandiose dream of a kingdom that will never exist. Even if he was still alive, I would never stand by and allow him to give up his happiness to serve a bunch of weak-willed sycophants who allowed their one true king to be routed from his home and chased like an animal." There was a sharp edge to his words. "Storm Keep deserves exactly what they got, a council that dictates their lives according to the rule of power."

Amelia stared at Kendrick as if she didn't know him. "You don't believe that."

Kendrick sneered at her. "Oh yes, yes, I do."

She shook her head. "No, you don't! If you didn't care, you wouldn't have deliberately chosen to live in Lower City where you could help the most people. You wouldn't have helped my brothers with the units. You wouldn't have sent spell after spell to witches outside the city to keep them safe. If you truly didn't care about anyone, you wouldn't have raised such a loving and kind brother. And you wouldn't have been my *athair*." Amelia's voice broke, and sobbing, she turned to Darian.

Darian glared at Kendrick. "You've hurt her."

Kendrick shrugged. "She's a crybaby; she's been hurting for other people her whole life."

Amelia wailed harder, and Darian ground his teeth together. "You and me, outside. Now!"

Kendrick twirled a hand at him. "Sorry, old man, I don't have time for a macho showdown."

Anne twisted her hands in her lap. She had to believe that Kendrick was doing this for a reason, but what reason could he have to hurt Amelia? She looked over at Meryn. Meryn was watching Kendrick closely and not saying a word. It was as if she, too, was trying to figure out what Kendrick was doing.

Marshall stood, eyes blazing. "You've gone too far! How dare you hurt my daughter? You'll make time for me, young man!"

Kendrick smiled lazily. "What do you care? You couldn't protect your king, and you abandoned your own daughter in the process. Tell me, why I should take you seriously? What are you going to do?" Kendrick stood, knocking his chair over. "Well? Your king is dead. You have no idea who your enemy is. You're clearly outnumbered and outmatched. What. Will. You. Do?" Kendrick drew out each word mockingly.

Marshall roared. "I'll fight! I will uncover the truth, and when I do, I will destroy the ones who killed our king. I will make our people face the truth. I will erase every assessment test and protocol our council has put forth!" Marshall drew in a shaky breath. "We'll start over."

Kendrick let his head fall forward, when he raised it back up, there was warmth in his eyes again. "Then it sounds like you have a plan." When he smiled, it was no longer empty or sardonic.

Amelia turned in her chair to face him. "I hate you!"

Kendrick winced. "Oh, my darling girl, I am more sorry than you will ever know. But I had to know how far your father was willing to go. You know I didn't mean any of it."

Amelia glared at him. "You called me a crybaby."

"Well, you are." Kendrick said, looking confused.

"I am, but you said it to be mean," Amelia pointed out.

"I said I was sorry."

"You owe me two rides," Amelia sniffled.

Kendrick sighed. "Fine. Two rides."

"Rides?" Anne and Meryn asked at the same time.

Amelia wiped her face with her napkin. "Kendrick can fly."

"Seriously?" Anne and Meryn asked in unison again.

Kendrick nodded and picked up his chair. "I picked it up somewhere." He sat down and placed his napkin in his lap.

Marshall remained standing, he stared at Kendrick as if he had never seen him before. "Who are you?" he asked in a raspy voice.

Kendrick shrugged. "I'm just a poor archivist from the Lower City."

Meryn gasped and covered her mouth with her hands.

Kendrick shook his head. "I should have known you'd figure it out first. What gave it away?"

"Your name. Beth and I are doing the census; of course, I paid close attention to the family histories of everyone in this house. Keelan's was the only one that came up with a dead end. I was going to ask you about it later but..." Meryn blinked. "Holy shit balls," she whispered softly.

"Oh, Gods!" Gavriel and Beth exclaimed at the same time.

Anne turned over everything in her mind. The one word that popped out at her from the jumbled mess of confusion swirling around her mind was, *heika*. It meant...

"Your Majesty," she whispered.

There was a look of pride in Kendrick's eyes when he looked down at her. "I knew you'd get it."

"Holy shit balls is right," Colton echoed.

"How?" Aiden asked, looking from Meryn to Kendrick then to Marshall.

"Your Majesty!" Marshall exclaimed and bowed so deep Anne thought he was going to fall forward.

Kendrick shook his head. "Please don't call me that."

Lily stood quickly and curtsied low beside her mate. "Your Majesty, please forgive us."

Ryuu swept in from the kitchen and looked around. He turned to Kendrick. "You finally told them?"

Kendrick grimaced. "Sort of."

Ryuu placed a bowl of soup in front of Lily then Marshall. "You may want to get up; he really doesn't like that." Ryuu refilled their water glasses and walked around the table to check on Meryn.

Marshall and Lily straightened then looked at Kendrick who motioned to their chairs. They sat down, looking completely dazed.

Aiden stared at Meryn. "How did you figure it out?"

Meryn smirked. "Their last name. Ashwood. He combined the names of the two loyal houses. Ash from Ashleigh and Wood from Ironwood, Ashwood. There are no documented births or deaths of anyone with that last name in any of our records."

Marshall stared at Kendrick. "Prince Julian?"

Kendrick nodded.

"Julian?" The question was echoed around the table.

Kendrick shot Anne an apologetic look before facing everyone. "My name is Julian Stormhart, son of Kiran and Celeste Stormhart of the witch's city of Storm Keep."

Meryn turned to Anne. "This definitely increases his rank."

"Meryn!" Aiden covered her mouth with his hand.

Kendrick winked at the small troublemaker.

"But you were lost to us, how? When?" Marshall stuttered.

Kendrick threaded his fingers together in front of him on the table and took a deep breath. "I never really fit in among the noble families. I didn't look like mother or father; the rumors the nobles allowed a young boy to overhear were hurtful. So, I left as soon as I was old enough. Father had mastered mind magic before I was born and was an expert dream walker. Even though I travelled all over the world, he would reach out to me at least once a month to see what I was up to."

Kendrick smiled at the memory. "For over a thousand years I trained with shamans, priests, monks, keepers of knowledge. I was in what is now called Japan when news of the Great War reached me. My father had kept all knowledge of the War from me to keep me out of the fighting. He insisted I stay away, so, of course I wanted to come home, but I was too late. When I finally returned home, a new city had been formed, a castle built, and my parents were missing." He took a deep breath.

"Since I had been gone so long, no one recognized me. I wandered around the city for days looking for clues to what happened. When I heard about the deaths of my father's most trusted and closest friends and their mates, I knew I had to leave the city. I traveled for weeks before my father reached out to me in my dreams. He said that they had been betrayed and could never return to the city. I argued and told him I would fight, but he said no. That it was impossible to fight an unknown enemy.

"I had no idea what he meant at the time. I was young and angry, but I did as my father ordered and I stayed away from Storm Keep. Over time, my parents were forgotten, and we settled into a peaceful life. I still travelled, and they built a tiny cabin in the woods."

His expression softened. "I think that the years they spent alone in that cabin were the happiest of my parents' lives. They weren't a king and a queen, they were simply Kiran and Celeste."

He shook his head. "Anyway, everything was peaceful until the twins were born. Father didn't realize how much power they were giving off. It made it easy for our enemies to find them. One night, during a dream visit, I finally was able to meet my baby brothers for the first time. Gods! They were so tiny and helpless, I fell in love the second I saw them." He swallowed hard. "Mother dropped out of the dream first, to put Kendrick to bed. Keelan stayed with my father since I was still playing with him. We heard a loud noise and a scream. I'll never forget the look on my father's face when he realized my mother had been killed." He squeezed his hands together tightly in front of him.

"When my father realized that my mother was already dead and Kendrick along with her, he made a decision. He pulled out his dagger and sliced open his wrists. He called upon the Gods to grant him one final wish. Instead of using his vast power to fight his enemies, he offered up his life and pushed the baby and his grimoire to me. I remember screaming at him to fight, but the look he gave me was so peaceful and serene, I knew he wanted to be with my mother and brother more than he wanted revenge. He didn't want them facing death alone.

"When I woke, Keelan was in my arms, and my father's grimoire was on the floor. My father made history that day as the first witch to pass physical matter across great distances in a dream state, but no one would ever know.

"To keep us safe, I bound Keelan's powers until he was old enough to do it himself and we moved back to Storm Keep. I figured that the enemy didn't know that Keelan or I even existed, and if we did, what were the odds we would live right under their noses? I took my brother's name, so that, in some small way, I could honor his memory and settled in as lowly archivist. I could monitor the council closely and slowly destroy the books of powerful spells my father was forced to leave behind."

"You don't look like a Julian," Meryn announced.

Kendrick gave her a grateful smile. "That's because I'm not, not anymore."

"But Your Majesty, this changes everything," Marshall started.

Kendrick shook his head. "This changes nothing. Without cutting off the head of the snake, history is doomed to repeat itself. I won't reveal myself and put my loved ones in danger for nothing. Only after we identify our true enemies can we hope to make any changes."

"Not to sound like a smart ass..." Meryn began. She had to stop when almost everyone around the table snorted. "As I was saying, I don't want to state the obvious, but aren't the ones in power now the ones who are responsible? Can't we just go kick their asses and call it a day?"

Lily shook her head gently at Meryn. "You are truly my niece. I'm afraid the answer isn't so simple, or I would have done just that years ago."

"Well, why not?" Anne demanded. She didn't like the idea that Kendrick was in danger.

"Because, Your Majesty, the ones in power were most likely manipulated in the same way as the people." Lily explained.

Anne blinked.

All at once, the implications of Kendrick's royalty hit her. "Oh, my."

Kendrick reached over and began rubbing her back. "It's okay, everything is the same as when we sat down for Ryuu's wonderful soup. Breathe."

Anne turned and slapped at him with both hands. "Don't tell me to breathe, you royal pain in the ass! I'm fine!"

Meryn cackled. "I knew I liked her."

"Actually, Anne, you're hyperventilating," Rheia called out from the end of the table.

Anne took a deep breath and held it before exhaling slowly. She did that a couple more times all while glaring at Kendrick.

"Where's my levelheaded nurse?" he teased.

She flipped him off, and he chuckled. He winked at her and lifted his wine glass. She narrowed her eyes and leaned in close enough so only he could hear. "Keelan showed me a dream where I had triplet boys."

Kendrick sputtered in his wine glass and began to choke, which caused him to inhale more wine. Smiling sweetly, she now rubbed his back. "There, there darling, everything is okay. Just breathe."

Meryn licked her finger and drew an invisible line in the air marking Anne's victory over Kendrick.

It took a couple minutes for Kendrick to clear his airways. His chest was still heaving as he stared at her in wonder. "Truly?" Kendrick grinned at her with a goofy look on his face.

"Maybe."

"Well, I know what I'm doing tonight," he announced.

She gulped hard and stared at him. The dark, heated look he was giving her reminded her of the way a jungle cat watches its prey.

"So what do we do?" Lily asked.

Kendrick broke eye contact with her and turned back to the others. "Do exactly what you have been doing. This secret cannot leave the room. If you don't think you can carry on as you always have, you need to let me know, and I'll erase it from your mind."

"I think I speak for all of us when I say that we will, of course, keep your secret," Gavriel replied formally.

"Our mission is over." Lily turned to Marshall.

Marshall smiled at his mate. "And we have a daughter, a new son and niece to get to know."

Aiden cleared his throat. "Actually, if you could call Caiden and resume your Elder role, that would help us out quite a bit."

Marshall nodded. "Of course, but why is that a problem?"

"Because we have multi-flavor douchebags from each of the pillar cities trying to cause trouble," Meryn explained.

Lily smiled and tapped her lips. "Really? That sounds like fun."

"Oh, Gods," Aiden, Marshall, and Elizabeth said at the same time.

Beside her, Kendrick stood. "Aiden, I'll let you catch Marshall and Lily up on where we stand with the Committee. I have other pressing matters to attend to." Kendrick turned to Anne and bowed, one hand over his heart and the other stretched out to her. "My Lady, may I escort you upstairs?"

"Bow chica wow wow," Meryn sung.

Anne felt herself blushing furiously, but didn't care. She placed her hand in his and stood. Turning, she noticed that everyone at the table was grinning ear to ear.

"Good night everyone," she said.

"Sleep tight!" Rheia called.

"Don't let the bed bugs bite!" Amelia yelled laughing.

"But let Kendrick bite if he wants to!" Colton smirked.

Everyone was still laughing as they walked into the hallway. Kendrick was every inch the gentlemen until they stepped into the foyer.

"I will give you a ten-second head start." His eyes flashed with lust.

"Fuck!"

"Exactly."

Anne didn't waste another precious second; she ran.

CHAPTER ELEVEN

Anne ran as fast as she could, but he still caught up with her before she even reached the top of the stairs. She laughed as he swung her up in his arms and headed to her bedroom.

"Not to ruin the mood, but I need to check on Keelan," she said as they passed his door.

Kendrick stopped and set her on her feet. "Thank you for putting his needs above your own."

Anne opened the door and approached Keelan's bed. "He may not be my mate, but he is my best friend." She checked his feeding tube and his IV port and replaced his drip bag. "Does he know about your parents?"

Kendrick shook his head. "No. I never wanted to put him in any danger, he was better off not knowing."

"What did you tell him about your parents?" Anne asked.

"That they died in a boating accident trying to cross the river; neither one of them knew water magic. It was the most plausible explanation I could come up with." Kendrick smiled down at his brother.

"He didn't even think to doubt you, did he?"

"No. Growing up, he must have believed I walked on water. He was always following me around, getting into my spell supplies." Kendrick laughed suddenly. "When he was two, he ate almost an entire bag of saltpeter while I was engrossed in translating a manuscript. When I realized what he was doing, I ran around like a madman trying to find someone to help. The widow down the road laughed at me and gave him a liquid that made him start throwing up. I felt like the worst brother in the entire universe as I watched my little buddy empty the contents of his stomach for five hours. That episode made me want to learn about healing. I never wanted to stand by helpless when he needed me again."

"I can't wait to ask him questions about you." Anne held out her hand.

Kendrick took it and dimmed the lights in the room with a wave of his hand.

Arriving at her guest suite felt almost anti-climatic. When the door shut behind them, she sighed. Kendrick went to the dresser and turned on the small lamp. Its low wattage gave off just enough light to see but was easy on the eyes.

Kendrick looked up. "Do you want me to chase you around the bedroom?"

She laughed and shook her head. "It feels so obligatory now."

"Obligatory?" Kendrick slowly unzipped his hoodie. "I'll give you obligatory."

Anne watched him as he casually began to strip out of his clothing. When he was shirtless and unbuttoning his jeans, she held up her hand. "Stop."

Kendrick blinked. "Everything?"

She walked over and reached out tentatively. Kendrick's personality hinged on his brilliant mind, so she often forgot that he was extremely well muscled. The short auburn chest hair gave him a warm glow in the low light.

She started by placing her hands side by side in the center of his chest then moved them upward, caressing his muscles. She ran her hands down his sides and then around the front, tracing the indention his hips made, which led downward. His body, under her hands, was very still. She looked up and saw a look of wonder on his face. She leaned in, placed her cheek against his chest, and listened to his heartbeat. "You're beautiful, you know. You have one of the most perfect bodies I have ever seen."

She eyed the brilliant red, black, and silvery white tattoos on his right forearm and looked up at him. "Very nice," she murmured.

He winked at her and took both of her hands in his, kissing them gently. He let them drop, grabbed the hem of her shirt, and pulled it up over her head. "Do I get to return the favor?"

She nodded as he slowly and deliberately removed each piece of clothing. He stopped when she stood before him in just her bra and panties. "I think I prefer to take you slowly rather than in the heat of the moment." He slid her bra straps down before he leaned down to kiss her collarbones. "I want you to know that I am thinking of you and only you, every second I am making love to you. I want you to know that each touch, each kiss, and each caress is deliberate. I don't want you to give in to mindless passion, because your mind is the thing I love the most about you." He undid the clasp and let the bra fall to the floor. "I want to explore every inch of you. I want to memorize every bump, freckle, and scar. I want to burn into my memory how your body feels against mine so that it never feels complete without you."

Kendrick pulled her close and the heat of his skin against her sensitive nipples caused her to shiver. He looked down and it was almost as if his amber eyes were glowing like molten gold. "Would you rather I throw you on the bed and pleasure you so much that you don't know your own name? Or would you rather I love you tortuously, drawing out every single wave of ecstasy until my name is the only thing you know?"

Anne wrapped her arms around his neck and looked up at him. "The second one, then the first one twice, then the second one again," she grinned up him.

Kendrick looked up at the ceiling before smiling down at her. "You will be the death of me."

"Always," she promised.

Kendrick stepped backward and unzipped his jeans. When he let them fall, Anne began to have serious regrets about asking for multiple sessions. She doubted she was going to survive the first round.

His cock was erect and reached his belly button. As if she wasn't worried enough about the length, the rounded head capped a shaft that she knew she would barely be able to wrap her hand around.

"It won't kill you," Kendrick said laughing.

Anne scrunched up her face. "It might."

"Let's see." He knelt down in front of her and rolled her panties over her hips and down her legs. She stepped out of them, and he threw them across the room.

"Have you ever made love to a witch before?" he asked as he used his thumbs to part her folds.

She shook her head. "You know I haven't."

Kendrick looked up at her with an impish smile on his face. "Then let me introduce you to benefits of being mated to a witch."

One second she was standing, the next she was on her back, floating in mid-air. "Kendrick?"

"I've mastered air magic my love, you won't fall."

He floated her over to the bed, but instead of letting her fall onto the covers, he kept her floating three feet above them.

She raised an eyebrow.

"The better to eat you, my dear." He spread her legs wide and ran his tongue up her slit until he was teasing her clit with his teeth.

Gasping, she threw her head back. Over and over he alternated between sharp bites and rapid flicks of his tongue. With her legs straining, she reached for him, chasing the pleasure he promised.

He drew back and dropped her gently on the bed. She whimpered at the loss, and he chuckled.

"It gets better," he said as he reached down and began to enter her slowly.

She knew she was right to be concerned. He was stretching her too much. She began thrashing her head from side to side. "Kendrick!"

She was about to tell him to stop when she felt his hot mouth on her clit again.

Huh? How could he be pleasuring her with both his mouth and his cock at the same time?

She opened her eyes, and he was smiling down at her. "How?"

"Fire magic."

The heat twisted and turned. She clenched down on his invading cock, trying to capture that one thing she was desperate for.

He leaned forward and leisurely licked and nibbled on her left breast. When he pulled back, an icy biting sensation distracted her from the overwhelming sensations around her clit.

He surged deep, filling her completely before igniting his fire spell to send her into the stratosphere. He mercilessly kept her on the brink of climax and then brought her down with a bite of ice. Back and forth, he used the dueling sensations to drive her out of her mind.

Just when she thought she couldn't take it anymore, he was leaning over her, thrusting into her over and over again. His gaze was filled with love and his eyes with tears as he began to recite words that she somehow knew; it was as if they were written on her heart and only he could see the words to unlock her soul.

"As there is a sun and moon, a sky and earth, and a Lord and Lady, so there are two pieces to this one soul. Let us be complete once more, never to be torn apart. I give everything I am into my mate's keeping, let my love protect and guard our joined souls."

He thrust deep one final time, shuddering with his own release, which triggered her orgasm. As her heartbeat began to slow, she began to feel a gentle, warm wave begin to engulf her. It wasn't forceful or savage. It was kind and patient as it slowly invaded every cell in her body. She felt new connections as awareness flooded her senses. She was now tied to nature itself; it was so humbling and beautiful, and she began to cry.

Kendrick withdrew from her body and rolled them onto their sides, wrapping his body around hers. He held her close as the waves began to dissipate.

She wasn't able to speak for a few minutes. "What was that?"

Kendrick kissed the side of her neck. "That was my magic, my connection with nature. I'm closer to Her than most witches. She was very happy to meet you."

Anne could still feel his power trickling through her body. "Am I a witch now?"

Behind her, she felt him shake his head. "No, you're still human, but you'll gain the ability to do certain things."

"Like what?"

Kendrick shrugged. "It's different for every couple. Usually a male witch and a female witch will exchange aspects of the magic they are best at. For example, a fire witch may gain the ability to call a breeze from his mate who can work with air spells."

"But you don't do just one thing."

"No, I don't."

"So, you really don't know."

"No, but doesn't that make it exciting?"

She laughed and then gasped. She could definitely feel the aftereffects of his lovemaking.

"Did I hurt you?" he asked immediately, sounding concerned.

"No, not really. I'm just slightly sore. It's more of a nuisance than pain."

He didn't say anything.

"Are you grinning?" She reached up behind her head to feel for his face.

Laughing, he fake growled and nipped at her fingers, causing her to squeal. "Careful love, you'll poke me in the eye."

Anne went to turn so she could face him and realized how big a mess they had made. She sat up and grimaced, looking at the covers.

Kendrick shook his head, went to the center of the room, and picked up his clothes, which now resembled a long gown.

"Didn't you have pants?"

Kendrick nodded. "Yes, but if I don't have them on for a certain period of time, the garment returns to its original state. Come here."

Anne gingerly hopped off the bed and stood in front of him.

He unbuttoned the gown and laid it across the bed where they had just made love.

"Kendrick! It's going to get dirty." She went to reach for it, but he stopped her.

"And for my next magic trick." He swept the fabric off the bed and it was as clean as it was at the beginning of the night. Anne sniffed; actually, it was cleaner. It now smelled like it had just come in off the line.

He pulled her close and wrapped the gown around them. Seconds later, her body was clean and even her teeth felt brushed. She stepped out of the gown and spun around check her body.

"That is amazing!"

"Now, I believe the order was second option, first one twice, and then back to the second?" Kendrick stalked toward her.

Giggling, she ran for the bed. His magic clothes were going to get quite a workout.

The next morning, they had already checked on Keelan and were just sitting down to enjoy their first cup of coffee when Anne heard loud footsteps racing down the stairs. Anne looked around, and only Darian and Amelia were absent.

The door flew inward, and a completely panicked Darian ran in holding a bundle of clothes.

Aiden stood. "Darian? What's wrong?"

Darian just stared in horror as the lump of clothes began moving. Seconds later, the head of a puffy German Shepard puppy emerged. It gave the cutest bark and looked around the room, tail wagging.

"Oh, my god! It's so cute!" Anne exclaimed.

Meryn had already hopped out of her chair and had raced over to Darian. "He's so cute!" Meryn gave him no choice and tugged the puppy out of his arms. She rubbed her cheek over the puppy's head over and over again. She turned to Aiden. "Can we keep him?"

"No!" Aiden and Darian exclaimed together.

Darian tried to get the puppy back, but Meryn kept turning her body. "Meryn, give her back!"

Meryn ignored his request. "How do you know it's a girl?"

"Because that's Amelia!" Darian shouted, chest heaving.

Lily set her cup down on her saucer. "Amelia Violet Ironwood, what have you gotten yourself into?"

Darian whirled to Kendrick. "Fix her, please!" he begged.

Meryn laughed. "She's so fluffy, I'm gonna die!"

Kendrick frowned as the puppy licked Meryn's face repeatedly. "I've never seen this before."

"Never?" Darian asked, looking ill.

Kendrick shook his head. "Nope, never."

They both stared at Meryn and puppy Amelia, and finally, Kendrick turned to Darian. "Do you like dogs?"

Darian's mouth dropped open. He turned from Kendrick to Amelia and back again.

Marshall chuckled. "Amelia, doing spells like that, you'll have people thinking you're a shifter's daughter."

Rheia's look became thoughtful. "Or if she's pregnant right now, she could end up having puppies, then everyone will think they're Colton's."

Darian pulled at his long blond hair with both hands frantically.

Anne finally took pity on him and turned to her mate. "Is there nothing you can do?"

Kendrick sighed. "I suppose, but she is awfully adorable this way."

Crestfallen, Meryn looked at him. "Do we hafta?"

Kendrick stood and gathered up the forgotten clothing from the floor and walked over to Meryn. "You'd miss your cousin eventually. May I?"

Meryn kissed Amelia on the top of her fuzzy head and handed her over to Kendrick.

Kendrick lifted the puppy to eye level. "You never stop getting into trouble, do you?" He carried her out into the hallway, Darian right behind him.

Anne felt a surge of power, and a minute later, Kendrick was walking back into the dining room. "Back to normal," he announced.

"How did she manage that?" Marshall asked.

Kendrick rubbed his chin. "Evidently, both she and Meryn inherited their empathy from your mate's side of the family. Ever since Amelia's magic broke loose during the battle, her empathy has been fueling her earth magic. I'm guessing that she'll be able to do a lot more with her magic than she ever has before. Her empathy is acting like a nuclear reactor, generating more and more power due to everyone's high stress levels."

Lily looked at Meryn. "*My* side of the family? But we're human."

Kendrick shook his head. "Mostly human. I'd bet you have a witch dangling somewhere in your family tree."

Meryn waved her hand. "Can I do spells?"

"No!" Aiden answered.

"But..."

"No." Colton repeated.

"Now, that's not..."

"*No*, Meryn." Elizabeth and Rheia said firmly.

"Y'all are no fun!" Meryn paused then looked up at Aiden. "Can I have a kitten?"

Aiden nodded then stopped. "What?"

"I've been thinking, I want a kitten, like a baby lion or bobcat." Meryn sipped from her cup.

Aiden began shaking his head. "No. What? Why? Baby lions and bobcats aren't called kittens they are called cubs, and they would grow bigger than you!"

Meryn shrugged. "So would any boy we have; you don't seem to mind that idea."

Elizabeth turned to her friend. "What brought this on?"

Meryn shrugged. "I've never had a pet before. When I was growing up, no animals were allowed in the house. Holding the puppy version of Amelia made me realize how much I missed out on." She held up her butter knife like a sword. "It could be a battle cat for Felix, like Cringer from He-Man."

Colton shook his head. "No sweetie, it would eat Felix."

Meryn frowned. "I didn't think about that." She turned her head. "I'd rather have you than a cat any day of the week, Felix."

Lily looked at Meryn worriedly. "Is something there?"

Marshall leaned forward eagerly. "She has a sprite, doesn't she?"

Meryn smiled. "Go on," she said encouragingly.

The air shimmered around Meryn's head and Felix appeared. He ducked his face behind her ear.

Lily inclined her head. "Very pleased to make your acquaintance, Felix. Thank you for looking after my niece."

Felix blushed furiously, nodded, and then disappeared again.

The dining room doors opened. Darian had his arm around Amelia who was grinning sheepishly. "Sorry about that everyone, I think I'll be able to shift back on my own next time."

Darian collapsed into his chair. "There won't be a next time. Never again, Amelia."

Amelia looked up at the ceiling. "Sure."

"She's lying." Lily and Marshall said at the same time.

Darian buried his face in his hands. "I can't, I just can't."

Ryuu walked in carrying a large basket. "This may cheer you up; we received a gift basket from the fae queen. The crew that will be fixing the town square delivered it this morning. I'm told that your favorite crumpets are in here, Darian." Ryuu set the basket in the middle of the table.

Darian perked up immediately. "Really?" He stood and used a pair of metal tongs to begin sorting through the assorted pastries.

"I can see how worried he is," Anne teased.

Amelia rolled her eyes. "I swear they're all ruled by their stomachs." She pointed to Aiden and Colton who were looking in the basket of goodies.

Anne turned to Kendrick. "Aren't you hungry?"

He smiled. "What would you like?" he asked.

"A cinnamon roll, if we have any."

Kendrick waved his hand, and three pastries floated out of the basket and landed on their plates.

"How'd you do that? I thought you had to see what you were aiming your magic at?" Colton asked.

"That varies from spell to spell, in this instance, I used my earth magic to identify the apple turnovers and the cinnamon rolls, and called them to me. Apples and cinnamon are gathered from plants." Kendrick lifted the powdered turnover and bit into it. He sighed happily as he chewed.

Anne dug into her cinnamon roll and wasn't disappointed. It was the best she'd ever eaten.

Kendrick looked down at his pastry. "I see that Cord still serves at the palace."

Darian looked startled. "How did you know that?"

Kendrick raised the turnover. "I would recognize his pastries anywhere."

Darian smiled. "He is a master at what he does."

The dining room became quiet as everyone enjoyed the unexpected treats.

Anne was sipping her tea when she noticed that some seats at the table were empty. "Where are Penny, Jaxon, and Noah? Did they already eat?" she asked.

Rheia leaned forward. "Mina is visiting a friend so she isn't able to teach Penny today; Noah and Jaxon volunteered to look after her. They raided the basket before we came down and have taken over command central for the day."

Anne had to smile at the image of those three together. "They are good boys."

Meryn nodded. "They make perfect minions."

Beside her, Kendrick began to choke. He reached for his coffee and gulped a few times to clear his airway. "Minions! I completely forgot. Basil will be coming by today. I'll be showing him how I set up the tests for the different necklaces."

Aiden looked over at Kendrick. "Thank you for teaching him. It really went a long way soothing hurt feelings about advancement. You wouldn't consider teaching a class or two to all of the unit witches while you're here, would you? I know that Noah is behind in his studies as well. When his parents kicked him out, his lessons stopped."

Kendrick nodded slowly. "I could easily do that." He turned to Elizabeth. "You're the planner, aren't you?"

Elizabeth laughed. "Yes, would you like some help?"

"Yes, please."

Elizabeth pulled out her day planner. "Do you need help organizing the class list, location or syllabus?"

Kendrick winced. "All of it."

Elizabeth stopped writing and closed her planner. "Got it. I'll just let you know where and when to show up and what you'll be talking about."

Kendrick looked relieved. "Thank you! Teaching isn't really my forte."

Elizabeth eyed Meryn. "I can understand that."

Rheia looked down the table at Anne. "Anne, Meryn and I will be heading to the clinic for check ups, would you like to come along to see the location and meet Adam, our other doctor?"

Anne nodded eagerly. "I would love to."

Kendrick leaned in and kissed her neck. "Look at you, so excited at the thought of organizing latex gloves and tongue depressors."

Anne turned quickly and licked his nose. "You're geeking out just as much at the thought of teaching Basil testing procedures."

Kendrick wiped off his nose. "Touché."

Amelia turned to her parents. "I'd like to visit with you as much as possible while you're here."

Lily hugged Amelia. "Of course, Meryn, too. When she's ready."

Meryn played with her danish. "It's not like I don't want to talk to you. I just don't know what to say. The only thing that comes to mind is, 'Your mother was a hateful bitch, and I'm glad she's dead,' but that doesn't seem like something you say over tea."

Lily covered her mouth with her napkin her eyes dancing with laughter. "Oh Meryn! You could most definitely say that over tea, at least with your uncle and me. Remember darling, we knew her, too. I had to practically drag Marshall away from her house. He wanted to turn her into a toad, but I stopped him since she was still raising Violet."

Meryn thought for a second. "No, not a toad, a slug. That would have been better."

Marshall winked at Meryn, causing her to blush. "I agree one hundred percent. We could have taken turns with the salt shaker."

Meryn laughed then stared down at her plate. "Perhaps later, after my appointment, we could visit together. Maybe talk about my mother."

Lily's smile was wobbly as she blinked back tears. "I'd like nothing more."

Aiden grumbled under his breath. "The more I hear about this woman, the more I support the idea of moving her grave to Lycaonia."

Meryn laid her head contentedly on her mate's shoulder. "I don't think so. I wouldn't want her fouling the place up. Maybe somewhere nearby."

Anne couldn't imagine what this woman could have done, but by the support the idea to move this woman's grave was getting from around the table, she was glad she had never met her.

The doorbell rang signaling an end to breakfast.

Anne stood with Kendrick. "You have fun today training your minion. Try not to blow anything up while I'm gone."

Kendrick sighed. "You're taking the fun out of my morning." He rubbed noses with her. "Have fun counting bandages and taking everyone's temperature."

"You know us nurses, we love to take temperatures," she teased.

"Love you."

"Love you, too. And seriously, no blowing anything up or destroying the house."

"I'll do my best." Kendrick said magnanimously and swaggered to the door to greet Basil.

CHAPTER TWELVE

They ended up taking Anne's CRV to the clinic since it hadn't been assigned a parking spot yet and was still out front. Meryn argued with Ryuu that she didn't need a babysitter, and she didn't want him in the room when someone was looking up her hoo-ha. Ryuu managed to look annoyed and worried about his charge at the same time as he helped her put on her coat.

Once in the car and on their way, Meryn exhaled. "Freedom!"

Rheia laughed. "Have you had a moment alone since you moved in?"

Meryn shook her head. "Nope. I could kiss the one who cast the spell to put up the perimeter. Maybe now I can go to the city on my own and visit Sydney and Justice."

Anne glanced to her right where Meryn sat. "I've heard their names before, who are they?"

"Sydney and Justice run the coffee shop in the city called The Jitterbug. They're both sinfully gorgeous and so lovey-dovey it should be illegal."

Amelia's ears perked up. "I think I watched an anime that had two men that ran a coffee shop in it. I'd love to meet Sydney and Justice, they sound fun."

"They are awesome peeps. Too bad I can't sample any of their newest creations," Meryn sighed and rubbed her belly. She looked down. "You better be worth it, kiddo."

Rheia cracked up in the backseat. "She will be."

Anne smiled. "You're having a girl?"

Meryn shrugged. "I don't know. I told Rheia not to tell me. So she keeps changing up the pronouns to confuse Aiden."

"What about you Rheia, do you want to know?" Anne asked.

"I wouldn't mind one way or the other. It might make it easier to decorate," Rheia replied.

"So. You got claimed huh?" Meryn asked out of the blue.

"Meryn!" Rheia gasped, sounding mortified.

"What? She said she didn't mind telling me," Meryn pointed out.

Anne couldn't keep the smile off her face. "Yes."

"And?" Meryn fished.

"And... it was magical, for lack of a better word."

"My claiming was hot, but I don't think I would use the word magical. I got bit though." Meryn pulled down the collar of her coat to reveal two shiny pink scars.

Rheia sighed. "I got bit too."

Anne frowned. "I didn't get bit. Was I supposed to get bitten?"

Meryn tapped the door. "I don't think so, maybe it's a shifter thing."

Anne followed the road. "Maybe."

After another couple minutes of silence, "Do you think I could use my sonic screwdriver as a wand?" Meryn asked.

Anne could practically feel Rheia staring at Meryn. She looked in the rearview mirror.

Yup. The I-don't-know-what-to-do-with-you stare.

"What's a sonic screwdriver?" Anne asked, breaking the silence.

"It's something the Doctor uses in that show I was telling you about. Keelan made me a magical version of one. Since Kendrick says I have some magic in me, I was wondering if I could use it as a wand to, you know, cast spells."

Anne thought back to every instance she had seen Kendrick use magic. "Meryn, I don't think real witches use wands like that. I've never seen Kendrick use one."

"I've never seen Keelan or Quinn use one either, Meryn," Rheia added from the back.

"Hmmmm." Meryn stared out the window.

"Besides, you're forbidden to use magic, remember?" Rheia reminded her.

"If Amelia didn't get in trouble for turning herself into a dog, I think I'm okay," Meryn protested.

"Is this it?" Anne asked as a large building came in view.

"Yup, that's it," Rheia answered.

Anne parked by the door and they got out. Rheia pointed out the different exam rooms and testing equipment as they walked by them.

"What are all these boxes?" Meryn asked, pointing into the supply room.

"Those are gifts from Éire Danu and Noctem Falls. A little birdie by the name of Elizabeth Monroe made some phone calls, and suddenly, I'm knee deep in much needed supplies," a warm male voice answered.

"Hey Adam!" Meryn yelled, running up to the large stranger.

Adam swept her up into a tight hug. "Hello, baby sister!" He set her down and looked at Anne. "And who's this? A new patient?"

Rheia wrapped an arm around her shoulders and walked her forward. "This is our new nurse. Adam meet Anne Bennett, Kendrick's mate. She was the one who helped me with the casualties from the hostage situation. I swear she was amazing. She always seemed to be exactly where I needed her. She's also the one taking care of Keelan for us at the house."

Adam stretched his hand out, and when they shook hands, she noticed he had calluses on his palms.

Adam rubbed the back of his neck when he caught her staring. "I started training with the Beta Unit. After the past couple attacks, I wanted to get back into top fighting condition."

"Who in the hell would want to fight you? You're huge." Anne asked, looking up.

Adam's booming laughter made her smile. He was so much more open and friendly than his surly younger brother. Then again, Adam didn't have a mate like Meryn to keep an eye on, either.

"You'd be surprised how many ferals don't pay attention to such things." Adam held up his arm. "Ladies, let's get these exams over with so I can check on my little niece or nephew."

Rheia turned to her. "Anne, could you go back to the supply room and try to get it organized? If we have enough supplies to spare, can you pack up some basics to take back to the house?"

Anne nodded. "Sure thing. Kendrick's joke about me counting tongue depressors has come true."

"Thank you so much. We won't be long, so don't feel like you have to organize everything. We'll leave the bulk of it for Adam to finish, but anything you can do to get him started would be a help." Rheia looked back to where Meryn waited for her in the hall.

Anne shooed her away. "Go on, I'll be fine."

Anne walked down the hall and went into the supply room. After about an hour, she had grouped boxes together and had opened enough of them to put together four field kits. If they needed anything else, they could grab it later. She swung the backpack full of supplies on her shoulder and stepped out into the hallway.

The hairs on her neck began to stand straight up. Trying not to be too obvious, she stopped at the water fountain and turned her head to look down the hall. It was empty, but then, out of the corner of her eye, she saw the air shimmer. It was a cross between what the air looked like before Felix had appeared and the heat waves that rose off the road on a summer day. Something was stalking her.

She turned and fought every instinct screaming at her to keep her pace normal. She walked as normally as she could until she was in front of Adam's office door. "Guys, all clear to come in?" she yelled.

"Yup, our legs are closed and we're clothed," Meryn quipped.

Anne forced herself to laugh. She opened the door and closed it quickly, throwing the lock. Swallowing hard, she felt like her heart was in her throat.

Adam stood. "Anne?"

Anne shook her head, pointed to the door, and mouthed the words, *Something is out there.*

Adam picked up the receiver on his desk phone and lifted it to his ear. Seconds later, he put it back on the cradle and shook his head.

Meryn dove into her backpack and pulled out her phone. Her tiny fingers began moving. Seconds crawled by like hours. With tears streaming down her face, Meryn shook her head. "I never had this problem when Keelan was the one answering Aiden's phone," she hissed.

Anne looked at Adam and Rheia. "Cell?" she whispered.

"I left mine at home," Adam confessed.

"Mine's in the car," Rheia said, her voice shaking.

Anne was about to respond when the doorknob jiggled. Seconds later, something slammed against the door. Adam jumped over his desk and braced himself against the door.

"Adam!" Rheia screamed as the door was hit again.

Anne took a deep breath and thought of Kendrick. She found that warm energy from the night before and began to follow it. Slowly, very slowly she floated back toward the Alpha estate. When it came into view, she passed through the walls to the second floor.

Kendrick was smiling and talking excitedly to Basil who was holding a crystal in his hands.

Kendrick!

Kendrick turned quickly in the direction of the clinic; there was no trace of laughter on his face now.

Kendrick! Help!

That was all she could say before she felt herself being pulled back. When she opened her eyes, Rheia cradled her in her arms.

Anne looked around. "What happened?"

Suddenly, Adam was jolted against the door. Whoever was out there was trying very hard to get in.

"You collapsed. I thought you'd fainted, but your eyes were open." Rheia helped her to sit up.

"I think I was able to reach Kendrick." She put her hand over her chest. "I'm sure of it."

"I hope to the Gods you're right. This door won't last forever," Adam said, repositioning his feet.

Rheia looked across the office to the window. "I suppose putting bars across the windows seemed like a good idea at the time?"

Adam grinned. "We can open them from the inside, they can't be opened from the outside."

Rheia stood. "Then why don't we just go out that way?"

Adam shook his head. "That's how they lost you last time. I have a feeling we'd be running right into a trap. It's better to hunker down here." He looked at Anne. "How sure are you that help is coming?"

Anne stood and faced the doctor. "Kendrick is coming for me."

He nodded. "Then the best thing I can do is hold on. The only way they are getting to my baby sister is by walking over my dead body."

Meryn smiled weakly at Adam then glared at her phone. "When I see Aiden, I'm gonna kill him."

Behind Adam the door began to crack.

Kendrick! Hurry!

"Do you see why we use quartz now?" Kendrick asked.

Basil nodded, his eyes glued to the crystal that was changing colors.

Basil had soaked up everything he had taught him that morning, including the warding spell on the door. He couldn't have picked a finer student.

Kendrick!

Kendrick turned and looked around. He could have sworn he just heard Anne.

Kendrick! Help!

There was no doubt in his mind; that had been Anne.

He whirled to face Basil. "Anne's in trouble. I need you to stay here. These tests are about finished. I need you to stay here and record the results for me; can you do that?"

"Of course!" Basil looked scared.

"Good lad!" Kendrick turned and ran from the room. "Sei!" he yelled as he ran down the stairs. Stress had him reverting to calling Ryuu by his first name.

Ryuu appeared below him in the foyer. "Something has happened hasn't it?"

Kendrick nodded, and they both ran for the door. They headed to the open field where the unit warriors were training. "Aiden, to me!" he yelled.

Aiden's head snapped up. He saw Kendrick and Ryuu running toward him and roared. Kendrick knew that the commander had figured out that if they were running to them, then the women were in danger. Some of the men ran to the small back building and others ran to the garage.

Aiden checked his sidearm. "What do we know?" he asked.

"Nothing, only that Anne called for me."

Ryuu looked at Aiden. "*Denka* is scared, but also angry at you."

Aiden groaned and ran back to his bag. He dug around and pulled out his phone. He put it on speaker. "Baby, I am so sorry."

"Later. Where are you?" Meryn demanded.

"We're leaving here in about two minutes. What's your situation?"

"Rheia, Anne, Adam, and I are trapped in his office. So far they haven't been able to get through the door."

Kendrick felt his impatience building. He wanted to leave already. Behind them, SUVs began to roll up as the other men jogged forward carrying bags of tactical gear. In less than a minute, the men had mobilized. Normally, he would just use his magic, but there were too many men, and he'd never been to the clinic before to gauge the distance.

"Anything you can tell us about the enemy?" Aiden asked.

"We think they are invisible ferals. They are being persistent and fucking annoying," Meryn yelled.

"There's my Menace," Sascha said, nodding at Aiden.

"Hey guys, you need to hurry, no shit," Meryn said. The hiccup in her voice had the men scattering.

"Wait! Tell them that they are invisible but are shimmering, as if they are giving off heat waves," they heard Anne yell into the phone.

Heat waves?

"Let's move it! Lorcan, your unit is assigned house detail. We don't know where these bastards could pop up next," Aiden yelled.

"Yes, sir!" Lorcan yelled back, and began positioning his men around the house.

Kendrick, Gavriel, Colton, Darian, and Ryuu jumped into the SUV with Aiden. All Kendrick could think about was Anne. If anything happened to her, he didn't know if he would be able to follow her peacefully into the afterlife. He was seriously scared for the men he rode with. Beside him, Ryuu was vibrating with energy. He knew that the squire would be focused on one thing and one thing only, Meryn. Between the two of them, their enemy didn't stand a chance.

When the men arrived, they simply kicked the door in and flooded the halls. When they got to the hallway leading to Adam's office Aiden held up his fist.

Kendrick and Ryuu looked at each other and stepped in front of Aiden.

"Wait, we don't know what's out there!" Aiden hissed.

"Doesn't matter," Kendrick said and turned his attention to the hall. Thanks to Anne's description, he knew what to look for. To Anne's untrained eye, the invisibility spell through his magic looked like heat waves, which meant that he would be able to see them. "Can you detect them?" He asked his friend.

Ryuu's hair floated around his body as if ebbing back and forth in the water. He shook his head. "No, but my magic can follow yours. What is the plan?"

"Kill them all," Kendrick said without emotion. Unlike Ryuu, Kendrick's element was fire, and the air around him began to crackle.

"What the hell?" Colton yelled.

Kendrick turned to look behind him. The unit warriors were backing up from the heat. Movement caught his eye from outside the window of the room they were standing next to.

"Aiden, we have company outside. It would be safer for you and your men to handle them. Let Ryuu and I take out the ones in the hallway."

Aiden hesitated. "That's my mate in there."

Kendrick let his power rise until Aiden stepped back again. "My mate is in there as well. Now go!"

"You heard the man!" Aiden led the men outside to deal with the ferals trying to flank them from behind.

Kendrick turned his attention back to the hallway where the hazy shapes were advancing on them. "Good, they want to play."

He raised his power hand. "*Inferno!*"

The hall was engulfed in heat and flame. The figures before him began to scream and fall to the floor.

"Oh, my fucking god, that is rank! What the fuck are you doing out there?" Meryn yelled.

Ryuu smiled. "And there is the helpless maiden," he said before lifting both hands. A wall of water rushed down the hallway extinguishing the flames that were climbing the walls.

Soot and ash covered bodies making them visible. They littered the hallway, blocking the way to the women.

"Can you remove them? *Denka* and Rheia have such sensitive stomachs these days," Ryuu asked politely–as if there weren't half burned corpses melting right in front of them.

"It would be my pleasure." Kendrick raised his hand again and floated the bodies down the hall and out the door where he flung them against a tree, creating a pile of smoldering flesh and bone.

"Is it safe to come out now?" Meryn shouted.

"No." Ryuu swiftly walked down the hall. When they were in front of the door, he knocked. "It is now safe, *denka*." The door opened slowly.

When Meryn saw Ryuu, she threw herself into his arms. "I'm so sorry! I never should have left without you!"

Ryuu picked her up as if she weighed no more than a child. "I am entirely to blame, *denka*. I forgot my first duty is to protect you. Like the others, I was lulled into a false sense of safety by the perimeter. But I can assure you, I won't let that happen again."

Meryn wiped her nose on her sleeve. "You can watch me pee for all I care."

Ryuu smiled softly. "I'm sure that won't be necessary."

"Anne?" Kendrick looked around the room.

Anne stood on shaky legs, her hands balled up into fists at her side, her face surprisingly calm. "I told them you would come for us."

Kendrick strode in and simply pulled her close. "This can never happen again. Never, do you hear me?" he managed to choke out. He was having a hard time speaking past the lump in his throat.

"Rheia! Rheia!" They heard Colton yelling.

One second he was in the hallway the next he had his mate in his arms swinging her around. "That's it! That! Is! It! No more clinic!" Rheia shook her head, laughing at his antics, but Kendrick noticed the tears streaming down her face.

Kendrick pulled back and looked at Anne. "Are you okay?"

She nodded. "I may freak out later, but right now, I think I'm okay."

"Okay? She was amazing!" Adam boomed. "This girl has nerves of steel. She kept Rheia and Meryn calm and helped me brace the door. She was also the one to notice that they had snuck in, and by remaining calm, she was able to get in here and lock the door without letting them know she saw them. That's one hell of a woman you got there."

"Meryn? Meryn!" Aiden's shouting had Meryn wiggling to get down. Ryuu set her down and stepped back.

Aiden came barreling through the door and scooped Meryn up in his arms. "Baby, I'm so sorry! I swear I'll wear my phone around my neck from now on!" Aiden buried his face in her shoulder.

Meryn wrapped her arms around his head. "I will kick your ass later. Right now, just hold me."

Anne looked up at Kendrick. "How'd they get in? I thought the perimeter kept these things from coming into the city."

Adam came back in from the hallway, waving a hand in front of his face. "I don't think I'll ever get this smell out of my nose." He sneezed twice and looked at Anne. "I think the perimeter is working fine. I suspect this was a sleeper cell. They were hiding out waiting for a chance to attack." He turned to Meryn and Rheia. "They saw the two of you without escort and moved in. It was probably their last ditch effort to get to you."

Meryn paled. "They were after our babies."

Kendrick gasped as pieces began to fall into place. He had to step back while everything processed.

"Kendrick?" He heard Anne call out.

"Leave him! He's working something out," Meryn exclaimed.

Souls, shifters, abilities, necklaces, couples, recruit, babies...

Kendrick shook his head. He looked around to find that he had backed himself into a corner and everyone was watching him intently.

His eyes met Anne's. "I know you need me, but I have to go. If I'm right..."

Anne pointed out the door, her eyes perfectly serene. "Go! I'm fine. Go check the tests, I'll be right behind you."

Kendrick turned to leave but had to kiss her first. He walked back over to her, kissed her urgently. He turned to Ryuu then Aiden. "I am trusting you both to bring her home safely."

Ryuu bowed and Aiden nodded. "You have my word."

Kendrick looked at Anne a final time and raced out the door. Once clear of the building, he took flight.

Just this one time, please. Just this one time, let me be wrong.

Kendrick flung the door open and ran up the stairs.

"Meryn? Rheia?" Amelia yelled.

"Fine, both fine!" he answered and kept going.

He opened the door to Keelan's room and Basil jumped.

"What colors did you see?" he demanded.

Basil picked up his notebook. "The crystals testing for abilities turned different colors based on the ability of the bead. Crystals one and two turned red. Crystal three turned green and crystal four turned blue. The last one that tested the container's make up, well..."

"Well what?"

"Sir, it g-g-glowed," Basil stuttered.

"Glowed?" Kendrick began to pace. He stopped and returned to the table. "That can't be right. Basil are you sure?"

"Yes, sir. I'm sure, it glowed white," Basil answered.

Kendrick froze, and his heart seized. "Why didn't you say that at first?"

Basil frowned in confusion. "Sir, the crystal is white."

Kendrick dropped to his knees. Of course, a novice wouldn't be able to determine the difference between a regular glow and a white light. He had been testing for centuries and had never seen anything glow white, because there was nothing on this earth pure enough to hit the scale and register white.

"Sir! Sir, are you well?" Basil circled him worriedly.

"Basil, can you wait downstairs? As soon as the others arrive, can you send Ryuu directly to me and have everyone else assemble in the front room? I'll need you and Noah to watch after Penny; she doesn't need to hear this," Kendrick whispered trying to keep his voice even.

"Yes, sir, anything you need." Basil ran out the door so fast he didn't even stop to remove his lead testing apron.

Kendrick stared at the floor. What had their world come to?

Minutes began to blur, because the next thing he knew, Ryuu was kneeling beside him. "*Heika*, are you hurt?" Ryuu asked sensibly.

"My heart hurts Sei. I fear for our future, I don't know if I want to live in this world anymore. I am so tired," Kendrick admitted.

"You have a very good reason to live *heika*; she is waiting anxiously for you downstairs." Ryuu put a hand under his arm and helped him to his feet.

"I'm glad Meryn has you, I am. But I would give anything to have you as my squire." He looked his oldest friend in the eye.

"I understand and I am flattered." Ryuu bowed.

Kendrick refused to give in to this sorrow a second longer. He straightened his back and took a deep breath. "They will need you, especially Meryn and Rheia." He opened his pouch and pulled out a small leather bag. "This is blessed chamomile, a little goes a long way. It is spelled to bring peace. Make a couple pots of tea for us throughout the evening; we'll all need it." He handed the bag to his old friend.

"*Heika*, one thing I have learned living with my *denka* these many months is that humans are stronger than we give them credit for."

Kendrick inclined his head. "I imagine they are. I'll let you go down first to start the tea, then I'll go down to the front room."

Ryuu placed his fist over his heart, bowed, then left the room.

Kendrick waited five minutes then made his way downstairs. With each step he took, his feet became heavier and heavier.

When he walked into the front room, he looked around at the people who had quickly become his family. Quirky Meryn and grouchy Aiden. Fun-loving Colton and his serious mate, Rheia. His kind-hearted godsdaughter, her noble mate, and her parents. Elegant Elizabeth and her dark and mysterious mate, Gavriel. Off to one side, sitting quietly was Jaxon, who, surprisingly, met his gaze unflinchingly.

"About damn time!" Meryn groused.

Kendrick looked in her direction but didn't say anything. He took another deep breath and exhaled slowly. "Some of the things I'm about to tell you, you either already suspected or knew. I am simply able to confirm them based on the tests I conducted. First, I can confirm that each bead is an individual soul. That being said, I can also confirm that each bead resonates with a different shifter ability."

"What didn't we know?" Aiden asked. He sat beside Meryn, holding her hand.

"The beads themselves are an impossibility. Up until today, I didn't think there was any way to create something that had the ability to contain a soul; unfortunately, I was wrong.

"Our enemy has figured out a way to harvest the purest of souls to act as containers." He looked around the room. The men figured it out first and held their mates closer. "They are killing unborn babies and newborns to use their pure souls to house the souls and abilities of the murdered shifters, their own mothers and sometimes fathers."

Sobbing, Amelia and Rheia turned to their mates. Elizabeth looked so pale that Kendrick thought she was going to pass out, but Meryn's reaction gave him hope. She wasn't crying; in fact, she didn't even appear to be outwardly upset. Nevertheless, Kendrick could tell by the look in her eyes that she was already mentally killing her enemies. Yup, she was picturing herself knee-deep in entrails.

Kendrick turned to Anne. She was pale, yes, but her eyes were tranquil. She watched him with a steadfast faith that humbled him. He could see in the way she looked at him that she believed he would stop these atrocities from happening. And she was right. As much as he wanted retribution for his parents, his father would never forgive him if he didn't do everything in his power to stamp out this insidious evil and protect not just his people, but all paranormals.

Elizabeth drew a shaky breath. "It's why they went after expecting couples. They would get the baby's soul as a container, the ability of the shifter, and possibly a new recruit for their army."

The sound of snapping wood drew Kendrick's attention to Gavriel. He had broken off both chair arms and his eyes were glowing bright red. "No male would move on to the next world honorably and leave their mate and unborn child trapped in endless torture. They would start out wanting to destroy the ones that killed their family but become lost in the bloodshed until they became mindless drones."

Ryuu pushed a cart into the room and silently began serving the fragrant tea. Ryuu held a cup out to him, but he shook his head. Ryuu didn't move, he just kept his hand extended, holding the cup. Kendrick relented and accepted the offering from his friend. As everyone sipped their tea, their breathing slowly evened out and their muscles relaxed. The sadness was still there, but the mind-numbing terror was fading.

Elizabeth set her teacup down on its saucer. "Ryuu, where did you get this amazing blend. I'm still horrified of course, but I feel like I can breathe again."

Ryuu bowed. "*Heika*, thought that this tea would help everyone with the tragic news he had to share."

Meryn allowed herself to topple to one side and hugged the sofa pillow to her face. "I don't want to face this right now." She peeked out and looked at Anne. "Do you know of any happy anime shows we can watch? I wouldn't even mind a lot of pink and glitter right now."

Anne nodded. "I think that's a great idea. Let's just spend the afternoon relaxing; we can face reality in a little bit."

Lily looked at her mate and they both stood. "We'll go to the council and update them on what we've learned here today. You kids take it easy." Lily kissed her daughter's tear-streaked cheek before going to Meryn to kiss her temple, and hand-in-hand, she and Marshall left.

Aiden stood. "I'll be right back baby, I'm going to ask Lorcan to escort them into the city." He rubbed her back and jogged after the older couple.

Gavriel shook his head. "Kids? I wonder if they realize most of us are older than they are?"

Darian shrugged. "I don't think it matters. Adelaide treats us like her boys, and she's much younger than most of the warriors."

Colton tugged on Kendrick's sleeve and jerked his head toward the door. "We're running out for a bit, but we'll be right back." He announced to the women.

Kendrick set his tea down and reluctantly followed the wolf shifter out into the foyer along with Gavriel and Darian. He noticed that most of the women were so out of it that they didn't even wave goodbye.

Aiden shut the front door, and when he turned around and saw them standing there, he frowned. "What do you all want?"

Colton brought a finger to his lips. "Shush, the women will hear."

"Hear what?" Aiden asked.

Colton pulled them into a huddle. "I have discovered something that is guaranteed to make the women happy, but we have to go to town."

The men were smiling as they looked at each other and then turned to stare at Kendrick. Aiden's smile was more like a smirk. "Well Kendrick, do you think you're ready to take on the Duck In?"

CHAPTER THIRTEEN

Kendrick glared at Colton. "You're lying, there's no such thing."

Colton shook his finger at him. "Oh, ye of little faith. I am mated to a human so I have been reading up on them. Rheia herself told me about these tiny warriors; she said that they also bake and sell cookies that are–and I quote–'better than sex'."

"Maybe better than sex with you," Darian muttered.

Colton kicked the back of the seat, pushing Darian forward into the dash. Colton continued as Darian cussed. "As I was saying...They train these girls to be like tiny ninjas. They have to earn special badges for the survival skills that they learn, kinda like how we teach the cadets. Now to balance out all the weapons training and harshness of wilderness survival, they also teach them to bake cookies."

Aiden nodded. "Humans are impressive creatures. Do you think we should enroll Penny in one of their programs?"

Colton shook his head. "Rheia says that Penny would have to leave the city for meetings and she doesn't want to risk them getting attacked."

Darian frowned. "That's too bad; this ninja program sounds promising, especially for young females. Maybe we could talk to your mother about it, Aiden."

Aiden snapped his fingers. "She would love getting involved in a program like this."

Kendrick frowned. "How are we supposed to find these elusive ninjas?"

Colton beamed at them. "Evidently, this time of year they don't even practice subterfuge, they are out in the open so that civilians can see them. Rheia said that they set up stands outside of supermarkets and practice their interrogation techniques on those going into the store, to try and get them to buy their cookies."

Gavriel looked over at Colton. "Are we sure they are human?"

Colton nodded. "Yes, this is a human program. It's extremely popular; in fact, it's a nationwide program."

Aiden pulled into the parking lot of the Duck In and parked far away from the building so they could scope it out.

Colton pulled out a pair of binoculars. "I have a visual. They are kinda cute, though there's one with metal attached to all of her teeth that looks frightening. I think she may be the leader."

Aiden turned to Kendrick. "The Duck In can be frightening, but it's the only place close by that sells tampons to help keep women from bleeding to death and condoms to help create children."

Kendrick blinked. "Aiden, I don't think that's how it works."

Aiden held up his hand. "Trust me. I am an expert."

Right.

"Okay, so let's go." Kendrick leaned forward and grasped the door handle.

"Wait!" the men yelled in unison.

Kendrick jumped back. "What?"

Colton turned to Aiden. "We need a plan of action. I have a feeling these warriors only sell their valuable cookies to those who have proven themselves in battle."

Darian nodded. "That makes sense."

Kendrick shook his head. "No, seriously guys, I think we can just..."

Colton shook his head. "Quiet Kendrick. You're the new man on the team." He then turned to Aiden. "What kind of firepower are we keeping in the SUVs now?"

Kendrick's jaw dropped.

Gavriel bent over the back seat and lifted the lid on their arms cases. "We have two grenade launchers back here," he called.

Aiden nodded, smiling. "I think we should go big. The more impressive we look, the easier this will be."

Kendrick shook his head repeatedly. "No, no, it won't."

"Okay men. Mission is to negotiate with the ninjas, secure the cookies, and take them back to the women." Aiden met the eyes of each man in the SUV. "Remember, we don't leave our people behind. If one of us is outmaneuvered, fall back to the SUV."

"Yes, sir!" Colton, Darian, and Gavriel yelled.

They all turned to Kendrick. He sighed. "Yes, sir."

As they were climbing out, Aiden turned to him. "I'm not feeling the team spirit here."

Kendrick pointed to the men who were putting on every piece of tactical gear they owned. "We're about to go negotiate with ninjas in front of a supermarket; I'm not seeing this ending well."

Aiden smiled wide and clapped him on the shoulder. "Dealing with humans is my forte." Humming, he walked past Kendrick.

Didn't Meryn beat him with a toilet?

Kendrick walked behind the four men as they approached the tiny ninjas. Immediately, Kendrick got the feeling something was very wrong.

Aiden stepped forward. "We would like to negotiate."

The ninja with metal in her mouth looked up. "What's negotiate?"

Aiden leaned back and winked at him. "Evasive answering. They are professionals. Look, she has the most badges, she is clearly their leader."

He then leaned down and got right in the ninja's face. "We want your cookies."

That was when she and the three other ninjas began to cry.

Colton looked at Aiden and frowned. "Commander?"

Aiden held up his hand. "This is a negotiation technique, it's meant to evoke feelings of pity in their victims."

Colton brightened. "Oh."

We're going to jail.

"What in the Sam Hill is going on out here?" Kendrick looked up to see an older man shuffling toward them.

Aiden smiled. "Bart! Good to see you again, friend."

Bart looked at their group then over to Kendrick. Kendrick just shrugged, lifted his hand, and wiggled his fingers at him. Bart turned back to Aiden. "What is wrong with you boys?"

Aiden frowned. "Sir?"

"Why are you harassing these sweet angels?" Bart demanded.

Aiden snorted. "Sweet angels? Ha! They have you tricked, my friend. I will let you in on a secret." Aiden leaned in close to the old man. "They are actually ninjas."

Bart didn't say anything right away; he just stared at Aiden. "Son, did your wife hit you with that toilet again?"

Aiden shook his head. "No, sir."

Kendrick pushed his way between Aiden and Colton. "Sir, what I believe my well intentioned, well armed friends were trying to do was buy some cookies."

By this time, angry looking mothers were swooping in to stand by their daughters.

Darian leaned into Aiden. "Abort mission, sir, abort!"

Aiden shook his head. "No! We came here for cookies for the women."

"Bart, get these maniacs away from my daughter before I call the police!" one especially shrill woman demanded.

Kendrick watched as each man took in the scene in front of them.

Crying baby girls, check.

Murderous mothers, check.

Angry mob forming, check.

Slowly, each one began to pale.

Kendrick turned to the furious mothers. "We want to buy your cookies."

The women looked at each other. "How many?"

"All of them!" Aiden blurted out.

Good answer, Commander!

Kendrick watched anger slowly ebb away as cash began to exchange hands.

It took all five of them to carry the ninjas' entire stash of cookies to their car. Once inside the SUV, Colton wiped his brow. "Those women were grown ninjas; you could tell."

Gavriel glanced down at his orange and green boxes, looking a bit harried. "I do not ever want to face them again."

Aiden was in the driver's seat, drawing deep breaths. "Good job, men. Though it may look like we got away easily, we can't be too careful. Darian, I want you to watch behind us to see if they try and tail us."

Darian quickly crawled into the backseat. "Yes, sir!"

Colton looked a bit wild around the eyes. "She had metal in her mouth. Are they supposed to have metal in their mouths like that?"

Gavriel shuddered. "I am going to have nightmares tonight for sure."

Colton nodded.

Aiden gripped the steering wheel. "It was worth it, for the women."

All around him, the men nodded.

Kendrick stared out the window.

Keelan, how did you do this all the time?

"Where do you think they went?" Elizabeth asked.

"No telling. Colton had that look in his eye." Rheia smiled.

"The one where he thinks he's being clever, but really he's being an idiot?" Meryn asked.

Rheia nodded. "Yup, that one. He's so adorable when he does that."

"Papa is silly," Penny chimed in from her mother's lap. After the startling revelations about the necklaces, Rheia went to command central to get Penny, she had been cuddling her ever since.

Basil turned to Noah. "So Tezuka really does like Yuri, he's just pretending not to?"

Noah nodded and passed him the bowl of popcorn. "He thinks he is protecting him."

Basil looked confused. "But isn't he hurting Yuri by denying their love?"

Anne leaned forward. "Ahhh. That is the crux of most anime. Hurting the one you love by denying them, so that others don't hurt them, finding out that you were hurting them all along, leaving them, causing them more hurt and then almost dying."

Meryn frowned. "Wasn't that *Twilight*?"

Elizabeth laughed and threw popcorn at her friend.

They heard the door open and close, and they all turned to see who had come in. Seconds later, Lily and Marshall came into view.

"Well, the Committee is now dedicated to finding out who cast the perimeter spell and used black magic. Kendrick did such an amazing job refuting their allegations, they have given up altogether. Though to be honest, if they had just walked through the city, they would never have wasted their time. The people absolutely adore you and your mate, Meryn."

Meryn bobbed her head. "They are good peeps."

Lily sat down with Marshall and looked at the television. "What are we watching?"

"One of my new favorite shows," Amelia answered.

Lily smiled. "Well, they certainly are handsome."

The women all sighed.

About an hour later, they heard the men return.

"Hold the door Aiden!" Anne heard Darian yell.

The women all looked at each other.

"Need any help?" Anne called.

"No!" The men shouted.

A few minutes later, the men walked in and began passing out brightly colored boxes.

Kendrick passed her two. She looked down mint and peanut butter cookies? She dropped the boxes to the floor and threw herself at him. "My favorites! How did you know?"

Kendrick chuckled. "I didn't, I guessed. I hope you know how difficult these were to obtain."

Anne kissed him soundly then immediately picked up her treat and tore into the box of mint cookies. Around the room, the other women were reacting in much the same manner. As each woman took their first bite, blissful sighs filled the room.

Colton eyed the cookies Rheia and Penny were eating. Rheia rolled her eyes and gave him his own sleeve. Shrugging, he opened the package and popped one in his mouth. His eyes widened and he began to chew faster. He quickly finished his pack and then hopped up to go get two more boxes.

Seeing Colton's reaction, the men scattered, each grabbing their own boxes. Anne lay back on the sofa and watched her favorite anime. She snuggled close to Kendrick, who had also broken down and was indulging in the sweet treats.

Around the room, everyone was floating in a happy sugar haze, deliberately trying to forget the ugliness of that afternoon. Ryuu clucked his tongue at their food choices and began carting in pots of tea and sandwiches for dinner in an effort to get them to eat something substantial.

"Oh dear! An elevator cable snapped in Spain; thirty people plunged to their deaths!" Amelia exclaimed, looking at her phone.

Darian plucked her phone from her hands. "We're doing happy time now."

Amelia buried her face in his chest. "Sorry, you're right. Happy time. I was just doing something for Meryn."

"How do you fit thirty people in an elevator?" Meryn and Kendrick asked at the exact same time.

Anne hid her smile at Amelia's incredulous expression. "That's what caught your attention?"

Meryn nodded. "Well, yeah. I mean how big was the elevator? Maybe it was a freight elevator," she suggested, looking at Kendrick.

Kendrick frowned. "If it was meant for freight why were thirty people in it?"

Aiden popped a cookie in his mouth. "You know, having Kendrick here makes me worry less about Meryn."

"It doesn't worry you that we now have two people who have a skewed sense of reality?" Colton asked.

Aiden shook his head. "No, because they're on our side."

Colton brightened. "Oh, yeah."

Anne tilted her head back and kissed Kendrick's cheek. "I love the way you think."

Kendrick leaned down. "You'd love it even more if you could see what I was thinking," he teased.

She laughed and hugged him tighter.

"Amelia, did you help me out like I asked?" Meryn said with a mouth full of cookie.

Amelia sighed. "Of course I did, though I don't know how you've leveled up so much in such a short amount of time."

"My furries on Facebook help me." Meryn popped another cookie in her mouth and tapped away on her phone.

Aiden sat up. "Her what?"

Elizabeth shook her head. "Never mind, Aiden, lost cause. Trust me."

"All your fields are belong to us," Meryn said in a robotic tone.

Everyone looked at Amelia who winced. "I introduced her to FarmVille."

"I will take over the world. Ma-ha-ha-ha!" Meryn shook both fists in the air.

Anne laughed at Meryn's quirky excitement over an Internet game.

When the doorbell rang, Anne wasn't the only one who looked around and mentally did a head check. Who could be at the door if they were all here?

Meryn hopped out of her recliner and headed for the door.

"Meryn," Aiden called.

Meryn froze and turned to him, tapping her foot. "Well, come on."

Aiden walked past her as everyone got up to look into the foyer.

Aiden opened the door. "Can I help you?"

"I was told the Sei Ryuu served in this household," a male voice stated in accented English.

Aiden held the door open, and a small man in traditional Japanese dress entered slowly, taking in his surroundings.

Anne watched as Ryuu walked in from the hallway; his eyes looked haunted. Kendrick walked past Colton and Gavriel to stand next to his friend.

The small man began to speak in Japanese.

Ryuu shook his head. "Out of respect for the owners of this house, please speak in English."

The man inclined his head slightly and continued. "Sei Ryuu, your services are required in the main household. Your contract is still valid." The man held up his arm and pulled back his sleeve. A faint grayish-blue tattoo wound around the man's wrist and up his forearm.

Ryuu bowed at the waist, apparently returning the man's gesture, and shook his head. "I was banished, I cannot return."

The man stepped forward. "You will do as you are ordered. It is disgraceful that you would come here and serve such as these."

"*Mizushima-dono*, how did you find me?"

The man's eyes flashed. "You dare address me in this way? Have you forgotten your purpose? Your friend at the main house was so excited to hear from you, he had to let everyone know that you were alive and doing well here in Lycaonia. How dare you serve anyone other than your master? Come!" The man pointed to the space next to him as if he was calling a dog to heel.

Ryuu looked down at Meryn. "Maybe this is for the best. My poor judgement almost got you killed today. I don't deserve to be at your side."

Meryn gave a low cry and flung her arms around Ryuu. "No!"

"*Denka*, please."

"*Denka*? This lowly creature? She is human." The man spat every word.

"*Denka...*" Ryuu tried to disentangle Meryn's arms from around his waist.

She shook her head back and forth. "No! No! No! No! You're *mine*." She looked up, tears streaming down her cheeks. "Do you hear me? You're *mine*! You're *my* family, you and Felix." She held up her arm where her own tattoo was blazing a bright royal blue. "You promised." She looked at him, unable to catch her breath. "I love you."

Those three words straightened Ryuu's back. He wrapped an arm around Meryn and looked at the small man. "I have bound myself in service to *denka*. The contract I had with your family is completed. It ended the day you exiled me from my country. The mark on your arm will continue to fade as will any power that was attached to it. I wish you luck in your future endeavors." Ryuu bowed, clearly dismissing the man, then stood tall.

Anne felt like jumping up and down. Meryn was a sniffling mess. She'd never be dignified or elegant, but it was clear to everyone that Ryuu cherished her love more than any prestige that could be found by returning to his old family.

The small man's face turned a dangerous shade of red. He held up his wrist and whispered a word. Ryuu jerked forward slightly, a pained expression on his face.

Meryn stood back. "Ryuu?" She turned and saw what Ryuu's former master was doing. She moved until she stood in front of Ryuu and held up her wrist. Whatever had been pulling Ryuu forward was negated by Meryn's tattoo.

Kendrick stepped between Meryn and Ryuu, and the outraged man. He shook his head at Aiden who had been reaching for the interloper. Kendrick grinned.

"Mizushima, was it?" he asked.

"Do not speak to me, dog." The man righted his robes.

"You showed me yours, now let me show you mine." Kendrick rolled up his right sleeve. His muscled forearm was encircled by a red, a black and a silvery white bands that formed intricate knot work. A phoenix, a black tortoise, and a white tiger wrapped around his wrist.

The man began to shake and took a step backward. "Impossible! You're a foreigner!"

Kendrick cracked his neck. "I don't see how that has anything to do with it." He walked slowly up to the man and grabbed his right wrist. Seconds later, the man was screaming as smoke rose from where Kendrick gripped him tightly. He released the man, letting him fall to the floor. He stood over him, a cold expression on his face. "All those years ago, I had to stand by and watch you treat my friend like a dog, and I could do nothing. He is free of you and your ilk, and I don't have to play nice anymore. Whatever hold on him you had is gone." He pointed to the mangled mess he had made of the man's arm. "That is your one and only warning: Leave. And never come near my family again." Kendrick waved his hand and the front door swung open violently. He crossed his arms over his chest. Mizushima scrambled on all fours out the door, which slammed behind him.

"And *that* is how you kick ass," Colton said grinning from ear to ear.

"*Kono-yaro*!" Meryn called after the man.

Ryuu looked down at Meryn in shock. "*Denka*, where did you learn such language?"

Meryn whirled on Ryuu "Anime." She began poking him in the chest. "Where in the hell did you get the idea I'd be better off without you?" Meryn continued poking him while he smiled down at her. "Forget I said anything, *denka*."

Aiden walked over to the squire and clapped him on the shoulder. "We couldn't live without you; you're family."

Ryuu stepped back, placed his fist over his heart, and bowed low. "I swear to serve your house for as long as there are family members to serve."

"And cook yummy food!" Colton added.

"And be someone to have tea with." Rheia smiled at the squire.

Darian and Amelia nodded. "It wouldn't be home without you Ryuu," Amelia said gently.

Ryuu kept his head down, but Anne guessed it would be so that the others wouldn't see how much their words affected him.

"Now, time for your punishment." Meryn rubbed her hands together.

Ryuu stood straight, a faint smile on his handsome face. "Oh, and what would that be?"

"I want all that yummy Japanese food you promised us. Actually, Meryn two-point-oh really wants it." Meryn rubbed her stomach.

Anne turned to Kendrick. It had taken every ounce of self-discipline not to jump him after the door closed. He still stood with his feet planted shoulder-width apart, his arms crossed across his chest. The tattoos coupled with his stubble made him look dangerous and sexy. He caught her looking at him and gave her a questioning look.

She smiled sweetly and mouthed the words, *I want you.*

Colton must have seen what she said because he cracked up laughing. Kendrick grabbed her hand and made a beeline for the stairs.

"*Heika*, aren't you hungry?" Ryuu called, amusement in his voice.

"I'm going to eat upstairs!" Kendrick called down.

That sent Colton into convulsed laughter.

Anne gasped and ran to keep up with him.

They checked on Keelan and then headed to her room. Never in her life had she wanted anything as much as she wanted her mate. As soon as she closed the door, she began stripping. Kendrick hurried out of his clothing and waited for her on the edge of the bed. Anne looked over at him and saw the smug expression on his face. She let her panties drop and was rewarded when his eyes began to darken. She could feel his magic now; it was racing through his veins like lightning.

Deliberately, she picked up her clothes and folded them into a neat pile on the dresser. When she bent over in front of him to pick up his magic clothes, she smiled when she heard him groan softly.

She carefully folded his clothes and laid them next to hers. She then turned and walked toward the bathroom.

"Anne, love?" he called.

She turned. "Yes?" she asked innocently.

"Where are you going?"

"To take a shower. The smell of burnt flesh from the clinic is in my hair."

"Oh."

"You're free to join me."

He stood up. "Thought you'd never ask."

She walked into the bathroom and went directly to the shower. She turned it on to the hottest setting. When steam was pouring out, she backed it off a little and stepped in.

Kendrick stepped in behind her and moaned when the water hit his back. "This feels like heaven."

"It's going to get even better," she promised.

Kendrick pulled her wet, naked body against his. "You know, I've never done this before."

"What, shower?" she asked playfully.

He tweaked her nose. "No. I've never bathed with a woman before."

Anne reached for the soap and began to lather up the washcloth. She took the cloth and began to work small circles over his chest, slowly moving downward. When she dropped the cloth and used her soap-slicked hands to stroke him, he swallowed hard.

"Gods woman!"

She worked him fast, then slow, torturing him in the same fashion he had her the night before. When she dipped her thumb into the tiny slit, his breath exploded from his body, and he slammed both hands against the tile on either side of her head.

He looked down at her. "Please tell me you're ready."

She nodded. Wielding so much power over him had tightened things low in her body. She was aching for him.

"We're going to make a mess again," he said, lifting her up and wrapping her legs around his waist. He turned off the water.

When her hot core made contact with his stomach, she began to grind against him, trying to find relief. "I don't care; that's what magic is for," she panted.

Kendrick walked out of the shower and went directly to the bed. The water from their bodies dripped onto the covers but neither of them cared. Without warning, he struck. He plunged so deep, she screamed out her pleasure. He took her wrists and pinned them over her head. Again and again, he slammed into her. She lifted her hips with each thrust. When he began to increase his pace, she knew he was close.

"Please," she whispered.

Grinning, he moved his hips, and suddenly, heated friction from his magic was twisting and teasing her clit in time to his thrusts. It didn't take long until her body was exploding in waves of pleasure. He thrust twice more before he yelled out his own release, collapsed on top of her, and she held him close.

"I'm dead; you've killed me," she whispered hoarsely.

"It's the mating heat," he managed to say between gasps.

"We mated, shouldn't it be dying down?"

Kendrick shook his head against her neck. "It gets more intense as the years go by."

"I'll never make it." Anne pushed his bangs back and kissed his forehead.

He pushed himself up and slowly slid from her body causing them both to moan. On shaky legs, he walked over to the dresser. "You have to get up, love."

"Put caution tape around me; I can't move." Anne said, still trying to catch her breath.

Chuckling, he waved his hand and she began to float over to him. He righted their bed then used his magic clothing to clean them up. When she was tucked in next to him, her head on his chest, she sighed happily.

"Now that the tests are done, I can try to track down the witch responsible for the necklaces," he said quietly.

"I support you, no matter what." She placed her hand over his heart.

When he didn't reply, she sat up and kissed his lips. "Tomorrow. Worry about it tomorrow."

"Thank you."

"For what?"

"Being a mate I can lean on."

"You deserve no less." She kissed him again and lay back down.

"Very fitting for a queen."

She bit him gently, and he laughed. "I'm just a nurse."

"Yes ma'am." His arm tightened and she fell asleep to the beating of his heart.

CHAPTER FOURTEEN

They stayed in bed until noon the next day. Every time one would go to get up, the other one pounced. Laughing, they walked hand-in-hand into the dining room just in time for lunch.

"They live! Good," Meryn teased.

Anne dropped into her chair and yawned. "I'm starving."

Kendrick sat down beside her and stifled a yawn.

Aiden pointed to the mountains of sandwiches in the center of the table. Anne reached for the sandwiches then stopped and pointed. "What's that one?"

Rheia let out an exasperated sigh then pointed at Colton. "His own special creation. It's mayonnaise, peanut butter, beef jerky, pickles, and cheese."

"Yummy!" Penny crowed, waving her sandwich about.

"They are delicious," Meryn chimed in taking a huge bite out of hers.

Anne looked over at Kendrick. "Be my guest. I'll pass." He pointed to the pile, wondering if she would really try such an odd sandwich. Anne picked one up, looked at it, and then took a bite. At first, her expression was one of horror, but the more she chewed, the less panicked she looked. She swallowed. "It's actually not that bad."

"Wonderful. Another convert." Ryuu sighed and placed a large bowl of fruit salad on the table.

Kendrick searched the large pile until he found a boring ham and cheese sandwich and dug in.

"Kendrick?" Meryn called his name.

"Yes?"

"Can I ask you something?"

"Of course, Meryn."

"Since you have three tattoos, does that mean you have three squires?" It was an innocent enough question, one he didn't mind answering because he knew she was genuinely curious and not seeking more power.

He shook his head. "No, they weren't squires, they were my best friends."

"Were?" Meryn's eyes filled with sympathy.

"A long time ago, we traveled together. When they faded from this world, they left me their power. It took me thousands of years to master each one, but it was worth it. Every time I use their magic, I feel like they are watching over me."

"Why did they fade?" Anne asked.

"I think I may know," Gavriel said quietly. "When you live for so long and you see so much pain and mindless evil, it becomes hard to find a reason to get up each day. The longer you live, the more you just feel like resting and letting everything disappear." He turned to Elizabeth and smiled. "That is why, when you find something to live for, you fight for it."

"Gavriel is right. They were very, very tired and their souls were weary." Kendrick rubbed his right wrist.

Meryn turned in her chair and poked Ryuu in the stomach. "No fading."

He nodded. "I don't see how anyone could get bored with life around you, *denka*."

"Good! Wait..." She eyed him. "Was that a compliment?"

"It was," he answered.

"Okay then." Meryn turned back in her chair and resumed eating her monstrous sandwich.

Kendrick waited until everyone was mostly done with lunch before he decided to bring up the topic of necklaces.

He looked over at the Unit Commander. "Aiden, now that the tests are finished and we know what the necklaces are, I could attempt to try and trace down the witch responsible for their creation."

Rheia turned to Noah and Jaxon. "Boys, can you take Penny to command central?"

Noah stood. "Of course. Come on squirt, when you get asked to leave the table because the adults want to talk, you get two desserts." Noah stacked up plates with slices of pie in his arms.

"Yay!" Penny cheered. She climbed into Jaxon's lap and the three of them left the dining room.

"Thank you, Rheia," Kendrick said.

Aiden sat back. "What are the risks?"

"To trace the magic to the witch who cast the spell, I'll need to break every bead in every necklace we have to get a strong enough trail. If we do that, no more different types of testing; that's the trade-off."

Everyone was quiet.

"Let's do it," Amelia said firmly. "Now that we know what they are, there's no reason to keep them trapped. Let's set them free."

Aiden looked around the table. Everyone nodded.

Anne spoke up. "Is there any danger to you?"

Gods bless her! She always thought of him first.

He shook his head. "I'll follow the trail using my magic, my body remains here. It's safe."

"Should we alert the council to what we're doing?" Elizabeth asked.

Aiden shook his head. "My father and the rest of the council are obligated to pass on everything they learn to the Committee. In this instance, we're better off asking for forgiveness than for permission."

"Agreed," Gavriel said.

Kendrick looked over to where Ryuu stood behind Meryn. "I'll need your help, old friend."

Ryuu bowed. "Of course, whatever you need."

"I'll need to use you as an anchor."

"It would be an honor."

Aiden stood. "Let's get started."

Kendrick was upstairs gathering the necklaces when Anne placed her hand on his arm.

"You weren't lying were you? There's no way that you'll get hurt?"

Kendrick stared down and saw real fear in her eyes. He cupped her face with his hands and kissed her gently. "I was telling the truth. When you were in danger at the clinic, how did you reach out to me?"

Anne frowned in thought. "I recalled that warm feeling I got when I touched your magic during our claiming. Once I touched it, I was able to follow it back to the house. Oh! Is that what you'll do?"

Kendrick nodded. He kissed her again before he picked up the necklaces. "Ready?" He extended his hand. She took it and they walked downstairs to where everyone was waiting in the front family room.

"So what exactly is gonna happen?" Meryn asked.

Kendrick waited until Anne was seated before he started his explanation for the group. "Do you remember the conversation we had about how higher magic works? That a witch must form a contract with a higher being or offer something of themselves up in exchange?"

Everyone nodded.

He held up the necklaces. "When I break these beads, the piece that the witch offered up will be freed and temporarily connected to the witch. I will follow that connection back to the caster. With any luck, they won't be too far away, and I'll be able to identify them. Worst case scenario, I'll have to do a sketch of the person I see, but at least it's a start."

Aiden stood next to Ryuu. "It's more than we have now."

Kendrick winked at Anne, who rolled her eyes. Smiling, he walked over to Ryuu. "I'll need you to attach your magic to me so that I can find my way back. There's no telling how far or how fast I'll fly when these beads are broken."

Ryuu reached out and encircled Kendrick's right wrist with his hand. Where they touched, blue light flared. "I am ready, *heika*."

Kendrick took a deep breath, and using his magic, he crushed the beads in his hand. Green light flared and he concentrated on finding that sliver of magic. He saw two strands, one thicker than the other. He grabbed onto their faint pink glow and raced after the receding light. He flew past trees and through the woods. He was surprised to see that he was heading right for Lycaonia. As he whizzed past businesses and houses, he had a sinking feeling he knew where he was heading. He looked up as the pink strands snapped in front of him. He could go no further; the building where both strands disappeared into was warded.

He turned and tugged on the blue light that secured him to his body. Ryuu began to reel him back. Buildings and streets raced by, and trees were nothing but a blur. Suddenly, he was back in his body.

Gasping, he opened his eyes and stepped back from Ryuu. "Gods!"

Aiden appeared beside him and helped him to a chair. "What did you see?"

Kendrick took a deep breath. "I wasn't able to see their faces; there are two of them."

In the background, Kendrick heard a cell phone ringing.

"Two of them? What does that mean?" Colton asked.

"It means that there was more than one witch creating necklaces," Kendrick answered.

Anne took his hand. "Why couldn't you see their faces?"

Kendrick looked up at Aiden. "Because the building is warded. I ended up at Council Manor."

The room was silent except for the faint ringing sound.

"For the gods' sake, Aiden, answer your damn phone! You never answer your phone!" Meryn exclaimed, throwing her hands in the air.

Aiden growled and pulled his phone out of his pocket. "What!" His face instantly cleared. "Father, I'm sorry, I... What! When?" Aiden swallowed and collapsed into his chair. "Father, I'll have to call you back." He ended his call and stared at the floor.

"Aiden?" Gavriel called.

Aiden looked up. "Elder Adalwin is dead. They were in the middle of a meeting when he began to scream and age right before them. Father said he looks like a dried up mummy. The other committee members are in an uproar. They believe that he was murdered using black magic and they want units out there ASAP to start an investigation, and of course to protect them."

Kendrick nodded. "That would make sense. If he was one of the witches who had cast the spell, then when the beads are broken, the years of his life he offered up would be collected." Kendrick looked over at the broken beads. "He must have created a majority of the ones we broke."

Elizabeth frowned. "But you said there were two threads."

Kendrick nodded. "That means there is still one more rogue witch in Council Manor, and we have no idea who it is."

"Well, fuck a duck," Meryn exclaimed, throwing herself backward on the sofa.

Kendrick couldn't have agreed more.

"I'm telling you it has to be that douchebag, Réne!" Meryn said, coming to her knees on the sofa.

Elizabeth pulled her back down. "Meryn, we have to look at this from every angle."

Meryn gave her friend a flat look. "Douchebag vampire is evil bad guy. We kill evil bad guy, save the day, come home, and eat cake!"

Kendrick found himself siding with Elizabeth. "Meryn, we have to go in with an open mind. I'm all for getting rid of the bad guy, but I want to make sure that we're getting rid of the true evil one, not the guy that just acts like a douchebag. Besides Réne is a vampire, not a witch."

"I think it's Daggart," Elizabeth suggested.

Meryn became thoughtful. "Damn, now that's difficult. He was a douchebag, too. I bet they are in on it together."

Anne cleared her throat. Kendrick looked to her immediately. "I know I'm new here, but do you think that's why Adalwin wanted to know if the ferals would accept anything else in trade for the hostages? What if they never really expected the perimeter to be lowered? It's like when you're a kid–you ask for something completely outrageous, so when you're told no and suggest something reasonable, the parent is more inclined to say yes, since they shot down your first idea."

"Gods, I did that to my uncle so many times!" Elizabeth exclaimed.

"Réne backed the idea to give up the necklaces," Colton growled.

Gavriel tuned to Aiden. "What do we do?"

Aiden stood and reached for his phone. "I'm going to request a council meeting with just father, Rowan and Celyn. Since Réne was picked up to be the Lycaonian committee member, we can justify his exclusion since his loyalties are divided. Gavriel get on the phone. I want Beta and Delta here at the house guarding the women, and I want Gamma to go in with us. They've been included in every meeting thus far; we can use that as an excuse to get them into the council chambers."

Gavriel stood and pulled out his cell phone as Aiden made the call to his father, requesting a meeting.

Anne went to him. "I'm not going to ask if you'll be safe, because I know you won't be. But I am going to make you promise to come back."

Kendrick stood and pulled her close. "Not even death could keep me from you," he whispered in her ear.

Grinning, she pulled back. "I know you meant that to sound romantic, but after all these talks about souls and mummies, it was kinda creepy."

"I can always rely on you to keep me grounded." He kissed her forehead.

"I'll be waiting right here for you to come back. That means you walking up those stairs unhurt and very much warm and alive. None of this 'not even death could stop me' stuff." She shuddered. "You know how I feel about zombies."

"You have my word," he vowed.

Aiden tucked his phone away. "Gamma will be here in five minutes. Let's get our gear on."

Kendrick kissed her forehead again and joined the men as they headed to the door.

"You gonna gear up?" Colton asked.

Kendrick shook his head. "No, but it's always amusing to see how much stuff you manage to cover yourselves with to go into battle."

Behind them, the women giggled. Colton gave him a grateful smile and a thumbs up.

Keelan, I swear, we'll all make it home this time.

Heads turned and people whispered as the two units jogged from the parking garage to Council Manor. Kendrick's long legs ensured he was able to keep up. Elder McKenzie met them at the door, a grave look on his face. "What's this all about, son?"

"Let's talk inside, Father." Aiden walked side-by-side with his father through the halls. They passed the normal meeting chambers to a smaller room meant for more intimate conversations. Sascha closed the door behind them, and Kendrick cast a soundproofing spell.

The Gamma Unit arranged themselves toward the back of the room while Alpha stood in front of the three council member chairs. Elder Vi'Ailean was already seated when Elder McKenzie sat next to him.

"We're just waiting on Rowan; he had to talk Daggart out of the rafters when Adalwin, uh, petrified." Elder McKenzie explained.

"Elder McKenzie, I ..." Kendrick stepped forward.

The elder held up a hand. "Please, Kendrick. While we're in this room, let's not be so formal. I've had enough of formality to last me into the next century," Byron said sourly, referring to the recent meeting with the Committee.

"Of course sir. I..." The door to their right opened, and Elder Airgead hurried forward. Kendrick watched as he made his way to his chair. His normally dark hair looked lighter at the temples and there were more lines on his face than when they had met earlier.

Kendrick recalled how haggard Adalwin had looked as Aiden's voice rang through his mind.

We've already broken a few. One by accident and the others because they were hurting Amelia.

Kendrick felt his heart stutter as he stared at the witch elder. The second trace had been to him! Rowan must have been the creator of at least one of the necklaces he had broken earlier, that's why he looked older.

Rowan caught him staring, and his eyes widened.

Kendrick growled. "It was you!" He raised his hand, but he wasn't quick enough.

Rowan raised his hand, "*Debilito!*"

Kendrick felt his awareness freeze within his own mind. He couldn't see or hear anything. He struggled to bring his magic to the surface but couldn't. Every time he thought it was within reach, his mind clouded and it slipped away.

What was Rowan doing? Was Alpha safe? Kendrick screamed internally, until even the feeling of helplessness began to fade away.

Kendrick.

Who is this?

Réne Evreux, I got suspicious when Rowan called a meeting and I wasn't invited.

He's one of the ones responsible for making the necklaces!

I know; I was the one who sent you the necklaces to get the evidence we needed. Listen, I can only free one person, and it will have to be you. You're the only one strong enough to beat him. The committee members won't believe me if I tell them what's happening.

Call the Alpha estate, ask for Anne; she's my mate. Tell her what's going on. She'll get Meryn to mobilize the other units.

I will. Good luck.

He felt as if Réne used a fresh breeze to wipe his mind clear. He looked around. Rowan was approaching Aiden with a dagger. Centuries of frustration, the acidic burn of betrayal, and the fear of losing another loved one fueled his anger. He leveled his hand and whispered, "*Praemorior*."

Rowan turned at the last moment, and the spell hit him full in the chest. He flew backward against the wall and slumped into a heap on the floor. He looked up at Kendrick, a thin trickle of blood dripping from the corner of his mouth. "Why? Why did you have to come to Lycaonia? I was so close, so close." He let his head fall backward against the stone wall.

"So close to what?" Kendrick eyed the other men in the room, all still frozen and unaware by Rowan's spell.

"It was all for nothing!" Rowan gasped for breath.

Kendrick watched dispassionately as Rowan's feet began to disintegrate and disappear.

"Rowan, you're about to face our Goddess. You will carry with you the weight of the unborn children you murdered, but you can do one final act of goodness. Tell me who is behind all this?"

Kendrick knelt beside the witch who had served their people selflessly for centuries. "Tell me," he begged.

Rowan's smile was kind. "My master has no name, at least not one that he shared with me. He is beautiful, he tempts you with the very thing your heart desires. You can't say no."

Kendrick looked down at him in pity. "Whatever he promised you, he lied."

Rowan shook his head back and forth slowly as his legs began to fade. "That's just it. He doesn't have to lie. The way he operates, he doesn't have to, therein lies the treachery."

"What was the deal?" Kendrick prompted.

"I would help him in Lycaonia. I let him use my mind, my memories, and my long-standing relationships with the people of this city to dream-walk into the minds of the matriarchs and plant the seed of panic regarding their sons' mates being killed. He wanted all of the warriors mated." Rowan drew in a ragged breath.

"Why?" Kendrick took Rowan's hand in his. "Focus. Why did he want the unit warriors mated?"

"Mated paranormals are needed to make his army. Vampires... blood. Witches... fuel. He can steal their children." Rowan coughed and blood spewed down his chin. His lungs were disintegrating.

Rowan laughed and gasped for breath. "He never counted on the females. Gods how they managed to unravel things so quickly."

Kendrick gasped. "Meryn, Elizabeth, Rheia, and Amelia."

Rowan nodded. "He thought that by mating the warriors they would gain a weakness, or what he perceived to be a weakness. I could have told him that a man fights harder when he has something to protect and a woman even more so. Women are more fierce, more ruthless."

"It's over now. Aiden destroyed the factory..." Kendrick stopped when Rowan shook his head.

"You have no ... idea ... how far up this goes, how wide. I never knew who to trust. Like the beads on the necklace, we were kept separate from one another, our only connection was to him." Rowan gripped his hand tightly.

Kendrick held on to Rowan's hand. It wouldn't be long now.

"What did you wish for? What did he show you?" Kendrick asked softly.

"His necklace. I wanted... his necklace. The first one made, the one I had to save, no matter the cost." Rowan's face relaxed as his arms and chest slowly became transparent.

"He... fooled me. He said I would see my king again. I thought if I freed my king, Kiran would defeat him."

Kendrick's mind began to race. "Rowan! Rowan! Your king is dead, how could you free him?" Kendrick yelled.

"How... he... came to be. King Kiran, Queen Celeste, and their baby were the first bead created." Rowan closed his eyes.

"No!" Kendrick shouted.

"Promise me! Promise me, you'll free him," Rowan begged.

Kendrick felt his heart breaking into pieces as he nodded. "I swear to you on my father's soul, I will not rest until my parents' murder is avenged and this evil is banished from this world."

Rowan's eyes opened wide at his words, he looked at Kendrick as ghostly tears began to flow. "He was right; I got to see my king, after all." Rowan struggled to lift his other hand, but didn't stop until it rested on his vanishing chest. "Long... live... King Julian. Gods all bless you!" It was as if that declaration took the last of his strength. Rowan closed his eyes and was gone.

Behind him the men unfroze and began to shout orders. Kendrick knelt on the stone floor and began to shake.

"Kendrick?" Aiden came up behind him.

"Clear the building!" Kendrick screamed. He looked down at his empty hands. His magic was raging out of control with his emotions. Black electricity crackled all around him. He wouldn't be able to contain it, everyone was in danger.

Aiden didn't ask, he began barking orders, and the sounds of the unit warriors grew fainter and fainter.

Under his knees, the earth began to move, upset that it had been awakened so forcefully.

"Mother! Father! Kendrick!" He beat his hands on the floor.

All these hundreds of years, they had been trapped, forced into use by the very evil that took their lives.

Above him the ceiling began to collapse, large heavy stones fell dangerously close, yet he didn't care.

Kendrick.

He ignored the soft voice of his mate. He refused to let her see him like this.

Athair.

No! Not his godsdaughter, too.

Is this thing working, Ryuu?

Kendrick smiled through his tears. Even Meryn was trying to reach him.

Kendrick my love, it's time to come home. You've done what you can for the day, now it's time to rest. Come home to me. You promised.

"Anne, my sweet Anne. Steadfast and true. Patient and loving. Gods, my parents would have loved you."

Athair, we're all worried about you. Whatever you're facing, you don't have to face it alone. We're a family remember?

"I let my family die, Amelia. I don't deserve another one."

Kendrick, brother, I won't let you die like this. You're a member of Alpha now; that means you fight. Aiden, Gavriel, Darian, and Colton are in the hallway waiting for you. They believe in your strength, as do I.

Kendrick gasped and looked around. "Keelan?" He saw a stone falling and dodged it just in time. He staggered to his feet. He had never let Keelan down before; he wasn't going to start now.

Get your ass moving! I don't want Aiden getting squashed like a pancake!

Kendrick laughed at Meryn's chiding and ran for the door. He caught the doorframe with one hand and flung himself into the hallway. There, waiting for him, was his unit.

"About fucking time! It's getting dicey out here!" Colton yelled.

"My apologies," Kendrick flipped him off and ran past him.

"Hey!" Colton yelled.

The men laughed and ran between the falling ceiling pieces.

Kendrick felt the earth shift again and knew the building was about to go.

"Run for the door, don't stop! It's coming down!" he yelled.

They ran zigzag down the narrow passages until they reached the large receiving room by the door. They heard cracking and the sounds of explosions behind them. They dove for the exit and rolled down the Council Manor steps. Behind them, the five thousand-year-old building came tumbling down.

Kendrick stared up at the sky and noticed how very blue it was. Colton's dirty face appeared grinning over him, then Aiden's, Gavriel's, and finally Darian's. Kendrick held up his hands, and they hoisted him up.

Sascha came up behind them. "Guys, we don't have to pay for this... right?"

Kendrick laughed, because he was either going to laugh or cry. Knowing that his mother, father, and brother were out there, trapped, had opened old wounds, but unlike the time when he'd first sustained them, he now had family around to help get him through.

Aiden was still chuckling when he ordered the men to return to the Alpha estate. Kendrick wasn't certain, but he was pretty sure he heard Elder McKenzie say, "fuck this" before he also left. They walked to the parking garage and got into the SUVs. Like Kendrick, the only thing the Alpha Unit wanted was to get home to their mates.

CHAPTER FIFTEEN

Anne kissed Kendrick's forehead and eased out of bed. She quietly got dressed and left their shared room. All of the men had been exhausted when they returned from the Council Manor the evening before. Though not even the men had known at the time what had happened with Kendrick. They had stayed behind because he was a part of their unit, and they didn't leave men behind.

When a battered Kendrick walked through the door, he had shocked everyone by dropping to his knees and burying his face against her belly. Everyone left them alone, and when he was ready, Kendrick stood, took her by the hand, and joined everyone in the family room.

His voice remained calm as he told them what had transpired after Rowan cast the paralysis spell on the men. He explained about Rowan's betrayal and the startling revelations about his parents. It was no wonder Anne had felt his pain even though they had been miles apart.

She had turned to Amelia and Ryuu for guidance on the best way to reach Kendrick and talk him through his grief to get him moving. She didn't want to think about what would have happened to all five men if he had delayed a second longer.

Anne went downstairs looking for Meryn. She owed her a couple hours of watching *Doctor Who* this afternoon, since Meryn had watched anime with her. She walked into the office and stopped short. Meryn was in the process of trying to lift her legs and was using her hands to fold them together in front of her. Seconds later, Anne had to cover her mouth to keep from laughing out loud, the tiny woman had tipped backward and ended up on her back cussing.

"Motherfucker!"

"Meryn, give up; it's just not for you," Elizabeth murmured, her eyes locked on her laptop.

"Bullshit! I'm doing this 'Zen' thing if it fucking kills me."

Anne stepped into the room and helped Meryn sit up. "You know being Zen shouldn't lead to stress or death."

"I know. Okay, one more time." Meryn wiggled until her legs were folded in a scary position resembling a pretzel. She placed her hands on her knees, closed her eyes, and tilted her head back.

After a few quiet moments, Anne looked over at Beth. Beth was looking down at Meryn, a bemused look on her face.

"What exactly are you doing?" Anne finally asked.

"Ryuu suggested that I try meditating to relieve stress. He said I should try and find my inner spirit animal," Meryn said without opening her eyes.

"What? A Pikachu?" Anne asked, smirking. Across the room, Elizabeth began to choke on her coffee.

Meryn's eyes popped open. "Rude! And I'm not that short!"

Colton popped his head into the room. "Oh, ladies! News from the committee, come to the family room."

Meryn looked down at her perfect position. "Motherfucker!"

Elizabeth and Anne reached down. "Come on, Menace, you know you want to hear what they have to say," Elizabeth said.

"Why did they have to make it out of the Manor? I wouldn't have minded if they'd gotten squashed," Meryn murmured.

"Oh, Meryn," Elizabeth sighed.

They walked into the family room. Anne glared at Colton when she saw a sleepy looking Kendrick sitting on the sofa.

"You could have let him sleep." She sat down next to her mate.

Kendrick pulled her close. "I'm fine. Much better today after having gotten so much rest."

"What did the assholes want?" Meryn asked.

"The assholes, as you call them, are furious of course." Byron leaned down and kissed Meryn on the forehead.

Meryn blushed. "Oh, hi, Dad."

Aiden grinned at Meryn's discomfort and rubbed his nose against her neck, causing her to squeal.

"Children," Byron chided.

Aiden sat up straighter. "Sorry, Father, please continue."

"As I was saying, they are furious, but they can't say much since one of their own was working for the enemy." Byron looked at Kendrick. "Are you sure that keeping Rowan's involvement a secret is the right thing to do?"

Kendrick gave one short nod. "I'm not making excuses for him; his choices were his own. He, and he alone, is facing the Gods for his actions. But he wasn't always a bad man. He did a lot of good here in Lycaonia, and I didn't want to tarnish that. Besides, if the enemy, whoever he is, believes that we have no idea about Rowan's involvement, then he'll have no idea that we were told anything, including anything about his very existence."

Meryn smiled. "Twisted. I like it."

Kendrick chuckled. "Thought you might."

Byron shook his head. "Well, I'm on vacation until the new Council Manor is built. I will be at home enjoying my cake." He turned to leave and then turned back. "By the way Aiden, why is Sascha begging me to talk to you about removing him from patrol?"

Colton started laughing, and Darian gave him a high five. Aiden's grin was devilish. "Because for some reason, only Sascha is getting zapped by the perimeter, so we make him do perimeter sweeps."

Darian leaned back. "It's like Keelan is still with us."

Beside her, Kendrick tensed. "What did you just say?"

Darian's face paled. "I didn't mean anything by it, Kendrick. It's like I told you, they had a rivalry, and Keelan would always electrocute Sascha."

Kendrick sat straight up in his chair. "That little bastard!" He sprang to his feet and ran upstairs. Anne was right on his heels as was everyone else. Kendrick flung Keelan's door open and went to the antechamber that he had told her was Keelan's sacred ritual space.

They waited for him in Keelan's room as he rummaged around, knocking over boxes and glass bowls.

"He did it! He actually did it!" Kendrick ran into the main room, holding a leather-bound book.

"He did what?" Aiden asked.

Kendrick began to pace. "Someone... someone told me something..." He pointed at Darian. "You! What did you tell me the night I arrived? What was Keelan's message to me?"

Darian shook his head. "He... uh, he said, 'Tell my brother he was right, but this was the only way I saw where you all lived. Tell him I'm sorry for what I've done, but I'd do it again.' That was it."

Kendrick whooped and picked Anne up and swung her around! "He said he was sorry!"

Anne laughed. "Kendrick, honey, you're starting to scare me."

He put her down on her feet. "He said he was sorry for what he had done, but that he'd do it again. I always thought that he was sorry for joining Alpha, for staying with you all when he knew he was going to die, but that wasn't what he was talking about!"

Kendrick's excitement was contagious. Anne grabbed Kendrick's arm. "What was he talking about?"

Kendrick stopped and looked at their faces. "You don't get it, none of you? That's frightening. How do you get through the day?"

Ryuu cleared his throat. "*Heika...*"

Kendrick pointed to Ryuu. "Right. The day after I got here, I told you that the entire city was covered by black magic, right?" Everyone nodded. "That kind of grime can only be caused by human sacrifice, so naturally, I assumed it was our enemy. I was wrong! Gods! How often do I get to say that?"

"Kendrick!" Anne exclaimed, losing her patience.

"It was Keelan!" Kendrick exploded.

Aiden's face turned red, and he jerked Kendrick up by the collar. "Keelan would never in a thousand years kill anyone for magic."

Kendrick pried Aiden's hands off his collar and patted him on the chest. "You, my large friend, are absolutely right; he would never, ever kill anyone to cast a spell. But, what if...just, what if, he knew the exact moment someone was going to die?"

Anne reached around blindly with her hand until she found the chair. She sat down. "Oh, my god."

"He knew he was going to die! He's known it for centuries! He figured out how to make a perfect perimeter. Did none of you wonder why Keelan wasn't up and walking around?" Kendrick looked at the others.

"Because he lost his soul. Duh!" Meryn replied, pointing to the bed.

Kendrick held up a finger. "Then what about ferals? They have no soul and they're able to run, fight, drool, bite, you know, the normal feral behaviors."

Anne looked at her mate. "I said the same thing the first time I saw him, I said that it was like he wasn't even there."

Gavriel stepped forward. "Then where is he?"

Kendrick went to the window and opened it. He pointed to the sky. "He's out there! The missing component to any perimeter is intelligence. You can never cast a spell to, say, block all vampires. We have vampires in our units. How does this perimeter tell friend from foe?"

"Keelan," Meryn whispered.

Elizabeth pointed to the window. "Keelan is out there, right now?"

Kendrick nodded.

"Well, get him back!" she exclaimed.

Kendrick threw the book across the room. "I don't know how! For all I know, what he did was a one-way trip. He cast the perimeter spell the second his soul left his body and used his own death as the human sacrifice needed to make the perfect barrier. I don't even know where to start to unravel this."

Anne stood and cupped his face with both hands. "You have plenty of time to figure it out. It's not like he's going anywhere, is he?"

Kendrick blinked. She squeezed his cheeks together, squishing his face. "You keep forgetting you're not alone anymore. You even have a very dedicated minion who would eat glass if you asked it of him." She jerked her hands to the left. "Stop trying"–she jerked to the right–"to do everything"–she held him in place and looked him in the eye–"by yourself." She released his face.

Kendrick rubbed his cheeks. "All of these years looking after Keelan, I thought I was my brother's keeper. But you're the one taking such good care of the both of us. You're our keeper."

Anne laughed. "Arrogant jerk." She pointed to the sky. "Keelan is the one taking care of us. He is his brother's keeper, and it sounds like he always has been."

Kendrick smiled, and Anne noticed there was a light in him that hadn't been there before. Now that he knew his brother was safe, she knew there was nothing in this world that would prevent him from bringing Keelan home, no matter how long it took. And she would be right there beside him, supporting him every second.

EPILOGUE

Everyone was practically high on the good news that Keelan's soul had been found, no matter how impossible it seemed at the moment to bring him home. Elizabeth felt like she had aged centuries in the past week. So many things had been revealed, it was as if their world was a darker place now.

"What is wrong my love?" Gavriel asked, taking the seat beside her.

She leaned against him. "We don't know who to trust. I feel like our world will never be safe again. It's as if our family's happiness slips away more and more each day."

Gavriel raised an eyebrow and pointed to Meryn who was leaning precariously out the open window yelling at Keelan to shock Sascha again while a frantic Aiden tried to pull her inside. "You were saying?"

Elizabeth began to laugh despite her morose mood. "Thank the Gods for that tiny human. I don't know what this house would be like without her."

"You chose your sister well." Gavriel nuzzled her neck, causing her to sigh as electricity ran through her body.

She was about to invite him upstairs when her phone rang. She pulled it out and smiled. "Uncle!

How are things in the city of the night?" She answered cheerfully. Her uncle always made her feel better.

"Elizabeth Monroe, I am demanding your presence immediately and bring along that runt human friend of yours," her uncle ordered.

"Of course, Uncle, anything you say. I understand completely." She ended the call and looked around.

Everyone had stopped what they were doing when Gavriel began hissing at her phone.

Her mate stood, eyes blazing red. "Who does he think he is to make such demands?"

Elizabeth tapped her fingers to her lips. "What did he call me, my love?"

Gavriel stopped and turned toward her, his eyes now a deep burgundy. "Elizabeth Monroe."

"Oh shit! What's happening in Dracula Town?" Meryn sat down on the sofa while Aiden closed the window.

Gavriel looked over at Beth, and she smiled at him. "My uncle never even calls me Beth, much less Elizabeth, and he loves Meryn. He would never call her 'that human runt'. Something is dreadfully wrong and he's in a position where he doesn't trust anyone around him to speak openly." She looked at Meryn, grinning mischievously. "Well, you always wanted to see Noctem Falls; you up for a road trip?"

Thank you for reading!
I hoped you enjoyed My Brother's Keeper.
For a full listing of all my books please check out my website. **http://alaneaalder.com**

I love to hear from readers so please feel free to follow me on Facebook , Twitter, Goodreads, AmazonCentral or Pinterest.

If you liked this book please let others know. Most people will trust a friend's opinion more than any ad. Also make sure to leave a review. I love to read what y'all have to say and find out what your favorite parts were. I always read your reviews.

Don't forget to sign up for my newsletters so you will receive regular updates concerning release information and promotions.

Vanguard Novella Coming Soon in 2016!

Inception

Wander through the years while following one of Lycaonia's most dedicated unit warriors and discover how the Vanguard came to be.

OTHER BOOKS BY ALANEA ALDER

Kindred of Arkadia Series

This series is about a shifter only town coming together as pack, pride, and sloth to defend the ones they love. Each book tells the story of a new couple or triad coming together and the hardships they face not only in their own Fated mating, but also in keeping their town safe against an unknown threat that looms just out of sight.

Book 1- Fate Knows Best
Book 2- Fated to Be Family
Book 3- Fated For Forever
Book 4- Fated Forgiveness
Book 5- Fated Healing
Book 6- Fated Surrender
Book 7- Gifts of Fate
Book 8- Fated Redemption

Bewitched and Bewildered Series

She's been Bewitched and he's Bewildered...

When the topic of grandchildren comes up during a weekly sewing circle, the matriarchs of the founding families seek out the witch Elder to scry to see if their sons' have mates. They are shocked to discover that many of their sons' mates are out in the world and are human!

Fearing that their future daughters-in-law will end up dead before being claimed and providing them with grandchildren to spoil, they convince their own mates that something must be done. After gathering all of the warriors together in a fake award ceremony, the witch Elder casts a spell to pull the warrior's mates to them, whether they want it or not.

Each book will revolve around a unit warrior member finding his destined mate, and the challenges and dangers they face in trying to uncover the reason why ferals are working together for the first time in their history to kill off members of the paranormal community.

Book 1- My Commander
Book 2- My Protector
Book 3- My Healer
Book 4- My Savior
Book 5- My Brother's Keeper

LUST BY JAS T. WARD
Available on all digital platforms and print

Book One of The Shadow-Keepers, MADNESS revealed The Grid to the world. Ward gives us even more of the wild ride in book two: LUST!

Welcome Back to the Grid

McKenzie Miller is a tough, hardcore woman who had learned to shut anything out that could hurt since her parents were killed in a murder, suicide when she was a child. After living on the streets, she landed in a tolerable place in her life but happiness and love doesn't even come close to reaching her–because she refuses to let it.

There are greater powers always aware of Kenzie's existence and had been there all along with whispers in her mind and at times, rescues from more tragedy being thrown into her world. Kenzie made sure no one knew that she most likely had lost her mind, why add any more negative labels than she already had? But Kenzie's not going crazy, not even close. Lust takes care of its own. But other dark powers want to play and Kenzie's dull, loveless life is about to end ... literally.

Lana Penchez just wanted to dance. It's all she wanted to do for as long as she was able to walk. That want translated into an obsession with her parents and Lana strived to make them proud with each step she ever took in her ballet slippers. Sadly, they were taken away from the aspiring ballerina but their ambition to have their daughter reach a dream they demanded she have still drives the young woman. Love? Relationships? Who had the time?

All that changed one night when she's attacked and thrust into the secret war that is being fought right in front of mankind's eyes–hidden behind tattooed stamps of undercover soldiers, bad-asses and immortals. The memories of the events of that attack are all a blur to Lana, except for one very clear detail that seems to be branded on her mind–a beautiful, strong, lavender-eyed woman who saved her.

And then just disappeared.

Can love cut short in life still find its way in death?

Can someone learn to live despite being no longer alive?

And can a heartbeat be found, even when the heart lies still?

Welcome back to the Grid–
What Darkness Makes YOUR heart beat?

The Shadow-Keepers Reading Order:

Stories from the Grid: CANDYMAN
Book One: MADNESS
Stories from the Grid: BOUNCE
Book Two: LUST

Other Books by Jas T. Ward

What Makes Your Heart Beat?

Bits & Pieces: Tales and Sonnets Volume One

A collection of short-stories, poetry and other literally "bits" that the author had published on social media as a thank you to her fans. This book gave birth to both the Shadow-Keepers series and the upcoming Light and Dark Series in the form of short-stories included.

Love's Bitter Harvest

Romance- The Ward Way

Matt and Katherine McCall were high-school sweethearts and in love from first kiss. But time changes people and sometimes the strongest seed of love can only harvest bitterness. Fast forward four years–Katy has a new life far from the one she had with Matt. And she thought it was all worth it.

Matt McCall's last four years were full of loss, doubt and sorrow. And now? He's only half the man Katy left behind.

Can love survive in hardened, bitter tainted soil? Or does it eventually die under the coldness of heart-break.

Love's Bitter Harvest
Romance-The Ward Way

To Contact Ward:
Facebook:
https://www.facebook.com/AuthorJasTWard/info
Amazon Page:
http://www.amazon.com/Jas-T.-Ward/e/B00CJO70A8/
Website: http://www.authorjastward.com/
Blog: http://authorjastward.blogspot.com/
Pinterest: www.pinterest.com/AuthorJasTWard
Twitter: http://twitter.com/jastward

<<<<>>>>

Printed in Great Britain
by Amazon